Lock Down Publications and Ca$h
Presents

# SON OF A DOPEFIEND 4

Prostitution The Constitution

By

# RENTA

First Edition 2023

Printed in the United States of America

This is a work of fiction. Names, characters, places, and incidents either are products of the author's imagination or are used fictitiously. Any similarity to actual events or locales or persons, living or dead, is entirely coincidental.

Lock Down Publications
P.O. Box 944
Stockbridge, GA 30281
www.lockdownpublications.com

Like our page on Facebook: Lock Down Publications
www.facebook.com/lockdownpublications.ldp

# Stay Connected with Us!

Text **LOCKDOWN** to 22828 to stay up-to-date with new releases, sneak peaks, contests and more...

Like our page on Facebook:
Lock Down Publications

Join Lock Down Publications/The New Era Reading Group

Visit our website:
www.lockdownpublications.com

Follow us on Instagram:
Lock Down Publications

Email Us: We want to hear from you!

Dedication

This one's for Dunte. Thank you for the sacrifice you tried to make for me; you tried to trade your life for mine, and I love you for it. Twenty years later here we are still thuggin...getcha bread or play dead cause being broke is close to dying anyway.

# Chapter 1

Oakland California

Prostitution The Constitution

*1996 wasn't only the height of gang banging, but it was "one" of the last years of modern pimping! This day was gray; the sun hiding behind the clouds as beneath that drab sky, the city of Oakland, California thrived with illicit behavior. Messiah found himself valeted on 12th Street and 1st Avenue; not far from where the Economy Inn Motel was being used for the fuck for a buck. And it was there that he was able to peep the life of Oakland through the lens of his Cartier lenses. The blade, "hoe stroll", wasn't far away, and ever since he'd entered that city, Messiah had been swept up into the con and slippery game of the cut throats. He loved it! Though New York City, Detroit, and Milwaukee has three of the U.S. coldest strolls, Oakland was an entirely different animal. It had been a year since he'd entered the city, and as he reclined in the backseat of a fresh out the womb new Benz, he marveled at how far he'd come. He'd left Black Diamond back home, but with the game she and Pimpin' had invested over the years, he'd been able to up his stable to six of the baddest felines the game could gift him. Two sat in the front seat, trophy bitches for the lusting eyes of bigger fish. See, Messiah noted the change in the game, and had changed ones before he ran into a dead end. Only his newest freaks worked the stroll, and this was merely because he believed every hoe needed a taste of the blade to cut her skin before becoming a prostitute in pursuit of a big willy in a suit. Tutts, and Liberty "both" were his bottoms, and both had graduated from motels to hotel suites where men and women paid to see them freak. Toy, Tokyo, Snowy and Liz, were top shelf as well, but Moan and Exotic were two new sluts that he had to teach new stunts. He smiled at the thoughts of the two until the ringing of his new Motorola barked beside him. Retrieving the big block device, and assuming the caller was talking money.*

*"Articulate," he answered.*

*"What's the haps, daddy? I thought you were swinging through to rendezvous with a feline?" She purred.*

*A slight frown eased onto Messiah's face before recognition allowed him a smug smirk.*

*"Sassy?" He inquired.*

*"I'm in my panties and nothing else, baby, but you know dick is too cheap for his pussy, and if a nigga ain't talking about "something", he can't be talking about "nothing"! How are you?" Sassy jived.*

*Messiah chuckled. Sassy was a madam who ran whore houses from California to Texas, and was respected in the game of pussy and dick for being stomp down and finessively treacherous. Ever since Messiah had bumped shoulders with lady, she'd attempted to go into business with him. Her proposal being she'd open the doors for his lady's to work out of her brothels in exchange for a thirty percent tax, but Messiah knew there were no such things as partnership in "the life", and declined every time.*

*"I hear that, baby. I hear that." He was digging her vibe.*

*"And you know I stay ten toes as I win hoes, so if you're not calling to jump down with a real playa, what's the meaning of us talking shit and swappin' spit?" He smashed the friendly vibe.*

*Sassy giggled." Are you calling "me" a whore, Messiah?"*

5

Messiah's fingers traced his freshly trimmed goatee as he considered her question. "Sassy, "every" woman has some hoe in 'em. Some just settle for less so they can hide their hoism behind more tasteful titles."

"But are you callin' "me" a whore, baby?" Threat was a tinge in her tone. Messiah knew she had the power to touch him long distance; she came up in Pimpin's era, and had long money.

"A proper understandin' trumps an improper one any day, mama, and if you've "ever" used pussy as an allure, then you've exercised your hoism. No matter how much pussy you've managed, you have pussy in ya panties, so being whorish is second nature, Sassy. Seduction! Using what's between those pretty thighs to be freaky wit ya man, to entice a friend, or merely helping it stand out in ya pants, is all hoe tactics." He chuckled.

"You know I can have ya nuts sloshing in my champagne flute by tonight if I chose, baby?" Sassy's tone was feline; sexual.

"Cliche, Sassy, a hoe uses her seductions to get a nut out a dick, and here you are speaking of using my nuts as ice cubes in ya wine glass."

Silence! Then, deep laughter. Messiah glanced up, catching Tutts' eyes in the rearview mirror. She loved him, his game.

"Messiah." Sassy tamed herself. "I love it, honey. You're so refreshing to the life of a woman as myself. So, let's get to it. I want those two gals you have. In exchange, I'll give you a quarter million."

Messiah's vision drifted to Liberty; pretty in the passenger's seat.

"One condition and we have a deal." He proposed and could feel her surprise through the phone.

"Okay?"

"I get a full night with you."

Sassy giggled. "Oh no, honey, I'm—"

*"Only way,"* he concluded, *and after a brief silence, Sassy cast date to the Gods.*
*"Deal."* She agreed. *"But I must tell you. My pussy is a thief."* She giggled.

\*\*\*

*Back in Dallas, Texas, C-Bo was feeling good as he slid his new Delta 88 into the drive through. Eight Ball and MJG vibrated from his trunk as he bobbed his head. His vibe making the freak in his passenger's seat feel bossy.*
*"Welcome to Jack in the Box, can I take your order, please?"* Whomever was working the window asked.
*C-Bo leaned toward the intercom. Grateful to have beat the three cars behind him, he smirked.*
*"Yeah, let me get a number five with a curly fry and cheese."*
*"Would that be all, sir?"*
*"Hold up —"* C-Bo glanced over at his passenger. *"What you want, baby?"*
*"Umm, just get me two number threes, ten tacos, and five small drinks,"* she requested without having to consult the menu.
*C-Bo's face balled up. "Bitch, what?"*
*Shawty smacked her lips. "Whaaat? I have five kids, boo, don't play!"*
*C-Bo's mouth fell open in shock, but shaking his head. "Say, add five tacos to that,"* he spat when he turned back to the intercom.
*"Uh uh, nigga, what 'bout my kids?"* Lady protested.
*"Bitch, that's a taco for each one of them lil mu'fuckas."*
*"What 'bout me, I'm—"*
*"Gonna have to split a taco, bitch."* C-Bo laughed when Lady smacked her lips and crossed her arms over her chest.
*"Cheap ass nigga!"* She smacked her lips.

\*\*\*

*Nigga, you sure?" Sunjay was skeptical as he pulled the red bandanna out his pocket, and tied it around the bottom half of his. Reaching in the backseat, he snatched off the sawed off pump.*

*"Blood, I'm saying, it "looked" like the hoe ass nigga. I was checkin' the bitch on the passenger's side when I saw the boy, but Murda shrugged. "I could be wrong, but…" His words trailed. Sunjay was already gone.*

\*\*\*

*Pulling the car to the window to retrieve their food, C-Bo smiled up at the queen behind the register. She was dark as charcoal with big box dookie braids in her head; yet it was the gigantic, gold earrings dangling from her ears that let it be known the ghetto was her birth place.*

*"That'll be sixteen nin—" she was saying when the piercing scream from the passenger's seat snatched their attention. C-Bo's hand was on auto as he went for his fire, but—BOOM! The explosion from the gauge rocked the car as buck shots sprayed his companies face onto his shirt. He barely registered the red flag covering the shooters face before instinct kicked in. C-Bo mashed his foot down onto the gas just as Sunjay yanked down on the pump.*

*BOOM! BOOM!*

*Fire leapt from the pipe just as the car shot forward. A spray of crimson peppered the air in its wake and Sunjay knew he'd hit his mark. The lady working the window abandoned post; her screams hysterical.*

*"Fuck!" Sunjay spat, but paused when the sound of crushing metal hinted that even the devil grants blessings. Skiirrrt! The sound of biting rubber snatched his attention just as Murda swung the car around the corner.*

*"Come on, Blood, the bitch boy hit. He crashed into the Jack in the Box sign up front!" He shouted.*

\*\*\*

*She watched the black Crown Vic ease out of the driveway and disappear off the block before slipping out of the Toyota Celica she'd borrowed from a friend. Black Diamond was on a mission as she looked up and down the street to ensure he hadn't doubled back. Detective Spinx's modest home was a contradiction to his side hustle; the man was smart enough to not become obvious. Black was focused and as she made her way toward the three bedroom in Desoto, Texas. She had one thing in mind. I have to get into this house!*

\*\*\*

*The inhabitants of Butter Beans Apartments were outside, and though the sun was setting, there was no sign of turning down. In the midst of young niggas slap boxing, BBQ's and young tenders on their best thotish behavior, hustlers we're getting to it. Hand to hand combat with the exchange of vice for wrinkled bills. So, when the sounds of Spinx's car gave off that telltale sound the brakes makes when the police is lurking, all activities seemed to freeze! All eyes captured the car just as it pulled to a stop. When the window rolled down and Spinx shouted to Danny, all eyes drifted to the shade tree mechanic that could fix just about anything. Danny was beneath the hood of someone's car when he was summoned, and wiping his oily hands on a dirty rag, he glared at the dirty cop.*

*"What you want, Spinx? Can't a man make an honest livin' without ya harassin' 'em?" He spat, before looking to Spinx's Caucasian passenger.*

Spinx chuckled. *"Yeah, yeah, sho ya right, Danny boy. I was just stopping through to tell ya to let,"* His eyes touched a few known hustlers he knew, before turning to Danny. *"Let the hood know that today may be a good idea to get low. Ya never know when me and my boys may feel lucky."* He smirked with mischief in his eyes.

Danny shrugged before waving his hand in an arch. *"Never knew you gave warnings, Pig, but I'm sure your message was well received."*

Spinx's eyes drifted until he found a curious sight. Tweety was hugged up and leaning against a car with a man too old for her youth.

*"Ole KG, I see yuh still robbing the cradle, huh? You ever heard of statutory, punk? Tweety, baby, how old are you these days?"* Spinx chuckled. *"Fifteen? Sixteen?"*

*"Grown, nigga,"* Tweety retorted, and Box Head spat at the ground. Spinx nodded before easing his window up and finishing his rounds.

*"Did you really just warn those guys?"* Officer McHeney was flabbergasted.

*"Spinx chuckled. "It'll make our job easier if they expect heat. It's a good chance most won't be around.*

*"For?"*

*"You ask too many questions, McHenry. You act like the police."* Spinx laughed at his own joke.

\*\*\*

Black Diamond had entered the house by way of a side window, and after searching every possible place she could think Spinx would hide something he wanted kept secret, she was drenched in sweat.

*"I know this negro got the pictures in here, but where? Think girl!"* She whispered. *"Where would I hide them?"* She asked herself before back tracking to his bedroom. The place was spotless, and for some reason, her eyes kept

*drifting towards the closet. Yet, she'd searched it three times already! Intuition beckoned her in spite of, and that's how she found herself back inside the walk-in closet, where Spinx kept a locked filing cabinet. And even more, that's where she spotted a metal lock box, hidden in plain sight!*

# Chapter 2

*Oakland*

*The sun traveled somewhere across the world. The night hosted a crescent moon amongst thousands of stars, and as Messiah eased the Benz to a wrought iron gate, an iota of insecurity was birthed. As if by magic, the gates rolled open and allowed him to pull onto a sprawling estate with a vast, manicured lawn. Behind him, Liberty and three of his other girls followed him in his Jag, and when he pulled to a stop at the entrance of Sassy's mini mansion, he knew the night would be an odd easy. There were foreign and old school whips valeted out on the lawn, and after finding a place to park, Messiah glanced over to Tutts in the passenger's seat. After they'd ran the painting play, they'd link like a chain, but in spite of his mastery, Oakland's game was dangerous like an uncharted jungle filled with famished animals. Nonetheless, he nodded and Tutts opened the glove compartment and touched the button to unlock the trunk. Messiah chuckled. "Let's see if California is up to par." He jived, knowing Liberty had popped the trunk on the Jag as well.*

*\*\*\**

*The mansion was a brothel known as "The Honey Spot", and every six months, Sassy invited the choice playas of the game to rub shoulders amongst the finest. Each pimp paid a thousand dollars entry fee to bring their hoes to fuck and suck the tricks that mingled amongst playas. NBA players, a few NFL boys, and even big money femmies were present that night. The first floor of the two story dwelling was converted into a classy setting, complete with a stocked bar and sitting area. Messiah and company became the main attraction when they entered. Draped in matching, customized army fatigue hued mini dresses, all six of his girls sashayed in and lined up lengthwise. And only after all eyes were on them did Messiah slip in; camouflaged down to the butter Timbs on his feet. The man was exclusive! The army fatigue jacket he wore open; and shirtless beneath, his Rolex necklace brandished a medallion so diamond encrusted, it resembled a pile of glitter against his dark chest.*

*"You hoes at ease and go get ya hoe on, but just make sure when it's time to dip, my dough long." He jazzed before slapping Tutts and Liberty on their ass. With giggles, his lady's dispersed, and Messiah made his way to the bar.*

*"Good evening, handsome, welcome to The Honey Spot." The bartender purred before licking her lips suggestively. Though he didn't show it, Messiah was caught off his pivot to see that lady wasn't merely exotic, but was as naked as a Greek statue. "What can I do for you?" Her full lips offered, and when his eyes finished their exploration of her landscape, he chuckled.*

*"Anything wet will do, ma." He toyed.*

*"Her lips smiled. "Pussy perhaps?" She fed the innuendo.*

*Messiah chuckled. "Love, the only way pussy will ever touch these lips is if with a kiss, it'll make me rich, and the only way thangs I've ever seen pussy spit out is blood, cum, and babies." He adjusted his drip. "And neither of those things ever added to a nigga's piggy bank."*

*"No, honey," the lady giggled mischievously. "Pussy is a drink I created. It's gin, with a splash of pink lemonade and lime; clear like cum."*

*"Well, in that case, let me taste that."* He fed the vibe and when lady turned to fix his drink, a presence slid onto the stool besides Messiah.

*"If pimpin' weren't the profession, I'd give a confession, but since it is?"* The familiar voice snatched Messiah's vision from all that ass queen had. Pimpin Yella Shoe chuckled before extending his pinky to him. *"Proud of you, P."* He nodded, and Messiah was only vaguely surprised to see him there.

Messiah interlocked pinkies. *"For?"*

*"I seen ya entrance and how ya bimbos was ya projection. See, when I first rubbed shoulders with ya back home, I knew you'd be a star in this life, and I'm glad to see ya took my advice. It's not 'bout ya game, it's bout ya aim! What you "want" from ya hoes and what ya "can't" afford for either of 'em to be to you. And...* Yella Shoe paused as Messiah accepted his drink, and seeing as Yella already nursed a glass, the bartender winked before giving them their privacy.

*"And?"* Messiah sipped after the question.

*"And if you wouldn't have taken my jewels to heart, I would've taken offense, because my jewels expensive like a pink mink on the shoulders of an inappropriate white whore that only wants more."*

Messiah chuckled before lifting his glass in toast. *"The game is vast. So, what brings you here?"*

Just beyond his question, erotic moans serenaded the air. Yella Shoe spun on his stool to face the center of the room, where two felines intertwined, and when Messiah spun to peep the scene, for the first time since arriving, he took in his surroundings. The room had a lounge feel, with imported chairs and couches strategically positioned to face a floor bed that was positioned in the middle of the room. It was there that the two ladies; one Latin, the other vanilla, sixty-nined.

*"This here is The Honey Spot, Messiah, and only the top shelf is invited, and not to gander down on ya game, but I'm surprised to see you here. Which tells me you either added ten years to ya game or it's some shit in the game."* The man tickled Messiah's ego and to blanket his offense, he sipped and visually explored his surroundings. All around them were "naked" women, and while some disappeared up the winding staircase leading to the second level of the strange house, hand in hand with a date, others did vulgar things out in the open. He spotted Liberty in a far corner tongue kissing a part of a stranger that would've cursed them with an indecent exposure charge if the police were present. Finally, Messiah's vision found Yella Shoe. *"Are you sayin' my game ain't—"*

*"Excuse me."* They were interrupted by an Amazon goddess wearing nothing but skin and heels. *"The mistress of the house requests your presence."* She smiled sexily at Messiah, and all he could do was stare. The woman was a stallion with flawless yellow skin and long wavy hair. Gorgeous! Her hypnotic eyes found Yella Shoe, whom she'd been accosted by on numerous occasions to get down with his regime. Smiling, she slid her tongue over her lips.

*"Mr. Shoe,"* she greeted.

*"Paradise."* He nodded; on the verge of breaking on her, but taming the impulse. His curiosity of the happenings between Messiah and Sassy grew.

Messiah slid from his seat chuckling. *"I'll catch you in traffic, OG, I have…"*

*"Let me spit in ya ear real quick, P. Yella Shoe touched his arm before nodding for Paradise to give them some space.

She smirked knowingly before doing so, and Yella Shoe tapped in, *"Say, how you know Sassy, P?"*

Messiah frowned, not feeling the playa in his mix. *"I don't think that's none of—"*

*"Listen, lil nigga, now is not the time for arrogance!"* Yella's time took Messiah fast and his face balled up in anger.

*"Nigga, my daddy died back in the eighties!"*

*"Yeah, I can dig it, but listen while I pull ya coat so ya don't get played like a joke! Listen, P."* Yella Shoe glanced over at Paradise, knowing she was Sassy's lover and bottom bitch. If Sassy was playing slick, then that would explain Paradise's presence. His eyes recaptured Messiah. *"Pimpin and hoin' coincides like Bonnie and Clyde, but everything slick don't slide, so make sure you always got some extra slick to escape a sticky situation."*

Messiah shrugged the man's hand away.

*"As I said, P, my daddy got whacked back in the eighties,"* he reiterated before making his way into a spider's web.

***

The night was absolute in the city of The Triple D, and as expected, the hood had heeded Spinx warning! The Butta Beans was like a ghost town, save for a few fiends and young niggas that hustled the breeze ways. Yet, inside A234, Lil Zetti was gone off dro smoke and liquor. He and the little freak occupying his time were indulging in both. He'd heard Spinx threat and closed shop; having no worries cause the spot was no longer a trap, but more a stash spot they kept the money at.

*"Damn, Lil Zetti, I've been suckin' this mu'fucka for thirty minutes and it still ain't got hard!"* LaTosha whined, and Lil Zetti's vision fell to her. In his wheelchair with his pants bunched at his ankles, he smirked before tilting a bottle of V.S.O.P down toward his lap. The dark liquor splashed over his Johnson and family jewels, making the seat slippery beneath him.

*"See what's up now? You ain't ever sucked a dick that you can get you tipsy."* He laughed, but she didn't. Shouting to her feet, she crossed her arms over her perky breast. *"Don't play, nigga. Can the dick stand up or is it cripple like—"*

*"Say what, bitch?"* Zetti spazzed before hurling the bottle at her.

She'd touched his insecurity, and though she'd dodged the bottle, Lil Zetti was already going for the gun he'd rested on the table. She saw his intent and knew if he'd got his hand on that tool, he'd do something foolish, so she went for it. Zetti saw her and in a wild attempt, he rocked forward as hard as he could, to beat her to it.

*"Augh!"* He cried when he fell out his chair, landing ass up on his stomach. The girl snatched the gun and knowing it would take him a minute to get to it, she tossed it behind her.

*"Bitch, I'mma have my sister beat—yo—ass!"* He growled. LaTosha covered her mouth to stifle her laughter; the sight before her was comical. With his pants at his ankles, and his ass cheeks wet from the liquor, Lil Zetti fought to get himself together.

*"Yeah, whatever, nigga."* The lady laughed while going for her purse. *"Just make sure you dry ya ass before you do."* She hurried for the door, but when she threw it open, she ran into trouble.

*"Hey there, sweet thang. Where ya so in a rush to?"* Detective Spinx smirked.

\*\*\*

*The room Messiah had been escorted to was the size of a loft. Dim, it was tastefully decorated with cherrywood furnishings. An antique bureau, two chocolate hued love seats and an open terrace was merely eye candy compared to the most captivating fixture on display. Beyond the massive cherrywood, canopy bed Messiah's eyes found*

*Sassy, sitting with her legs crossed in one of the love seats. His inches stretched out in his boxers. Her chocolate skin glistened with oil, and outside of her sheer thong, her femininity peeked through; her skin was all she wore. Her double D's were surgically enhanced to sit up without support, and her thick, chocolate areolas were mouthwatering. Yet, the most beautiful vision to capture Messiah's fancy, was the duffel bag stuffed with pictures of a dead man's face! A quarter milli! Sipping from a champagne flute, Sassy smiled at the lust radiating from his stare off with the check. After glancing at Paradise, whom laid across the bed, Sassy recaptured Messiah with her orbs.*

*"All this pussy, and you're more interested in the money." She sipped gently. "Admirable." She whispered. Messiah's vision found her. Dark, hypnotic eyes, full lips, glossed with Marilyn Monroe mole just above them. Her hair was cut into a bob that was short in the back, but long in the front, and reminiscent of Chili's from TLC, and her thighs and hips bulged even while sitting down. Beside her pedicured toes, a black bottle of champagne made the view bossy.*

*"When was the last you've been fucked?" His question was left field, and caused her to pause, glass midway to her lips.*

*"Messiah, I'm a boss bitch. Sex?" She giggled before slipping from her seat and standing before him. "With beautiful women or gorgeous men, is "nothing". I sell—"*

*"Why haven't you answered my question, Sassy?" Messiah knew he had to crush her confidence in order to accomplish his goal. Sassy smiled, her eyes capturing his general's attire; his drip was official!*

*"Last night." She humored him. Messiah's vision slipped to Paradise laying on her side in the large bed, and she guiltily dropped her gaze to the comforter before smiling and running a hand over the mink material. Chuckling, Messiah found Sassy's weakness. With no for-warning, he slipped his dick out his pants.*

*"Get on your knees, Sassy,"* he demanded, *and evil spread across her face.*

*"No, yo young ass got me fucked up. This—"*

*"Bitch, we have a deal. The money "and" you, so either get on your knees and taste what only few has tasted, or—"*

*"I can have you killed, keep my mula, "and" the whores."*

*Sassy gave him a wicked smile that was somehow seductive.*

*"Then, there's that too," Messiah conceded with a nod, and releasing his control of his ism. His dick engorged. Sassy's vision captured it, and Messiah used the distraction to slip the duece duece from up his coat sleeve. He knew he'd be searched so he'd come prepared. "Or I can kill you for breaking your word?" He smirked. Sassy did too, before downing the rest of her drink.*

*"Touché," she murmured before refilling her glass and following orders. On her knees before his thickness, her eyes deviated from dick to face. "I'll play your game tonight."*

*Messiah smiled. Sassy's weakness was she'd been a boss bitch so long that she'd forgotten to feel feminancy. Being submissive! In her line of work, submission was a sin, but Messiah saw what hid just behind her seduction. Need! Want!*

*"Cool, now use your lips for something more than words." His demand was met by eroticism. Sassy took his dick and dipped it in her glass before sucking the champagne from his flesh.*

*SMOP! Her lips popped when she released him. "Like this, daddy?" She purred.*

\*\*\*

*"This ain't got shit to do with me, officer? Why am I cuffed?" The lady demanded.*

*Spinx and two of his "special" force boys had cuffed her and cuffed Zetti to his chair. And ignoring her, the dirty cop smirked down at Lil Zetti.*

*"Bad ass Zetti Jackson."* He shook his head bitterly. *"Look at ya, all shot up, and crippled and shit."* He chuckled.

*"Fuck you, Uncle Tom, mu'fucka!"* Zetti spazzed before spitting at him.

Spinx rushed him, and with both wrist cuffed to the arms of his wheelchair, he was defenseless against the punch to the face. His head snapped back and blood exploded from his nose.

*"Why'd you hit him, pig? He's cuffed!"* The girl cried in shock, but Detective Spinx was so busy spinning the wheelchair around that he paid her no mind. His fellow officers glanced at each other. They were there to rob the spot, not draw blood!

*"Y'all keep an eye on her while me and ole Zetti have a lil chat,"* Spinx spoke over his shoulder while wheeling Lil Zetti toward the back of the apartment.

*"No pork on my fork, pig. Suck my dick. I ain't telling you shit!"* Zetti spazzed.

*"Oh, you will, son, you will."*

***

Messiah had a fistful of Sassy's hair as she ate him up, and the vision had Paradise's twat saturated. Yet, just beyond the monster of lust, hid an iota of disappointment, and that's exactly what Messiah had anticipated! Sassy was a madame, and was so bossy that her girl's looked upon her as a goddess, and to see her submit to her lowest denominator, her power evaporated before Paradise's regard. Wet sucking sounds emitted as Sassy slurped, and Messiah clenched his jaws to prevent from exploding.

*"Come here, Paradise,"* he demanded, and Sassy's war against his soldier slowed until she popped him free and glared.

*"She has nothin' to do with—"*

*"Silence, bitch!" Messiah commanded before forcing her head back forward. "Or do you fear my ism, Sassy?" He smirked and just as he thought, the challenge motivated her. Returning his smirk, she suckled his head back into her mouth. Checkmate! Messiah thought as Paradise took that as permission to obey him.*

*She slipped from the bed and over to him; a stallion before a God! Jacking his dick, Sassy showed her work. Slurping, kissing, and sucking was only a measure of her arsenal, but when she popped him free of her lips, and began to stroke him feverishly while blowing on his wet head, Messiah's ism morphed into Jism. The first squirt painted her nose and just below her right eye, and feeling another round surging, she hurriedly buried his flesh inside her champagne flute. The tan liquid turned milky as he impregnated it, and when Sassy went to wipe her face, Messiah chuckled. "Naw," he paused her as his vision captured Paradise. "Clean her up for me." Paradise frowned, but squeezing Messiah's dick till the point of pain, Sassy merely smiled. Paradise turned to retrieve something to clean the mess, but Messiah grabbed her wrist. "Naw, baby, get on ya knees and "lick" my fruits clean." The suggestion was vulgar, intertwined with eroticism, and when Sassy didn't refuse, Paradise went to her knees and licked her face spotless. The whole time, Sassy never diverted her vision from Messiah's, and when Paradise had finished, Sassy showed Messiah that she was a step ahead of him. Lifting her tainted glass, she toasted him.*

*"To business." She smiled before swallowing the fruits of her labor. Messiah's dick regained life, and from there, he slayed both women, making sure his performance was artful.*

\*\*\*

*"I'mma ask yo lil ass one...mo...time, nigga. Where y'all keepin' the dope and money!" Spinx growled. The room was*

21

*dark, save for the light pouring from the open blinds, and as Lil Zetti blinked in and out of consciousness, Detective Spinx glared. Sweat glistened atop his bald head from the beating he'd given the boy, and when Zetti finally got his bearings, he smiled, revealing broken teeth.*

*"Sunjay i—sss, gon—na kill you," he spat before spitting a piece of his tooth at the man. The brave heart enraged the rouge detective and within a moment of evil, he slipped behind the wheelchair and put Lil Zetti in a chokehold.*

*"Where that money, lil nigga!" He gritted as Lil Zetti's gargled fights for breath filled the room, and just before the boy lost consciousness, Spinx eased the pressure of his forearm.*

*"Hhhaahhhh!" Sucking a lungful of air into his lungs. "Please?" Zetti finally broke, and Spinx smirked before lowering his ear toward him.*

*"I didn't hear you, gangsta. You said that mula where?"*

*"It's—it's in the bathroom toilet. The back of it." Zetti was defeated, and in shadows of that dark room; with sweat glistening on his face, Detective Spinx smiled sinisterly.*

*"Good boy." He chuckled, and that's when his crime transcended into pure evil. Lips close to Zetti's ear, Spinx squeezed as tight as he could, cutting off Lil Zetti's air supply. Cuffed to the chair and crippled, all he could do was scratch at the arms of his wheelchair as the cop squeezed life from him.*

*"Ahh-hhhh!" He cried. "Ple-s-ee?" He rasped, eyes bloodshot within the dimness.*

*"Shisssh!" Spinx hissed. "Don't fight it, baby boy."*

***

*Her light snores made Messiah smile in the dark; he'd punished Sassy! Erotically! Twenty years older than he, she'd been defeated by her youth, and as he slipped out the bed, Messiah only has one mission; finding Paradise! She'd retired after he'd proven that only a God could truly separate the waters from the earth. And that he did! Slipping out the room, and into the huge hallway, he was amazed at the size of the spot! Yet, he tiptoed to prevent waking the dead. On this wing, there were doors on both sides of him; most closed, but few cracked as if it's occupants "wanted" one to peek.*

*"Um—ummmmm, yes, daddy, take this pussy!" A gorgeous Snow cried in passion as she bucked atop a stranger. Messiah watched for a bit before moving along, shaking his head. This was a real life whore house, mane! He thought before pausing at another cracked door. Two men were having their way with a fluzzy, and no matter how hard they attempted to dominate her, lady took pipe in every hole like a sewage system! Messiah shook his head before tipping away; it never ceased to amaze him how the feminine body could turn the masculine one into a slave! He chuckled, until the next room he found himself before let him know it was game time. Paradise's room was dim, and though she donned a skimpy silk robe, her curvature was dominant beneath the soft material. She'd just showered, and with her damp hair slung over her left shoulder, she sat rubbing baby oil into her thick thighs. When Messiah invited himself in, she looked up, and the mischievous smirk she gave made it evident she'd expected him.*

*"Mr. Messiah?" She seemed to purr, and Messiah's vision found the tray of food beside her. A can of whipped cream and a bowl of cherries was her late night snack.*

*Messiah smirked before making his way over to her, "Get ya shit, you leaving with me." His demand brought a frown to her face.*

*Then, laughter! Paradise laughed until his lack of, made her regain composure.*

*"Okay. Okay" She patted the air before plucking a cherry from the bowl and nibbling its tip. "Does that really work with the girls?" She smirked while savoring the fruit. Her eyes took in the man's nakedness, but it was more of his*

*audacity that intrigued her. Standing before her in nothing but skin and jewels, Messiah's confidence was official. Taking up the can of whipped cream and a handful of cherries, he studied her.*

*"You calling me a molester of considering yourself a child?" He probed.*

*"Huh?" Paradise's eyebrow rose.*

*"You asked if my ism worked on all the "girls"."*

*Giggling, Paradise sucked juice from a cherry before crossing her legs. "Who are you?" She asked, and Messiah gripped his nuts.*

*"Bitch, you know my name is synonymous with game, so stop playin' lame and catch the money train before I leave you at the station bumpin' pussies with a feline that can never be the queen of the jungle cause there's no such thang!" He broke on her.*

*And though she seemed the rhyming of his macking juvenile, the paradox was—It intrigued her!*

*"But who are you? Who is Messiah?" Paradise nibbled the cherry while studying his vulgar image.*

*"I'm He, hoe. Now, why you investigating my history instead of diggin' our chemistry? I see it in ya eyes. You're seduced by the fancy life ya mistress provides, but just beyond it, this domestication contradicts ya education! You earned ya degree in hoism, and like a lioness going from the wild to the zoo, the kept life is killin' ya spirit."*

*His drip made her pause with the half-eaten cherry midway to her lips.*

*"Again," she spat, no smiles. "Who the fuck are "you." You don't know me!"*

*Messiah released his family jewels, and smirked. He needed her on the defense so he could play his offense.*

*"Bitch, I'm HE! "H"ere, and "E"verywhere, hoe! And a playa ain't gotta know you to see you. Mama, I'm certified like a vocation, and it's not ya pussyhole that generates a bankroll; it's the location of your presentation!" He waved a*

*dismissive hand around the room. "And for all this fancy shit, it can never compensate for where you "can" be in life, and Sassy," he chuckled. "Just proved before your pretty eyes that even a goddess bows to a God! My name is Messiah, love, the way, they truth, and the light, and I'm tryin' to lead you to all three if only you take the make believe from ya sight."*

*Paradise gently placed the half-eaten fruit back in the bowl before slipping from her seat, and standing before him.*

*"You don't understand, Sassy is good to—"*

*"Bitch, if God meant for same sex relations, he woulda given us both a pussy "and" a dick, so we can fuck or be ducked "without" having to be gay or partake of that fruit. So, yeah, Sassy may be good "to" you but what's unnatural ain't always good "for" you!" Messiah ran a finger down the crease between her breast. "Let me ask you something, Paradise."*

*"Sassy won't let me leave, so save your breath." Though she smiled, the bitterness in her tone was the tell all.*

*Messiah watched her nipples imprint her nightie. His touch was manipulative! Ignoring her, he massaged her flesh, "On a cold winters night, if a man offered you a full length mink, or a lay by a roaring fire aside his fireplace, which would you choose?"*

*Paradise's eyes drifted shut as she stifled a moan, "A lay by a roaring—"*

*Spisssh! The cool splash of whipped cream painted her face. Paradise went rigid as her eyes shot open in shock, "Wha—what the hell?"*

*"Bitch, wrong answer!"*

*"But, the—"*

*Spissh! Messiah sprayed her again. "Bimbo, a lay by a roaring fire will only keep you warm for a night, but what about tomorrow? So, you'd rather a warm night and a wet pussy than an asset!" Messiah growled, his vibe suddenly menacing. And without warning, he threw the cherry at her face. It stuck to the whip cream and made her face look like a pretty cupcake. "Hoe, "that's" what I'm telling you. Sassy is merely a privileged lame, and all a lame can teach another lame, is how to be lame!" He spat before turning and heading for the door. With his back to her, Paradise never saw Messiah's dick surge to life, but before he made his exit, he pimped hard. "If you woulda chose the mink coat, at least when the nigga puts you out in the cold, you can stay warm. And after the season ends, you can survive off the bankroll you get from selling it!"*

*"But you said a cold "night"!"*

*"Bitch, have you ever felt a cold night in the summer? I was speaking of the winter. See, a boss bitch you'll never be, cause you fear yourself more than you do Sassy's wrath! I just realized it." He shook his head before opening the door.*

*"Messiah," Paradise called to him, and...*

# Chapter 3

*Next Morning*

*The cool breeze wafting through the room aroused him from his slumber, and when his eyes cracked open, Messiah had to remind himself that after his convo with Paradise, he'd returned to slay Sassy's vagina before succumbing to the arms of sleep. Sitting up in the bed, the morning light filled the room and drew his vision to the open doh le doors leading out to the terrace. It was there he found Sassy, sitting pretty in a champagne hued, sheer negligée. Before her was a small table, set with fruits, eggs over easy, pitchers of coffee and juice, and strangely, a thick stack of money.*

*"He's aliiiive!" Sassy mimicked Frankenstein, before taking a feminine sip from her coffee cup. Messiah slipped out the bed and into his fatigues before making his way to the terrace. "Nice doin' bidness, lady, but—"*

*"Have a seat, Messiah, you can use a bit of protein to replace what you lose." She smiled with a nod toward an empty seat.*

*"I'm Versace on the breakfast, mama, and—"*

*"Messiah," Again, she interrupted, but it was callousness in her gaze that froze him. "What I have to tell you, you may have a seat for," she spoke before taking another sip, and it was something in her tone that made him comply.*

*"Sup, lady, pimpin' don't sleep, so I have to get my girls back to—"*

""My" girls, sir." Sassy's tone held an edge, and Messiah's astonishment. Two beauties stepped out the terrace. Though he hadn't heard them enter the room, the .38 special they aimed let him know "that" was the least of his worries!

"See, last night while we fornicated, a few of my girls engaged in yours with a little girl talk." Sassy smiled, and Messiah's heart dropped. It was a moment of de'ja vu; a revisit of Pimpin knockin' him a few years back. His vision recaptured the two women, one redbone with green eyes, and the other white with baby blues.

"Bitch, what you yappin' 'bout, and why you got these hoes out here on the extracurricular?" Messiah's inquisition was rhetorical, and they both knew it.

"I told you my pussy is a thief, but while you "assumed" I was speaking about what's between "my" legs, I was referring to all these pretty bitches I've groomed here." She nodded toward the two felines. "Femme fatales, baby, you familiar with the term?" Her words set both women into action.

"Fuck?" Messiah flinched when the redbone placed the tool to the side of his head and the Caucasian went to her knees before him. Messiah mugged her, on the verge of getting physical, but...

"Don't be silly, Messiah. Tracy and Stacy are sex symbols, but there is more blood on their hands than a doctor in surgery." Sassy warned, and the gorgeous snow bunny smiled up at him mischievously. When the barrel of the .38 kissed his crotch, he went rigid.

"Say, Sassy, what kinda shit you on!" He growled as the snow freed his flaccidness and began to lick and suck him.

Sassy shrugged before taking another sip of her cup. "Relax, honey, the guns are cautionary, and the head?" She shrugged, "It's a compliment." She giggled.

Though Messiah's nature rose against his will, his eyes were devious!

*Sassy ignored his menace, "When you leave here, baby, you'll leave with "one" girl versus the six you arrived with. As we speak, the other girls are receiving the house rules, and are now "my" girls."*

*Though the white woman's head bobbed feverishly in his lap, Messiah fought against pleasure—"Bitch, you just gone strong arm me for my ladies?" He growled as the pool his lap had become, became beautiful torture.*

*"Ah-uh." Sassy held up a hand. "I'm too much woman to be a brute! We're in the same business, love, and as you know, the game is by choice and never forced." She smirked. "See, M, most men's greatest mistakes are exposing women to the levels of the game they haven't reached yet. She waved a sweeping hand of the view of her thirty acre property. Just below them, shimmering in the mornings light, lay a beautiful Olympian pool, encased in and surrounded by imported marble. "Every woman wants to be spoiled no matter how much a trap nigga does for her, if given the chance, she'll cut throat him to slide with the plug."*

*Her truths were absolute, and Messiah flinched. Not only from the smack of the truths, but mostly from the demon surging from his nuts. He gritted his teeth at Sassy. Sassy smiled as she rested her cup and went for a vibe of green grapes. Human nature is stronger than human will, so even though Messiah willed himself not to relinquish his demon to that paled skinned woman, his body nature, silenced will as the lady licked and stroked him. Sassy savored a grape as Messiah fought the war. Will waved the white flag as nature broke through the front lines, and the whole woman popped him free just as that demon burst from his pisshole.*

*"Arrrrgh!" Messiah growled, body spasming as lady milked him. When it was over, his seed stained his lap and he knew he'd one day kill the bitch across from him. Fuck it! He finally concluded before pushing the white woman away and shooting to his feet.*

*"Bitch, I'm done playin' these lil black widow games. This ain't how it go. You gorilla'd my hoes and—"*
*"You're wrong, daddy," the redbone finally spoke and Messiah glared.*
*"That's their choosin' fees. Sassy doesn't "force" any of us to stay, you got knocked fair and square." The pretty bitch nodded to the money on the table, and it was then Messiah knew he'd copped, didn't lock, and so he blew his entire stable in Oakland, California. And to the surprise of his violators, he burst into laughter, all the while Black's past gem playing within his mental.*

"Tame that bitch in you, lil daddy. Every man has her somewhere in him. That bitch is your emotions! Envy, jealousy, and hate are bitch traits, Messiah! When Pimpin' knocked you for ya hoes, you should shared one of them ole cigars with him and congratulated him for takin them snake bitches off ya hands!" She'd jeweled.

*And with that, Messiah reclaimed his seat, before taking a plate of eggs and Turkey bacon. Dick still on display, he'd looked to the red bone, "That tool is too ugly to be grasped by someone so jazzy; how about you lose it and let me see if ya lips as skillful as the Caucasian persuasion's." He vibed before biting a piece of bacon. "For the road?" He chuckled, and the girl glanced to Sassy, whom stared at the man with respect. Sucking another grape between her full lips, she nodded her consent without breaking her gaze with Messiah. The redbone went to her knees and didn't waste time showing her work, and this time, Messiah sat back in his seat, real pimpish.*

*"Thank you." He told Sassy, and she frowned, confused.*
*"For?"*

*"For clearing my schedule, baby. The freaks you knocked for, sho nuff compliments you better than they did me, but never forget, love, either we cop, lock, or blow, but by no means do we sweat no hoe." He jazzed before resting his plate on the table and grabbing the pitcher of orange juice.*

*Taking a big gulp, he smirked. "Fair exchange ain't no robbery, and it's time to make my exit." He jazzed before dumping the pitcher onto the head of the lady that was topping him.*

\*\*\*

*In Dallas, two hours ahead of California's time, a crime scene was being taped off in the Butta Beans Apartments.*
*"Oh my Godddd, Nooo!" Tweety's hands flew to her mouth when the first body bag was carried out. The hood was out on that early morning. They'd just lost a real one.*
*"Come here, chile, come—here. Ms. Betty pulled her into her arms, troubled waters dipping from her own eyes, and in the midst, a burgundy road master screeched to a stop.*
*All eyes shot to him when Sunjay jumped out, eyes wild in panic. He'd been out all night and didn't know in his absence, Satan had come to visit.*
*"Fuck is—" He began until his vision captured the taped off apartment. Officers were in and out, but as if in slow motion, Sunjay's eyes drifted to the meat wagon. His heart pounded as his mind did a funny trick.*
"Nigga, you're gonna get him killed. You gotta give a fuck bout somebody, Sunjay!" Messiah told him. *And with those words, Sunjay's mental unfroze as the second body bag was carried out.*
*"Msssa. Bet—tyyyy, th—that's my ba—by brotha! They killed Zetti!" Tweety's cries was like voodoo to Sunjay's feet, and he rushed over, fighting past officers attempting to stop him, until he was standing over the body bag.*
*"Hey, son, you can't—hey!" An officer tried when Sunjay went to unzip the bag. Gripping Sunjay's arm, the man was firm. "This is a crime scene, are you immediate family of—"*
*"Get yo hands off me, pussy!" Sunjay slapped the man's hand away, and impulsively, the officer went for his weapon. Sunjay's eyes went black and mindlessly went for his own.*

*"Hey!"* Someone demanded before stepping into the storm. *"Hells going on here?"* Detective Spinx demanded. *He'd watched it all unfold.*

*"This scum is taunting a crime scene!"* The officer demanded, but Sunjay's eyes were trained on Spinx. The detective glared back, and with a serpentine smirk, he nodded to the other officer.

*"He's okay, Burt. This is "his" place, right, Sunjay Carter?"*

*"Hey, can we go now? This stuff isn't weightless, ya know?"* The coroner complained, and Sunjay turned back to his business. In his mind, the zipper came down in slow motion, and when his eyes met the wide open ones of Zetti's, a whimper slipped from his lips.

*"Uh."*

Before anyone could stop him, he'd yanked the zipper down midway, and went to pull Zetti out the bag. *"Get up, lil nigga, quit playin!"* He cried, his eyes becoming a gangsta's baptism. Spinx and the other officer restrained him as the coroners rezips the bag and hauled the fallen soldier off. *"He can't breathe in there, naw, nigga, naw"* ...Sunjay gave the world his pain, and Ms. Betty found her way to him.

*"Sunny, baby."* Her voice stole the energy from him, and Sunjay went slack. The officers released him, and to his knees he went. Gazing up at Ms. Betty from waterfalls for eyes, Sunjay spread his arms wide as if he'd fly away. *"See, Granny, God don't give a fuck bout us! Why he take Zetti, mama? Huh?"* He screamed so loud, spittle flew, and his voice echoed, and glancing up to the heavens. Sunjay let God see his tears.

***

Sassy stood surrounded by ladies, four of which she'd knocked from him, and as Messiah was making his exit. *"Hey, wait!"* Paradise screamed as she ran down the stairs, *lugging a small bag. Everyone glanced up curiously and Messiah paused in the threshold. Once at floor level, the beauty glanced from Messiah to Sassy before making her way over to the mistress of the house. Giving Sassy an unsure smirk, she leaned a placed a gentle kiss on her lips, "Sas, you've been good to me, but I—"*

*"Save it, bitch." Sassy flatlined her convo with a disgusted look. "Just a taste of some good dick and you're ready to switch sides." She shook her head. "That's a no, though, cause—"*

*"Well, love," Messiah intervened before turning and pulling something from his pockets. Assuming a weapon, Tracy, the redbone with the orange juice still dripping from her hair, stepped forward aiming her retribution. Yet, Messiah held up a thick knot of Ben Franks to dispel her intent. "That means, this choosing fee she gave me last night means nothing, which in turn means them lil cho-cho's you got from mine is just as meaningless? Or are your goals really captives trapped within a beautiful display of communism." He waved a hand toward the trappings of the house, and all eyes went to Sassy. She knew as well as he did, that Messiah's word play was manipulative. If she "forced" Paradise to stay against her will, it wouldn't do good for the other girls, cause prisoner whores don't hoe with the same enthusiasm as satisfied ones. And to add to the pressure, Yellow Shoe made his way down from the room he'd rested his pimpin' in. And oblivious, he stared in confusion at the standoff.*

*"What's the haps?" He inquired after descending the stairs. By that time, The Honey Spot was coming to life around them. Pimps, hoes, and tricks exited the rooms they'd used to sin the night before.*

*"Ain't shit, P, me and Sassy was just keepin it "P" and laughin' at swappin' hoes like we do clothes, ya dig." Messiah chuckled, knowing Sassy couldn't refute, or she'd fuck up her name in the game. Stuffing the bankroll back into*

*his pocket before tightening his clutch on the duffel bag he held, Messiah nodded toward Paradise. "Again, we either cop, lock, or blow, but we damn sho' don't sweat no hoe!" He reiterated his earlier sentiments. Sassy laughed bitterly, knowing with pimps and hoes, as an audience, it would be a sin not to show sportsmanship for the game. Though she smiled when she nodded her agreement, anyone that knew the feeling of blowing a bonafide hoe could see her facade. Then, a shocked expression fell over her face.*

*"I felt you leave last night, Messiah, butt naked. I didn't think you'd go too far." She laughed in amazement, before to everyone's surprise, she cupped Paradise's face, and pulled her in for a soft kiss. After she pushed lady towards Messiah, and though Tracy hated it, she lowered the gun nonetheless.*

*"What the," Yellow Shoe mumbled in shock as his vision bounced from them to the stuffed duffle in Messiah's clutch. Messiah turned to vamoose, but...*

*"Messiah?" Sassy called, and he paused, glancing at her from over his shoulder. Sassy nodded to Liz, a fresh out the womb bimbo Messiah had barely knocked before blowing her to the Honey Spot. "I told you you could keep "one", and—"*

*"Hoe", Messiah spat with a glare at Liz. He shook his head in disappointment. Bringing a newborn hoe to a den infested with soul snatchers, was a rookie move that he knew the game was spanking his ass for. Popping his collar, Messiah waved her off. "Hoe, you give freebies to kiddies, and my "P" been outta Huggies since the game showed me it can never love me. So save your gift pack for a new Jack, and "you" keep the hoe, treat the hoe, but please know not to get sweet on the hoe, cause if she's ever outta pocket, I'mma seek the hoe!" He jazzed before he and Paradise made their exit.*

*Yellow Shoe was too seasoned to look awestruck, but his expression read: "Aw Fuck!" To see junior pimp knock a seasoned madame he himself had been trying to knock for ages was funky! Sassy frowned in suspicion.*

*"Tracy?" She called, and the redbone paused drying her hair. "Where's the new dames, Tutts and Liberty?" Sassy inquired and Tracy's vision found Stacy, the snow bunny who shrugged.*

*"Last I seen them, both were escorting dates upstairs," she said, and Sassy's vision found Yellow Shoe.*

*"Tutts? Liberty? Messiah's freaks?" He asked, baffled.*

*""My" freaks," Sassy corrected before turning her attention to her girls. "Y'all go check on them," she ordered, and once they went to do her bidding, she shook her head. "You pimp niggas always tryin' a bitch."*

*Yellow Shoe chuckled. "A bitch was created for a pimp to try, cause if he didn't, hoin' would be obsolete and pimpin' would be incomplete."*

*"Nigga, hoes makes the pimp, and...*

*"Sassy! Sassy, come quick, it's some shit in the game!" Stacy shouted, appearing at the top of the stairs. Sassy's vision ricocheted from Yellow Shoe to her.*

*"Hell you talking about?" She demanded, and when Stacy held up a pill bottle, Sassy and Shoe starred baffled, never expecting what they'd find up those stairs!*

***

*It didn't take long for the Benz and Jag to valet at the National Lodge on 17th and International. The hotel was known for rampant prostitution, and when Messiah slipped from behind the wheel of the Benz, and motioned for Paradise to exit the Jag, she glanced around disgustedly. Sassy's opulence had spoiled her and she wrinkled her nose at the sight of the cheap motel.*

*"Surely, we're not staying in this dump?"*

*Messiah's vision digested her. Five-ten in height with long dark hair, and a body of curves, lady was a masterpiece!*

*Outside of the pale green mini she wore, the only things she'd packed were what meant most to her, and Messiah knew he'd have to introduce her to real pimpin' to break through her pacified ways. Yet, that would come later. Sticking the key into the trunk's lock, he smirked mischievously.*

*"Unlock the trunk of the Jag," he ordered.*

*"And bitch, we'll stay where "I" see fit, and if you ain't with it, then you'll get dismissed!" He jived before opening the trunk, and what Paradise saw, blew her wig back!*

\*\*\*

*"Bawhaha!" Yellow Shoe's laughter echoed throughout the room. He laughed so hard, tears ran down his face.*

*"Trazodone?" Sassy read the inscription on the pill bottle.*

*"An antidepressant, Sassy, that puts you in a dead sleep!"*

*Tracy shook her head as her eyes went to the man laying ass up in the bed, with his trousers down to his ankles. The window was open, and a mass of knotted sheets hung from its ledge.*

*"Sassy, you gotta see," Stacy barged into the room, but pulled up short when she spotted the sleeping trick.*

*Sassy, seeing the look on the girls face, shook her head in shame.*

*"Let me guess, Trazodone?" She summarized, but Stacy shook her head.*

*"No." She held up a water bottle and a small eye drop bottle. "Visine!" She revealed, and Sassy knew in another one of her rooms, a stranger lay asleep with his pants down.*

*"Bawhaha!" Yellow Shoe couldn't tame his laughter.*

\*\*\*

*Damn, bitch, you need driving lessons. You damned near killed me!"* Tutts rolled her eyes as she climbed out the trunk of the Jag. *Paradise's eyes were buck in shock.*

See, when Messiah had arrived at Sassy's place, the reason they'd popped the trunks were for the short con Messiah concocted. Liberty climbed out the trunk of the Benz.

*"Damn, Daddy, I almost suffocated in there!"* She complained while rubbing the wrinkles from her dress. Messiah wrapped his arm around her waist before beckoning for Liberty to slip into his other one, and he kissed both their foreheads.

*"You hoes are special talents."*

*"Daddy, I didn't know eyes drops would put a nigga to sleep until you put me on game. Hell, I wasn't sure that three drops would work, so I used half a bottle!"* Tutts admitted, and Messiah shook his head before bursting into laughter.

*"Tutts, you just killed a man just to sneak out a window!"* He informed her.

# Chapter 4

*Evening had set in and Justice had sat with her feet tucked beneath her on her sofa as she studied for tomorrow's exam. Since she started at SMU, she hadn't been able to get out much, but making her family proud would compensate for it.*

*"I hate Sociology!" She mumbled just as a loud knock made her flinch in surprise. Her eyes shot to the door before falling to the tight tank top and silk, high cut out shorts she wore. "Who is it?" She called as she rested her text book on the coffee table. Rather than answering, her visitor knocked again, this time more urgently. "Hold on, dang!" She called before slipping from the couch and making her way to the door. After a peek through the peephole, she flung the door open.*

*"Why they hell you banging on my door, Sunjay, you—" She was reading his rights before registering something amiss. "Sunjay?" Her expression was etched in worry. "What—"*

*"They took Lil Bro, Jus. Nigga ain't even make it out high school, and he dead! It's—it's my fault, tho." Water rolled over his lids and spilt down his face. Sunjay look like a madman! From his wild shag haircut, wrinkled Coogi shirt and down to the "sticky" splotch on his tan Coogi pants. And that's when Justice noticed his hands. In one, he clutched a bloody machete, and in the other was a leaking paper bag. Justice's eyes fell to the concrete below and when she registered the blood drops, her vision shot back up to Sunjay.*

*"Nigga, have you lost yo'"* —

*"My fault, Jus, I'm trippin, huh—"* He cut her off with a twisted laugh. Since she'd been back, their bond had grown thick, yet this was a side of Sunjay she always knew existed, but never got acquainted with. *"Sunjay Carter, what the hell?"* She treaded, but Sunjay ignored her and brushed passed her as he entered the apartment. Justice's eyes fell to the blood staining the concrete and knew Sunjay had just brought something dark into their world.

*** 

Though nowhere the size of Sassy's domain, Messiah's dwelling was still something to talk about. Two stories, red dirt brick, with Terra Cotta roofing. It was a four bedroom, honeycomb hideout! And as the sun traded places with the moon, four deep within the master room, the vibe was ceremonious. Lights off, and besides the glow of night from the curtainless sliding glass door that opened out into his backyard, nothing but the flickering flames of twenty candles disturbed the darkness. Messiah stood over his kneeling three women in nothing but his skin and jewels. They'd showered and had taken turns oiling each other, and as their bodies glistened beneath the glow of the candles flames, all three bodies craved becoming slaves to the sweet love of Messiah's ways.

A soft cloud of Kush smoke hovered around his face as he sucked the soul from the blunt between his lips, and after taking one last toke of the granddaddy, he made his way to the dresser and rested the half smoked cigar into an ash tray.

*"I blew my entire stable cause I know you hoes able,"* he spoke over lungs filled with smoke, before retrieving his golden goblet and the bottle of Crystal he'd placed there for that exact moment. After pouring a generous amount, he turned to face his ladies, and with a exhale of tainted smoke,

*he found himself back before them. Taking a sip from the cup, beneath the glow of dancing flames, he then lowered it before dipping his dick inside its golden interior. "On this night, I bring a new wife of the game into our folds, and in the names of all great pimps and hoes whom names are now in the scrolls, she must pledge to be the best hoe she can be! Yet, before her pledge, she must be blessed by my bottoms so there can never be a crack in my foundation. So," he ruled before gripping his Johnson and stepping closer to the first woman. Liberty, Tutts, and Paradise gazed up at him but it was Liberty whom he addressed. "If you take this woman to be your wife-n-law, without the jealousies of an average bitch, partake of the weakness of my nature and give me life," Messiah offered, and with a scrutinizing gander at Paradise. Liberty nodded before taking Messiah's flesh into her warm hand and lifting his flaccidness to her lips.*

*"I do, daddy," she murmured before downing him. Suckling his nature, it didn't take long for him to swell, and only after the taste of champagne was gone did, she free him. Again, Messiah dipped himself into the Crystal before stepping before Tutts.*

*"Partake of me if you accept, or deny me if you deny her."*

*Tutts didn't think twice before taking his masculinity by its base, and slowly inch by inch, sucked the liquid from him. Liberating him, she smiled. "I'll never deny you, daddy, so I can't deny her."*

*And with that, Messiah pointed his dick in Paradise's direction, "You've been christened by the stable, now I must ask you, do you bow to suck, fuck and slut out to make a playa rich? I"*

*Before he could complete his spiel, Paradise's mouth was filled with his flesh. She'd swallowed him whole and Messiah gazed down at her as she massaged his nuts, all the while nodding his answer.*

*"Damn, bitch, slow down before you choke!" Tutts burst into laughter, and though Liberty joined, Paradise sucked*

*without breaking eye contact with whom she'd just pledged her hoing.*

*\*\*\**

*And just like he said, I got Zetti killed, Jus."* Sunjay *concluded his tale. He'd given her his regrets, told her how he'd loved Lil Zetti and saw so much of himself in the boy. He'd told her how he'd always wanted a little bro to invest in. He'd told her how Messiah had prophesied of this exact conclusion. He'd even told her how they'd caught C-Bo down bad, and snatched him up at the Jack in the Box, and in the end, Justice had done the craziest shit one can do when dealing with an emotional rollercoaster; she'd brought liquor into the equation. Her and Sunjay sat on opposite ends of the sofa, him on his fourth glass of Alize, and her nursing her first. Yet, both their visions were fixated on the same focal point, the soggy bag Sunjay had rested on the table. Blood had soaked through and puddled beneath it.*

*"The great Messiah."* Sunjay *chuckled bitterly, and though she detected the envy in his words, Justice was just happy he'd left the long knife at the door. "Everybody's favorite. Messiah's so smart! Messiah's so playa. Messiah, Messiah! But what about me, Justice. Why nobody give a fuck bout Sunjay?"*

*Fresh tears flooded his eyes, and seeing him broken, touched her spirit. She sat her glass on the table before turning to him and, "I care about you, Sunjay." She reached over and cupped his face, and Sunjay's eyes took her in. At five-four in height, Justice was thick like Nicki. Cinnamon skin tone, with kinky hair; the girl was righteous work! His eyes fell to how her breast squeezed inside her muscle shirt, before reflecting on how her short shorts hugged her thighs and his dick swelled.*

*"Porsha cares about you. Dream does too. She was saying when treason was committed.* Before she knew, Sunjay had leaned forward and kissed her.

*"Sun—"she tried,* but his next kiss was a bit of tongue, and then the liquor spoke! She kissed him back.

\*\*\*

*Their bodies perspired as they freaked. Within that candlelit room, upon a bed Messiah had spread a quarter million dollars upon, their love sounds serenades the vibe.*

*"Mmmmahhh!"* Liberty moaned as she rode Tutts face. Gyrating her femininity on her wife-in-law's lips, her juices dropped down to where Tutts lay on her back with her own legs open like a Lambo. And below her, bent over with her face between Tutts thighs stood Paradise. As she sucked Tutts clit, her own pleasure surged through her as Messiah crashed that pussy from the back.

*"Umm! Umm! Ummmm!"* She cried in ecstasy as he stood behind her, delivering left strokes. The sounds of his pelvis slapping against her ass cheeks collided with the melody of sucking and moaning, and as Messiah gripped her waist and showed his work, his mental couldn't help but wonder if their juices would fuck up the money? He chuckled at the thought and sped up his pace.

*Smack... Smack...Smack...!* The sounds of her flesh against his echoed.

*"Ouuu, yas-sss, daddy, righ-t therrrre!"* Paradise spoke over a mouthful of pussy as her eyes rolled.

*"Give—me—this—cum, bitch!"* Messiah growled as his pace became savage. He was about to stain that money!

\*\*\*

*They'd stripped, and Sunjay had fell to his knees between her legs. Justice's pussy was fat! Juicy! Soaked! And as he tasted her, he never knew sumthin' could taste so good!*

*"SunJaaaay!" Justice cried.*

\*\*\*

*Messiah pulled out just in time, "Y'all come get this shit!" He growled, and all three felines hurried to the edge of the bed and he painted their faces. Tutts grabbed his strength and together, all three of them licked and sucked him until his knees buckled.*

\*\*\*

*Sunjay mounted her and had her legs spread wide. Justice allowed him to enter. His dick was a beautiful pain that she took like a big girl. He stroked deep, and she wrapped her legs around his waist.*

*"Damn, man, Justice, this pussy fire!" He gritted, pumping maniacally as they stared into each other eyes. Yet, even as pleasure high teens, Sunjay knew something was off.*

*"Sunjay? Sunjay? Boy, why yuh look like that?" Her question did something funny to him, and Sunjay snapped back to reality to find Justice still cupping his face. His eyes were wild as he realized their clothes were still on and it was all a trick of the liquor, but nonetheless, he leaned forward to make that fantasy official.*

*"Nigga, fuck?" Justice reared back in surprise, and as if finally realizing what he was doing, Sunjay shot to his feet.*

*"Man, Justice, I'm trippin', fam. My fault! It's just— just."*

*"You good, Sunjay, but I think it's best you leave." Justice climbed to her feet, cursing herself for giving him the liquor.*

*Running his hands down his face, Sunjay shook his head in embarrassment.*

*"No doubt, i'on even know why I'm here, fam. I—"*

*"Stop!" Justice held up a hand. "Sunjay, you like a brother to me, nigga. You can come by when you please, but tonight, you just need some rest."*

*Sunjay studied her with a crooked smile, "You still love him, huh?" He asked.*

*"Who?"*

*"Messiah, girl, quit frontin', you know who!" He laughed, but without having to think.*

*Justice nodded. "Yes, I do, but destiny may not favor our union," she revealed and the sadness in her tone was evident.*

*Sunjay pulled her in for a hug. "One thing I've learned, sis—" he began when they my separated, and Justice lifted a brow in question. Sunjay turned for the door, but paused, "You can't ever count that boy out! Ghoul ain't mean none of that shit I said about bro. One thang I've learned about Messiah is, he always ends up with a winning hand." He chuckled before opening the door.*

*"Sunjay?" Justice called him, and when he turnt to her, she nodded at the soaked sack on her table, "Ain't you forgetting something?"*

*"Oh snap, my fault, ma!" He laughed before retrieving the bag, but when he lifted it, the bottom fell out and C-Bo's head plopped back into the puddle it had made.*

*"Oops!" Sunjay's eyes grew wide, and Justice fainted.*

# Chapter 5

*They night was starless in Oakland, but the moon ruled like Nefertiti. A flock of bats flew over the gorgeous two-story Victorian, and within its main room, the twentieth and last candle winked out; leaving a black, snaking wisp of smoke in its wake. Messiah's night had been erotic and had rocked him to sleep like a baby, and maybe that's why he hadn't sensed evil slip into his home and commit sins only Satan could be proud of.*

*Yet, when he felt Liberty, whom had fallen asleep beside him, roll over in the bed, he subconsciously wrapped his arm around her wrist and pulled her to him. "You good?" He mumbled, before moving to kiss the back of her neck. His dick was throbbing for something wet, just not the type of wet that he found! While in the midst of reaching down to play with her kitty, the distinct smell of blood assaulted his nostrils, just as his lips and chin met something sticky and wet.*

*"Fuck?" He growled as his eyes shot open, and with the grayish light of night, spilling in through the glass doors of his patio, his eyes captured wickedness!*

*"Arrrugh!" He screamed as he shoved Liberty's headless corpse away and went for the thunder he kept on the night table, but when he came up empty, he knew he'd been caught with his pants down. Literally!*

*"Lookin for this?" A harsh voice snatched his attention toward the front of the missive room and Messiah gulped*

*audibly! A stranger draped in all black, stood clutching and admiring Messiah's gun with a wicked smirk on his face. "Forty calibers are beautiful guns, but their accuracy is a bit off; besides," He chuckled as his vision captured Messiah. "What good can it do you resting it where a killer can sneak in and disarm you in the wee hours of the night?" His teeth seemed to glow with his smile and recklessly, Messiah shot out the bed. Blood was everywhere, but being a stepper, the sustenance meant nothing! Yet, what the man held in his hand other hand, fucked up Messiah's pimpin! With her long tresses twisted around the strangers gloved fingers, her severed head dangled by his leg like a wallet chain.*

*"What the—" Messiah mumbled as his eyes went wild. When he'd fallen asleep, there were three women, but he woke up to a headless one! Seeing the question in his searching eyes, the killer shook his head sadly.*

*"Dead; all of them, but if there's any solace, they went quick."*

*His admission caused Messiah's vision to return to Liberty's face, frozen in a peaceful death mask. The killers low laughter was sickening.*

*"Rope saw," he whispered, and Messiah's vision lifted to him. "Very sharp bladed. A carbon steel chain that's really a chain saw without a motor," the man educated, and when he took aim at him, Messiah knew he wouldn't see the sun.*

*"Fuck are you?" Messiah spat as his vision drifted to Liberty's cold body. They'd all fallen asleep atop the money, and her blood had pasted many of the bills to her flesh.*

*"Me?" The man chuckled. "I'm the purged Messiah, and I was sent to execute you for angering a very powerful client."*

*Messiah's eyes shot to him. He'd done plenty within the game and though he could name many who'd want him dead. His gut spoke. "Sassy?"*

*The man smirked, and for the first time, Messiah registered though he clearly was a black man, his skin was so fair, he could pass for Latin.*

*"Maybe, but that's not the discussion for this day, "Pimp" The purge emphasized the word with soft laughter, and hope was born.*

*"This day?" Messiah asked shocked.*

*The man nodded, his eyes deadly as if considering his choice.*

*"Why?" Messiah didn't understand "why" a maskless man would allow his prey to come back as a predator.*

*The purge noted it and chuckled evilly, "Why would a man ask why God has blessed him?"*

*Messiah shrugged. God ain't ever gave a fuck 'bout me before, so when he finally tries, I wonder if he's toying with his food."*

*"God never toys, and when he sends the reaper, it's seldom one escapes his arrival. Yet—" The purge popped the clip out of the .40 before ejecting the slug from the head, and tossing the tool behind him. "Tell your friend Yellow Shoe we're even now." He chuckled. "You have to depart from this city, sir, never to return. By this night, leave Oakland behind you, or our next meeting won't be so cordial." He nodded before turning to leave.*

*"Say," Messiah called, and dude paused. "How you know I just won't relocate and come for yo' head?"*

*The purge laughed before disappearing into the night.*

# Chapter 6

*Three Weeks Later*

♫ *Slip on that red dress/ and put on your high heels/ some of that sweet perfume—it sure smells good—on—you/ slide on your lipstick, and let your hair down/ cause baby when you get through* ♫

*"Sang it, Johnny, you betta sang it, with yo' fine ass!" Black Diamond shouted as the music played from her stereo. Dressed in black silk pajamas, and as high as an astronaut, she swayed her hips as she inspected the smothered lamb chops she was cooking. Taking a drag from the Newport 100 she held between her fingers, she felt good! Though no longer a street walker, crack cocaine was a steady companion in her life. Yet, there's a big difference between a smoker and a crack head; smokers appease their addiction without the extracurricular, whereas, crackheads will steal and sell granny's insulin for a dance with the devil.*

*Before he left, Messiah made her promise to give up if not both, then one of her demons, and hoin was less addictive, so here she was! She'd even gotten a job at the post office, but with all bills being paid on the house he'd left her, and Pimpin' Maxwell taking her grocery shopping every two weeks with the mula Messiah left him for her, the occupation was merely for hobby. Black stayed to herself, and that's why when the doorbell rang, suspicion oozed in her bones. No one visited because only a few knew of the house. So, when Black made her way to the living room, a moment of deja vu enveloped her. Blow's sins remembered! She silently slipped a small .380 from beneath the cushion before making her way to the door, but after a peep through the peephole, she relaxed. And with a smile, she took a long drag from her cigarette; she'd been expecting the visitor.*

\*\*\*

*The morning was chilly, and reclined in the driver's seat of his jet black, 1966 Impala SS, that squatted on twenty three inch chrome Ds, Sunjay let the car's heat blow against the black and red velour, Fila unit he wore. Mr Lucci's, "Have You Ever", rumbled low in the trunk as he and Murda awaited their extorter. Sunjay waved off the blunt Murda tried to pass before tilting the bag of chili cheese Fritos to his mouth. 6:45 in the AM, the only South Dallasians lurking were the ever present fiends and a few early birds chasing their worms. Sitting crooked at the back of the car wash on MLK and Atlanta, Sunjay almost choked when Murda spoke over a lungful of smoke.*

*"Messiah wacked my twin, Blood." He chuckled menacingly, and Sunjay's vision shot to him. It was his second time speaking his gut and the look in his eyes was spooky!*

*"Wha—what?" Sunjay sputtered.*

*"Nigga, don't play like you unaware. I know you was the devil's advocate, cause of that shit that went down with Ms. Betty," Murda spat, his hand instinctively falling by his waist.*

*"You gonna smoke me, Murda?" Sunjay tool lay across his lap, and they both knew he had the ups.*

*Murda hit the blunt. "I'on give a fuck bout his bitch, but my twin? My granny? It's blood on that, Blood," he swore, ignoring the question.*

*"You threatening me, dawg?"*

*Murda's smile said, Gangsta's get their kick back! Sunjay shook his head contemplating doming family, but in the end, he fell back.*

*"Bam violated, Blood. That boy been having snake eyes ever since I came up, and you know it, but love makes niggas accept hoe shit from their people as long as it's not done to them!" He seethed. "You think his and Ms. Dorothy's blood on my hands?" He asked before filling his mouth with more chips, and just when Murda was answering, a black Crown Victoria pulled beside them. Chewing, Sunjay eyed the driver contemptuously, and Detective Spinx smiled before his window slid down. While letting his window down, Sunjay replaced the chips with his fire, and the detectives smile melted when the gun was trained at his top.*

*"Boo!" Sunjay taunted before retracting his aim and smiling wickedly.*

*Spinx spat out the window, glaring threateningly. "Let me get my dust, lil nigga."*

*Sunjay chuckled before Murda handed him a bundle of thirty bands, and in return, he tossed it to the rotten detective.*

*"After this, ain't no mo', so make it last," he informed, and the detective held the money beneath his nose and took a deep wiff.*

*"Ahhh, smells like success!" He laughed before handing it to his sidekick, McHenry, whom smiled from the passenger's seat.*

*"Listen here you lil punk, this shit don't stop until I say so, and if you try to get slick," Spinx chuckled, leaving his conclusion to deduced.*

*♬ Ouuu have you ever/ have you ever balled, wit' a playa of ya dreams/ ouuu have you ever/ have you ever, balled...til you falled— ♬*

*Sunjay's response was to unmute his bass and let Lucci talk his talk before his window eased up and the 23's twinkled with his departure.*

\*\*\*

*Cakes was a piss hued bitch, standing five six, with boomerang hips that switched to catch the eyes of the tricks. On that winter's day, as she sashayed in the midst of the hoes and pimps, she was being observed by a fella slick with his words. Cakes was a rouge hoe, and as beautiful as poetry in motion, "but" that's what made her strut down 22nd and Greenfield dangerous. In "The Mill", hoing was the main thing going, and though Wisconsin's Eastern district attorney aimed to shut it down, pussy's demand calls to the dicks of man, until he caters to supply and demand! And clad in a white tube dress and knee high white boots, Cakes did just that.*

*"Cakes, I see you still footin' it, when you pose to be a passenger slidin' in something pretty, with a playa that knows how to sell kitty! Quit standin' out in the cold, when you can be part of my fold." Fancy, a pimp from that land jazzed as he pulled alongside her.*

*Cakes rolled her eyes without giving him the decency of her gaze. "I'm selling my own kitty good enough, thank you, Fancy."*

*Fancy chuckled as he maneuvered the wheel of the teal green, 1979 Lincoln Continental. He spit his spit and talked his shit for blocks, until concluding he'd gave all he got, and after she'd made her way towards the bodega, he bade her farewell. Cakes was happy to see him go. He, like most of all the other playas from the city saw her potential and accosted her at every interval. Yet, Cakes wasn't like most prostitutes, she was soft at heart, but knew her exterior couldn't project that. She'd come to Milwaukee to run from her abusive husband, and penniless within a murderous city, she resulted* to the only job that generated income without her having to submit an application. *Hoin'!* This day, it was too cold for one to be out dressed as she was; the winters of Wisconsin were heartless! Yet, she'd rather catch pneumonia from showing too much skin, versus money passing her up for the next bitch who braved the wind. And just as Cakes was making her way down the Ave, a gray Jeep Wrangler eased to a stop beside her, and when her eyes chances a glance, she knew instantly the Caucasian fella was a trick. Though she'd made a nice bankroll that day, her residencies tag hotels were far from her ambition, so she nodded, and the Jeep pulled around the corner. Neither paid much attention to the cranberry Benz pulling up not far away.

***

♫ *Every woman need her own splackavellie/a brotha she can call when her man ain't doing her right/ he can work it all night until the morning light—* ♫

The music vibrated through the car as Messiah reclined in the backseat, sipping from a cup of Yac that put him in the mood to mack! And when his vision captured the two dames in his front seats, he had to appreciate the game for having mercy on a playa. Tutts sat behind the wheel and Paradise sat jazzy in the passenger. Messiah smirked at the memory of the night "The Purge" played with his psyche. That night, after hurrying into his clothes and tossing the soiled money into a bag, he'd packed everything worth taking and was on his way out the door before faint sounds gave him pause. Gun in hand, he'd followed them to one of the other rooms, only to find both women bound, gagged, and on their stomachs, with the word, "Purge", written in blood on the wall just above them.

"I think it's time, daddy." Paradise brought him back from the reflection, and Messiah's eyes found her, before *drifting to Tutts. She glanced back at him for confirmation, and Messiah witnessed the emptiness in her gaze; she'd taken Liberty's demise the worst.*

*"You good?" He asked, and she nodded, but he knew she was lying.*

\*\*\*

*Inside the Jeep, the trick hurriedly whipped out his Johnson, and Cakes eyes fell unimpressed.*

*"You're not the police, right, daddy?" She asked.*

*Dude rolled his eyes, "Come on now, sweetie," He nodded down at his exposure." Would a cop risk an indecent exposure case?"*

*"You haven't answered me, baby."*

*The trick blew a hot breath, "No, I'm not a cop, okay!"*

*Cakes smiled with a lick of her lips before reaching over and bringing him to erection with a vulgar massage. "Good, now what are you getting into, baby?" She purred.*

*The man groaned appreciatively as she manipulated his flesh. "Put those pretty lips on it, babe; just—wha what's wrong?" He sputtered when Cakes retracted her touch.*

*"Fifty measly bucks for my lips, daddy."*

*"Fifty dollars? For some head?"*

*"No, for me to suck yo' big dick until you erupt in my mouth, and I'll swallow for free!" She bit her lip.*

*"Thirty," the man bargained.*

*Rolling her eyes, Cakes hated cheap mu'fuckas! Tricks came to strolls asking for discounts like they had prostitution coupons! "Forty-five, baby, or I walk."*

*"Forty-five friggin bucks? Geesh!" He complained, dick throbbing. "Okay, cool, now let's see if you're worth it." He relented, but Cakes held out her hand.*

*"Money first."*

*"What? No, that's now how this works. I'm not gonna pay until—"*

*Before he completed his rant, Cakes was already reaching for the door. And that's when shit got funky!*

*"Bitch, you're not gonna tease me and just leave!" The man spat before snatching her by the arm, and just when Cakes was going for the cutter she kept in her boot. Smack! The back hand dazed her and the crazed trick grabbed a fist full of her hair. "Whore, you're gonna suck my cock first!" He roared before ripping the top of her dress, and making her breast spill out. Yet, Swish! The sound of a swinging razor cut through the air before a long split spit blood from his shoulder. He quickly released Cakes and spun to face the cutter.*

*"Get off of her, you sick trick!" Tutts shouted, tears spilling from her lids.*

*"What the—" the man spat and dodged as she went for another slice. Instantaneously, the passenger's door was yanked open and to Cakes' surprise, a beautiful Mulatto woman was there.*

*"Hurry before he recovers!" Paradise urged and as Cakes heeded the warning. The trick had gone for his own weapon. Before Tutts knew it, a .44 Bulldog was aimed at her face.*

*"Get the hell away from me, freak, before—" He was saying when the kiss of a barrel of a gun pecked his temple.*

*"Don't roll the dice, cause man isn't meant to live twice." Messiah had snuck in through the passenger's side. "Hand me that gun, white boy, and don't get slick cause this bitch has a sensitive clit!" He threatened, and after disarming the man, he addressed the women. "Y'all go to the car."*

*"What about her?" Paradise asked.*

*Messiah's eyes flickered to Cakes before recapturing the trick. "Take her with you, now go!" He demanded, and only after they'd gone, did the white man's expression of utter horror transform into one of anger.*

*"Okay, you can get the damn gun out my face now, dude!" He spat, and lowering the weapon, Messiah burst into*

*laughter. The tricks name was Mike, and though he was truly a customer of vagina, Messiah had given him a full night with Tutts and Paradise in compensation for the con they'd just ran.*

*"She fucking cut me, Messiah. That wasn't part of the deal!" He ranted while gripping his shoulder.*

*Messiah calmed, knowing Tutts had gone too far, and must've had, had flashbacks of Liberty's murder and wigged out. "Yeah, I owe you for that, Mike, and I'll give you a night with either one of my girls for the trouble."*

*Mike thought on it, lusting on the way Cakes' tits squeezed against the fabric of her dress, revived his erection. "You really think she'll go for it?" He wondered, and Messiah hurriedly turned his head.*

*"Aww, come on, Mikey, mane, get ya self together playboy!" He demanded with a wave towards dudes exposed dingaling.*

*"Oh, sorry!" The man turned pink as he fixed his clothes.*

*"Well, do ya?" He reiterated.*

*Messiah chuckled before returning his attention and aiming the gun at him.*

*"Wha?" Mike began.*

*"I never blow "before" I cop a hoe, but I need you to give me ten minutes after I'm back at my car before you leave."*

*"Huh?"*

*"Just trust me, Mikey." Messiah smirked before diverting his aim and aiming out his window.*

***

*In the backseat of the Benz, Cakes waved Paradise's hand away.*

*"I'm okay. I'm good, but who are y'all?" She asked. Paradise had dabbed at her busted lip like a concerned lover.*

*"You sure, honey?" She asked, and Cakes nodded. Paradise nodded.*

*"What were you thinking getting in that Jeep without protection!" Tutts asked.*

Cakes pulled the box cutter out her boot, *"I have some, he just lucky."*

*"That type of luck could've cost you more than some pussy, girl."*

Cakes shrugged, *"Could've, but y'all never answered my question?"*

*"Huh?"* Paradise gave her a strange look.

*"Who are y'all?"* Cakes repeated.

*"We're Messiah's girls.* Tutts answered from the driver's seat.

*"Messiah? The pimp?"* Cakes remembered the handsome man who'd just saved them. She'd been hearing a lot of the out of towner, and knew he was a strange one. Rumor had it that he only accepted particular types into his stable, and allowing her eyes to roll over Paradise's attire, she appreciated the view. In a midnight blue wrap around dress, Paradise slayed with the suede matching heels. Tutts matched her pretty with a yellow silk, one piece shirt set. Yet, it was the good necklace with diamond flooded apples around their necklaces that did it!

*"Whose your daddy?"* Tutts asked.

Cakes frowned. *"Daddy? You mean Pimp? Uh, not! I'm solo, honey. I can sell my own pussy."*

*"In an alley? With a box cutter?"* Paradise rolled her eyes with a suck of her teeth. *"Girl, palease!"*

*"Uh."* Cakes snaked her neck. *"Surely you hoes ain't turning ya noses up just cause I work solo, while y'all slave to line a niggas pockets? Why the hell would I need a pimp when—"*

Boom! The sound of the gunshot made her jump in surprise. *"What the—"*

*"That's what our daddy does when we're threatened, and we not only sleep in luxury, but our days of working the stroll are so through, but since your street walking ass still think fuckin' for crumbs in the backseat of tricks cars is worth your time. Bitch, get out!" Tutts spat.*

*And caught off guard, Cakes vision found Paradise, who crossed her arms before nodding to the door.*

*"Bye, bitch."*

*And though she hated to leave the luxury and wasn't of the Benz, Cakes rolled her eyes before slipping out. Winter's breath had no heart, and just as she slammed the door, Messiah made it to the car. Cakes' vision captured the blood stains smeared across his soft pink dress shirt and her eyes grew wide. Their eyes danced.*

*"You leaving with me or gonna chance this shit happenin again?"*

*Indecisive, Cakes stood, arms crossed over her exposed breast, as her vision fell to the chain on his neck. It was weighed down by a diamond encrusted apple; the same as his ladies except bigger!*

*"I don't need no pimp," she spat, and Messiah waved at the Benz squatting low on Lorenzo's. That, coupled with the Alaska glistening in his mouth was magic.*

*"And as you can see, I ain't in need of no hoe."*

*Cakes' eyes drifted toward the corner she'd just escaped.*

*"Is he dead?"*

*"As can be."*

*"Why you do that?"*

*"For you."*

*"You don't know me."*

*Messiah's eyes fell to his drip, and lifting the apple so she could see it's carats, he smirked. "That's" where you're wrong! See, Eve gave Adam fruit of knowledge, and so every nigga is in debt to the bitch for opening their minds to game, and since I'll never meet her, I bestow my appreciation on the next bitch that reminds me that I have Adam's apple."*

*"Huh?" Cakes was lost.*

*Messiah chuckled. "A woman's intuition is one of her most powerful gifts she can share with a man because she ate from the fruit first. Do you trust yours, ma?"*

*Cakes frowned. "Hell yeah!" She was sure, and without another word, Messiah turned and slipped into the backseat before closing the door on her. After a moment, Paradise slid out and made her way over to her.*

*"Here." She extended a shiny red apple to her. "Daddy says, at least Eve wasn't a liar like you. He says you can't trust your intuition if you find yourself in positions like this, and if you do trust it, you're just as foolish as Eve was when she accepted a piece of fruit from a snake, that cost her the entire garden of unlimited fruit!" She relayed before resting the apple on the ground at Cakes' feet. Paradise sashayed to the passenger's side and she slipped in. She shook her head in pity at the sight of Cakes rubbing her arms from the breath of Jack Frost.*

*"I'd love to have you as a wife-in-law, think big, baby." She blew a kiss before slipping into the warmth of the foreign.*

*The rear window eased down and Messiah gave her a flash of the emerald jewels dancing on his top and bottom rows of teeth.*

*"I see you're still leaving big game at your feet." He nodded at the apple. "Know what I find crazy, ma?"*

*Cakes rolled her eyes, but truth was, she was intrigued. "What, dude?" She fronted, and Messiah pulled something out his pocket she couldn't see.*

*"First, let me ask this; on this cold day, if I offered you a mink coat, or a night by a roaring fire, which would you choose?" He proposed.*

*Cakes was freezing, teeth chattering, "Can I get in and we talk about this?"*

*"Bitch, answer my question!" He growled.*

*"A stay by a roaring fire, damn! Now can I get in?"* She whined, trying to blow warm breath down her bare titties. Messiah chuckled. *"You said you don't need no pimp, well...what about a boss that can change ya life, and ensure you never end up standing titties out in 32 degree weather?"* He then looked down, and after a moment, tossed a burning hanker-chief out the window. *"You chose the roarin' fire, bitch, so warm yaself,"* he spat, and the car eased backwards.

Cakes' jaw dropped! Men were coming unglued for her to choose, but here was a nigga depreciating her beauty. *"Bitch,"* he called when the twenty threes paused in its rotation. *"I don't need no hoe like Eve, cause that hoe sinned twice! Not only did the bitch get played by a snake, but the hoe settled for a bite to eat instead of going for the tree of life! When I see you again, hoe, have that apple, and hand it to me like Eve did Adam, and I'mma give you more that the fruit of that tree gave her, and that's more game than yo' lame ass can fathom!"* He jazzed, before Tutts put her toes to the gas.

***

*"You know you hurt my baby, right?"* Black asked and Justice stared bitterly down at her hands. Sitting on her sofa, she still couldn't believe she'd went through with their visit. Porsha had informed her that Messiah was long gone, but Justice always knew how to find him. Though no one seemed to know where Black Diamond resided, Justice's ace in the hole was her father, and with JoJo being one of Pimpin's closest friends, it was nothing to get what she wanted. So, as she sat, eyeing the wax white rose she'd rested on the coffee table, she smirked at the thought of Messiah's reaction when he saw it.

*"I know ya heard me, Justice Andrea Kennedy!"* Black repeated, more authoritative. And when Justice glanced up,

*she saw the woman exit the kitchen with two plates of food. Handing one to her, Black took her seat across from her on the other sectional before crossing her long legs. Balancing her plate atop her knee, Black Diamond cut a piece of lamb with her fork before popping it in her mouth.*

*Her eyes were fixated on Justice, whose gaze fell to the fried, and smothered lamb, Velveeta mac and cheese, and buttery garlic potato wedges on her plate. "Yeah, I know Mama Ruth, but that wasn't my fault, even way back when, I never wanted to be away from Messiah, but—"*

*"Ya daddy." Black laughed and Justice eyes lifted to her.*

*"He didn't mean no harm, he just wanted to give his family a better life." She protected her hero, and Black Diamond laughed hard!*

*"What! Chile, I know you don't believe that shit ya just told me?" She asked, laughter subsiding. And when she saw the seriousness in Justice's eyes, Black smacked her lips. "Justice, you still havin' dem future dreams?"*

*Justice flinched in surprise, not many knew of her gift of the future being shown in her dreams, and though she knew Black and JoJo had come up together, she didn't think her father would reveal such a thing. She nodded her confirmation, nonetheless.*

*"Yes, Mama Ruth, but what does that have to do with why my father."*

*"Everything, silly girl!" Black Diamond jabbed her fork toward her, and suspicion bled in Justice's eyes.*

*"What are you saying, Mama Ruth?" She lifted a brow.*

*Black shook her head in pity. "Justice, ya daddy ain't never like Messiah."*

*"Huh? You're wrong, ma."*

*"Justice!" Black held up a hand. "Don't be so naive! Why you think that man knows most shit before they happen like he God or something?" She asked and a chill ran down Justice's spine, she'd "always" wondered that. "Why you think Pimpin's ass kept him so close?"*

*"I—"*

*"Girl—" Black waved her off. "JoJo's ass moved y'all away cause he and Pimpin' had a fallen out."*

*Justice began to tremble. "Wha—what?"*

*Black took another bite of her food, chewing as she studied the girl. "Jus, your father has the same gift you have. He sees the future in his dreams, and it was in those dreams where he saw my sons future."*

*Justice shot to her feet, seeming not to notice her plate as it crashed to the floor. "What de hell yuh talk bout, dats jus dotish!" Her Trinidadian grew thicker.*

*Black laughed. I'm talkin' 'bout ya pappy seein Messiah in his dreams, and knowin' my boy would grow to be HOH!"*

*"HOH?"*

*"Yes, Justice Kennedy, Hard on a Hoe!"*

# Chapter 7

*2 Weeks Later*

*The night was lit in the Triple D, and it seemed as if the entire city had turned out for Porsha's B-day bash. Club GiGi's was packed to capacity and with Trick Daddy scheduled to perform, the vibe was dumb dumb! In VIP, Porsha was surrounded by all her girls and they were on ten.*

*"Heyyy!" Porsha swayed her hips to one of Lil Kim's joints the DJ spun.*

*"Happy b-day, bitch!" Her girl Toya laughed before handing her her fourth shot of something clear. Porsha barely winced when she downed it. And though she was surely feeling herself, lady had no intent on turning down. Not too far away, Sunjay played the corner, mustering a bottle of XO.*

*"Damn, nigga, take it easy fo' you rot ya' liver!" Murda shouted over the music, but Sunjay ignored him. He was too far gone off the liquor and oxycodone pills to give any fucks about his health. Zetti's murder had rocked him, and though the police claimed the lady had strangled him before doming herself, the shit just didn't sit right with Sunjay. And seeing as though his mans didn't so much as glance his way, Murda shook his head before disappearing into the throng of party.*

*Sunjay ran the back of his hand across his mouth as he admired the way a freak on the dance floor shook her cheeks, and when the song ended, and the DJ announced the nights act, the crowd went stupid. The lights began to flicker, and*

*Trick Daddy hit the stage with the sauce of a nigga out the Pork-n-Beans bricks of Liberty City.*

*"Hoe, you don't know nann nigga, uh-uh! That'll represent like me," he rapped, gold teeth and wild hair making a statement.*

*"Nann nigga, uh-uh!" The niggas rapped along, but when the baddest bitch stepped out on the stage, the ladies lost their minds!*

*"Uh-uh, hold up, who the fuck this nigga think he is, I ain't ashamed of, nothin I do! Hold up, check this out. You don't know nann hoe, uh-uh/ don' been the places I been/ who can spend the grands that I spend/ fuck 'bout five or six best friends," Trina spit, and was echoed by the felines in the spot. And in the midst of the hype, Sunjay felt a presence slide up beside him.*

*"Sup, young blood?" Spinx leaned close to be heard. Sunjay merely tilted the bottle to his lips, bobbing his head to the music. The detective chuckled before stuffing his hands down into his pockets of his leather jacket. Ever since their first moment, Sunjay had changed his number, relocated his spots, and had been a hard man to link with. The shit left a bad taste in Spinx mouth, and Sunjay's attitude was making the taste fouler.*

*"You didn't show up to the last meet, playboy, and my boys and I need ours." The dirty cop leaned in to be heard, and just across the room, Justice was rolling her eyes at a pursuer that was feeling her fly.*

*"I'm saying, lil mama, you ain't gotta act like that. A nigga just tryin' to see bout you." He flashed her a smile. There's something cocky about Dallas niggas that radiates from their drip, and fella was no different. Clad in Coogi everything, playboy was fresh, but though Justice found him attractive, she had eyes for only one nigga. Yet, the powder blue spandex short suit that hugged for thickness, coupled with the lace up calves powder blue heels had niggas at her jugular about her attention. In the midst of it all, another bad*

bitch was generating her own groupie hype. The crowd parted as Keisha showed her work! Short, slim, thick, and with her hair twisted into long cornrows that cascaded down to the middle of her back, the Jamaican feline was a masterpiece. In a black tube shirt that matched her coo hue cutter leather shorts, and black sandals she sported, girlfriend popped her ass with so much vigor that women scrunched their noses and niggas gripped their dicks. Porsha wasn't feeling her shine being shared, and in a white halter top that was so small it resembled a belt wrapped around her titties, a pair of skin tight yellow leather pants, and white heels, she made her way to the dance floor.

"Aww shit, looks like we got ourselves a freak show!" The DJ shouted once Trick and Trina exited the stage. "Let's see what the birthday girl can do."

A lone spotlight suddenly glared down on Porsha.

"Yeaaa, mane!" He fed the vibe before mixing Shyne's, "Bad Boy", single— ♫ Now tell me who wanna fuck with us/ Ashes to ashes dust to dust/ I bang and let your fucking brains hang out/ snitches/ fuck Marla Maples/ bitches with riches. Keisha's chunky eyes closed; being full blooded rude gyal, dancing was her therapy! Yet, when her lids cracked to see diverted stares, she peeked over her shoulder to find Porsha giving her a mischievous smirk. ♫ What type of nigga slang bang in these streets/ what type of nigga stay in the trump for weeks/ Bad Boys/ what type of nigga." Shyne rapped.

Let me show you how a Dallas bitch do this shit!" She offered and Keisha returned her smirk before turning and waving to the space the crowd had opened for her.

"It's ya pardy, rude gyal, but ya ah can't she me ah not nothin, me from de island de wine was created. We ah dance before we den learn ta walk," she capped with a smug smile. Porsha's eyes took in lady's fit before registering how, though she was twenty pounds thicker than her, at five foot *four, chocolate, and hood that bulged as if all her food settled there, the bitch was nice work. Yet, at five nine, and with 140 pounds of thick thick stretching her equally motherland skin, Porsha felt no pressure.*

*♫♫ What type of nigga fly Bentley coupes/ Bad Boy."* Shyne gassed and Porsha put her hands in her hips and seemingly magically, her thighs and ass began to vibrate. Then, her hips began to wind, and only after she had their attention did she turn her back to Keisha and standing bowlegged. She bent at the waist without bending her knees and placed her palms on the ground. From between her legs, she smirked at Keisha before her ass cheeks began to clap so hard it could be heard! The crowd went stupid, but Keisha twisted her lips with her arms crossed. I'm not impressed! Her stance stated and when Porsha erected and turnt to face her, Keisha wasted no time hurting her game! Without changing stance, with her bottom lip poked out in a cute pout, and arms still crossed over her small breast, lady's body began a percolation that resembled boiling water. The exact move that Porsha had just done, but with less effort, and before anyone knew it; body still vibrating. Keisha walked it out until she was standing two feet away from Porsha. Then, her body stilled and with a wicked smirk, the girls leg lifted like a lambo door until she could rest her sandal on Porsha's shoulder. And again, crossing her arms over her breast, Keisha pouted as her thighs and ass jiggled—effortlessly!*

*"Awww shit! She did that, fam!"* A dude from the crowd lost it!

*"Sista girl bad!"* A female seconded.

*"Um hmmm!"* Her friend agreed. The vibe was live, but in that corner, Sunjay was still being harassed. Ignoring Spinx taunts, his hand absently fell to his swelling dick; he wanted to fuck Keisha with a vengeance, but rude gyal was team Messiah.*

*"So, this is how you wanna play it, Sunjay? This won't end well with you, playa. Dallas is my city, lil nigga, and robo cop ain't got shit on me!" Detective Spinx spat, and after another deep swallow from his bottle, Sunjay finally spoke.*

*"No pork on my fork, suck my dick, pig!" He spat with a chuckle, and the detective gave him an evil smile before leaning a bit closer.*

*"Funny, he must have got that slick shit from you," he whispered, and Sunjay's blood froze in his veins. Somehow, he knew what the swine would say even before the poison slipped from his lips. Sunjay tilted the bottle to his lips, but this time, he guzzled from the bottle as if it were a pitcher of Kool-aid. Spinx smirked. "That's what Lil Zetti said before I squeezed the life from his ne—"*

*Before he could finish his confession, the bottle of XO shattered over his head. Blood sprayed the air as the detective stumbled before crumbling to the floor.*

*"Awww shit, Sunjay just fucked Spinx up!" Someone shouted, and sloppy off the liquor, Sunjay didn't have no mind. He snatched the metal off his waist and took aim.*

*"Tell bro I sent ya."*

*"Sunjay!" Someone screamed, and Sunjay squeezed.*

*BOOM!*

***

*"Fuck, mane, nigga can't get no sleep round this bitch!" Messiah spat as he rolled over and snatched up the cordless phone beside his bed. "Fuck this is!" He growled into the mouthpiece. The familiar laughter made him tone down a bit, but he was still big mad! "Mama?"*

*"Nigga, pussy and dick don't sleep, so neither should ya pimpin'."*

*"Ma, it's four in the AM, what's up?"*

*"It's time for you to come back home."*

*"What? Mann, mama, I know you ain't call to—"*

*"Lil Zetti dead, Messiah, murdered. His funeral is in four days."*

*"Wha— stop playin, mama. That shit ain't funny!"* Messiah fumed, heart cracking as he shot up in the bed. The room was dark, a chill wafting in from the open door leading out to his terrace.

Black Diamond blew a long, sad breath. *"I wish I was chile, but you know I'd never play with the death of somebody's baby. Come home, Siah, Dallas need you."*

Was her parting words before the phone clicked on his ear. Messiah slipped out the bed, and careful not to wake his ladies, he slipped into his slippers and naked, stepped out into the freezing night. It had snowed earlier, and fifteen floors down, the ground was white with it. When he'd relocated to Milwaukee, knowing he wouldn't stay long, he'd opted to rent a condo near downtown, and gazing up at the hazy sky, Messiah allowed his diamonds to fall.

*"Damn, Zetti, I told you, fam, this street shit always costs a nigga more than it's worth."* He shook his head as his warm tears turned to ice water.

\*\*\*

*Thirty Minutes Later*

*"What the hell we're you thinking, dude! You almost killed a fucking cop!"* Justice raged as she drove. She'd been fending off another admirer when she'd caught the sight of Sunjay and Spinx' situation, and just after the bottle shattered, she'd made it just in time to fuck up Sunjay's plans. Now, thirty minutes later, she was pulling up to Sunjay and Dream's spot in the North. Sunjay slouched in his seat, head against the cold window, hoping the chill would stop his head from spinning.

*"Fuck em!"* He spat, and as soon as he spoke, he tried to push the door open but wasn't fast enough. He lost his stomach half in and half out the car.

*"I can't believe this shit!"* Justice slapped the steering wheel with each word.

*"My fault,"*Sunjay apologized once he was through throwing up. He let a leg dangle out the door as he slumped back in his seat. Wiping his mouth, he chuckled. *"Shit all fucked up, Jus, now that Messiah out the picture, Gator's bitch ass tryin' to tax on the work. I'd be wrong if I stung 'em for them stones though."* He laughed, but Justice was loss in the sauce.

*"Stones?"* She frowned. *"Stung him! Hell you talkin', Sunjay. Yuh drunk, boy, get on out my car before yuh gal comes out here trippin'"*

Sunjay laughed. *"Yeah, I fucks wit ya wheels, sis. It's smooooth!"* He drug the word with the liquor on his ass. *"And the stones? I'm talm bout the bag of diamonds Gator keeps in his wife's golden urn in his den. Them hoes worth some Ms, and his old ass just got 'em in his dead bitch's ashes like the kid won't take 'em down!"* He chuckled drunkenly, and that's when his porch light came on. Dream stepped out clutching his .40, and staring suspiciously toward the driver's seat.

*"Sunjay, nigga, I know you ain't brought one of ya hoes to my—"*

*"Bitch, shut up!"* Sunjay laughed when stepped toward the car.

Justice wasn't in the mood for more drama, and knowing Dream was for all of it, made her shake her head.

*"Nigga, I got yo' bitch,"* Dream spat when she made it to the car, but when she aimed he gun at Sunjay's chest, Justice had to intervene.

*"Nigga, I'll kill you and this—"*

*"Dream, it's me!" Justice slipped out the driver's side with her hands raised, and when Dream spotted her, her jaw dropped.*

*"Justice! Girl, when you get back in town? I didn't know." She lowered the gun, and Sunjay stumbled out the car. Swaying while trying to keep his balance, he glared at her.*

*"Bi—tch, it's cause it ain't ya biz-mess"—he slurred and that when Dream's nose scrunched from the smell.*

*"Boy!" She stank faced him as her eyes fell to the vomit on his pants. "You drunk!" She spat.*

*"Naw, hoe, fuc—k th—at, you pul—in guns on me, bitch, I'll break ya." And without completing his statement, Sunjay attempted to beat for her.*

*She weaved and his punch went wild, and being drunk, he fell on his face. "Bitch, when I get right, I'mma two piece yo' ass!" He spat from the ground. Yet, the cold earth felt too good to his spinning head.*

*Dream laughed. "It's been a long night, J, and I gotta take care of my man." She smiled over at Justice, and she took the hint.*

*Laughing, she slipped back behind the wheel of her gray Lexus that JoJo had surprised her with, and Dream stuck her head through the passenger's side.*

*"Ugh," she cried when the smell of vomit assaulted her. "You gotta get that clean."*

*Justice shook her head. "Yeah."*

*"Nice to see you back, girl. I'm sure Messiah is gonna come running back!" Dream smiled.*

*Justice started the car. "I doubt it. He may not even know I'm here."*

*Dream laughed. "Justice, you've been gone too long. Messiah knows most of everything going on in Dallas." She nodded as she knew for certain, "Yeah, he'll be back."*

\*\*\*

*Gazing down at the wax rose on the table, Black Diamond sat Indian style on the sofa, pipe to her lips and sucking tainted smoke into her lungs. She'd wanted to tell her baby Justice was back, but the girl had sworn her to silence! Echoing a thick cloud, Black rested her addiction before pulling the thick black book into her lap; she had a lot to record.*

***

*After showering him and getting him to the bed, Dream had laid beside her dude and tried to follow him to sleep, but it was a no go. All that night she'd anticipated his arrival and had planned to fuck him down, but as always, Sunjay had altered her plans. His loud snores made sleep impossible, and the call of her lower self was too loud to ignore. Laying on her side, she bumped him with her ass a few times to wake him. No avail! She even tried kicking him. No go! Finally. She just turned to face him, and from the light of the moon spilling in through the cracked blinds covering the window, she studied him. Laying on his back with drool leaking from the side of his mouth, his dark skin glowed with the moon's luminosity. She loved him, in spite of his imperfections, and though he hadn't fucked her in two weeks, Dream was the type of bitch that understood being a street nigga's gal. "Nigga, you got me fucked up!" She whispered as a mischievous smirk sneaked onto her lips. "You gonna give me my dick, Sunjay."*

***

*The moon was hidden behind a swirl of fog, and though it was below freezing outside, Messiah was oblivious as he stared wonderingly up at the heavens. Tutts stepped out onto the terrace wrapped in a thick blanket.*

*"Daddy, you're gonna freeze." She stepped behind him, and vaguely registered the full length mink she draped over his shoulders, before wrapping her arms around his waist, and resting the side of her face against his back. "Whatever it is, daddy, let God have it."*

*"Messiah stiffened. "Fuck God. That nigga ain't never gave a fuck 'bout us; look at us! You a hoe, Tutts! I'm a Pimp! "That's" what yo' God let us become!" He growled bitterly.*

*"Tutts sniffled. "Don't say that, Siah. Don't play with God."*

*"Bitch!" Messiah growled before slapping her arms from around him, and spinning to face her. "God been playin' with me my whole life. Fuck ain't nobody tell him to stop playing with me! Huh?" He raged and below the murky sky, the tears leaking from his eyes turned to ice, resembling little diamonds against his dark face.*

*Tutts' face balled up. "Nigga, you think you're the only one whose had to struggle? Huh?" She spat, her own river slipping from her eyes. "My own mama turned me into a whore! I've never been in love, and every nigga I've ever fucked wit sold me! But you know what", she roughly wiped her tears away before they solidified. "I have faith that God will come right on time to—"*

*Smack! Messiah slapped fire from her and her head spun to the left.*

*"Bitch look at the time and tell me how the nigga can be on time, when time is almost up! It ain't no God, and if you don't believe me, ask Liberty," he grit, glaring. "Ask my father and Zetti."*

*Tutts slowly turned to face him, and her glare was murderous. "Nigga." She hissed as her left eye leaked. "If you so worried 'bout death, you need anotha profession, because that's all that comes with this shit! We all got a day, and when mine comes, I'mma be right with my God," she whispered, her eyes staring knives.*

*Messiah laughed in contempt. "Only if that nigga a pimp or a square that don't care, because those the only kind of niggas that can have a bitch like you!" Even in his emos he was still hard on a hoe.*

*Tutts pulled the blanket tighter around her body. " A bitch like me, huh?"*

*Messiah chuckled, "Yeah, a bonafied hoe!"*

*Tutts nodded, her expression evident that his words cut. She back pedaled toward the door, but paused in the threshold.*

*"My God don't see hoes. He sees angels, and if you ever put your hands on me again, Messiah, as much as I love you, you're gonna earn ya wings."*

*With malice in his posture, Messiah stepped toward her, but Tutts didn't budge. And seeing the resolve in her eyes, he deflated before turning and gazing up at the moon. "I may take you up on that; me and whoever this sucka you call God need to face off. He's took too much from me, and I need my licks back."*

***

*Wet sucking sounds filled the room, and subconsciously, Sunjay responded to the thralls of pleasure. Dream had slipped beneath the comforter, sucked him to erection, and beneath the tent her bobbing head made beneath the cover, Sunjay's dick dripped with her saliva.*

*Muah! Smuah! The sounds of her kissing and sucking serenaded as she drowned his head between her lips. Suckling it, she jacked him feverishly. Sunjay stirred with a moan, but Dream paid him no mind as she sucked his mushroom as if it were a straw and she were attempting to suck his spirit from it.*

*"Damn," Sunjay mumbled as she massaged his nuts, before swallowing him whole. Though only seven strong, his muscle was thick, and stretched her lips, yet familiarity*

*helped her master it. Before long, she felt that distant throb of his nut surging toward the thick vein of him, and popping him free, Dream hurriedly slid from beneath the covers, crawled up to his body and reigned above him. And positioning his dick, she arched her back before arching down into him.*

*"Ahhmm!" She bit her bottom lip while his thickness split her open, and placing her hands on his chest, she rocked the boat. Back and forth, that pussy worked in a swinging motion; no up and down, just deep pussy punishment. "You gonna give me this nut, daddy, ummm!" She cried, and Sunjay's eyes cracked open to capture her juicy titties swinging in his face.*

*"Fuck?" He mumbled, but Dream had an agenda.*

*"Um! Umm! Ummmm!" She moaned, chunking that pussy as him. "Bout—to—give—youuuu—this cum, daaad—dyyy!" She cried as her pace became possessed.*

*Sunjay's toes curled as the liquor surged through his veins, and when the sway of her breast began to make him dizzy, he resulted to the only rationale of stilling them; he grasped her D-cups and squeezed.*

*"Ohhh, youuu, motha—fucka!" Dream cried as her storm came down in a sticky flood. "Cumming—on—my—diiick!" She screamed, and then, BLAM! The front door flew off its hinges.*

# Chapter 8

*Two Days Later*

*The day was gray, the snow blanked the ground, but on Milwaukee's south side, the game don't stop. And when the Benz and Jag slid into the lot of the bodega on Greenfield Ave., the thick crowd of pimps, hoes, and hustlers parlaying in its midst took notice. Coming to a halt, side by side, the foreigners were their own movie as Tutts and Paradise slipped from the driver's sides making a video. Both sported black full length minks with only the middle button fastened, and it was evident that beneath them, the only things they wore was skin, and the gold and diamond apple pendant necklaces. Not a mu'fucka present was naive to who they ho'd for, yet, just beyond the movie they made, what birth curiosity was the small shopping bags each woman held. Paradise strutted to the back of the Benz and cracked the door, and when the Texas nigga slid out draped in a tan and dark brown, leather Dapper Dan Gucci fit, complete with fresh Gucci boots, he killed 'em!*

*Flashing a diamond smile, Messiah took a bite from a green apple as his vision scanned the scene. Greenfield was a stock market for extracurricular! Pussy, dope, hope, murder for hire, or even a new born baby; if you had the loot or the con, you could find it on that sinful piece of land. Messiah spotted his prey standing outside the bodega, sipping a soda while being harassed by pimping! Cakes rolled her eyes as a pimp known as Gorgeous broke on her, and chuckling, Messiah listened as he made his way toward the only life he knew.*

*"Bitch, my game international like an airport! I've broke on hoes from Cuba to Aruba, Maine to Spain, blind, crippled, and crazy! I've had a white hoe with one leg that jumped for my bread until she amazed me...a black hoe that could suck a John's balls out through his dick head before she pays me...And even a Latin hoe, whose ass I kept my Gators in, cause she was wayyy too lazy! Hoe! I'm Pimp Gorgeous, game fast like the hare, because I ain't ever been slow like the tortoise! And if you can't see I'm the flyest nigga on the globe, you need to beg the hoe goddess for some new eyes cause ya vision distorted...I know you touching cause you've had ya heart broken, but," He flicked his nose. "Ya sob story you can save it! And put ya heart in ya pussy, cause I'm on that; fuck love, "pay me!" Loves for squares, and—"*

*"Pardon moi, Pimp friend, but let a sho' nuff mack feed this hoe some "P" for a few, ya dig." Messiah's interruption froze Gorgeous in place. With a jabbed finger poised toward Cakes, his eyes slowly found Messiah. Gorgeous was a light skinned "P", clad in a platinum silk shirt, white slacks, and platinum hued gators. And though his jewelry was H20, it was his green eyes that complimented his ism and long hair.*

*"I know you see me kickin' some "P" to this freak, so scram, Jack, and let me finish jackin' my slacks until I got this hoe flat backin' for my mackin'!" He spoke, still frozen in his uncle Sam's pose. Messiah took another bite of his apple as his vision captured Cakes in a black, tear away catsuit with buttons running up its side to hold it together, snow boots, and a quarter coat. Lady exuded sexy. Gorgeous notes her and Messiah's chemistry, and knowing he'd be shamed if he allowed the out of towner to steal his shine, he defrosted before facing off with him. "Say, country boy, let me talk my talk, and if I can't crack this hoe's code, you—"*

*"Country boy?" Messiah laughed before wiping apple juice from his mouth. "Nigga, I'm from Texas, where the*

*game futuristic like the Jetsons! And "how" you claim to be talkin' to this bimbo if yo' eyes on me?" He smirked before patting the fluff of his freshly cut, drop shag.*

*Gorgeous waved him of., "We "were" talkin' before you came cock blocking."*

*Messiah shrugged indifferently. "So talk."*

*"Listen here, "P", my daddy was a rolling stone, and my mama was the hoe who let him exercise his pimpin', so I've been the only authority in my life since the game taught me to never accept a penny pinching! So, I talk when I'm ready."*

*"That's a lie, P. You talk when "I'm ready." Messiah chuckled.*

*Danger bled into Gorgeous's stare as his hand dropped to his waist. "Playa, you got Gorgeous fucked up!"*

*"Naw, "P", not fucked up , but I can get you fucked "down" for the right price." Messiah chuckled, before his hand fell to the grip of the P.90 jutting his pocket. Gorgeous noted it, and the fear blossoming in his orbs unveiled his bluff! He was a lot of pimp, but zero gangsta, and smirking to show him he knew it, Messiah winked. "Yet, why we talkin' when you just claimed to be talking to the lady?" He nodded towards Cakes.*

*Sweat beaded against Gorgeous forehead. "I—I told ya, champ. I talk when I'm ready!" He sputtered.*

*"And I told you otherwise."*

*"I'm done talking, P."*

*"Shut up then, nigga, you ain't talmbout shit anyway!" Messiah baited, and just as her expected, Gorgeous bit.*

*"Nigga, I talk when I'm ready!" He stomped his foot in frustration.*

*Messiah laughed. "Thought you were done talking, but I see you're just good at talking backwards." He jived before biting a chunk from his apple.*

*"Fuck?" Gorgeous spat before recapturing his fly. Fluffing his permed hair before gripping his nuts, he dropped his ism, "P, hoes talk backwards when they're lying,*

*and ain't a hoe gene in my pimpin'! I talk how I get money."
He waved a hand before his face. "Face to face." He jazzed
before glowering at a humored Messiah. "Fuck so funny,
P?"*

*Messiah was beside himself with laughter. "P, how you
talk face to face when you "just" said you was talking to this
hoe, and she's behind you? You didn't even feel when she
squirted that soda on the back of ya slacks!"*

*It seemed inhuman how fast Gorgeous head spun to see
what he was referring to, and lifting his slacks to inspect, he
spoke from over his shoulder, "Nigga, ain't shit on my—"*

*"See!" Messiah taunted with a jab of his finger. "There
you go again, P. Talkin backwards! First, ya goofy ass was
lookin at me, but talkin' to her, but now you looking back, but
talkin' to me! Damn, errythang you do is backwards, "P"!"*

*His psychological play made Gorgeous the joke of the blade,
and even Cakes burst into laughter! Gorgeous lost it, and
went for his burna, but Messiah tossing the apple into the air
did it to him! "Catch this," he offered and when Gorgeous'
eyes followed its ascent, Messiah upped his tool and had it
trained on his target just as the gravity brought the fruit
down on the man's head.*

*"Not over no bitch, P. Let's keep it playa and let the hoe
choose her own poison," he bargained, and Gorgeous's
hands shot into the air.*

*"Naw, you got it, P. I'm cool on the hoe." He blew trail.*

*Messiah smirked. "Cool, Mack buddy, but I can't risk you
sneaking me while I break on her. He nodded toward Cakes.
"So, I'mma need you to strip down to ya undies, P."*

*"Huh?" Gorgeous was baffled until—"*

*BOCA! Messiah shot by his feet, and the man leapt, man's
height!*

*"Strip, P!" Messiah demanded, his facial revealing his
animal.*

*"Aight!" Gorgeous relented, and in seconds had stripped
down to his tightie whities! Shuffling from foot to foot as his*

*teeth chattered, the man was freezing! "Come on, P, this ain't how it go," he whined, but Messiah was so shocked, he had to shake it off. There, standing with his toes in the snow, Gorgeous wore a pair of Fruit of the Loom undies with the little pocket in the front.*

*Messiah shook his head. "Not the Fruit of the Looms, P!" He disdained, and the crowd was wild in laughter. Yet, Messiah knew a scorned man is worse than a bitter bitch, so he had mercy. "Cakes," he called before nodding to Gorgeous pile of clothes. "Get that gun for me, ma."*

*She wasted no time complying and only after she had the tool in her mitts, did he address his man. "Get ya shit and split, P," he ordered, and Gorgeous moved at God's speed! Gathering his attire, without bothering to dress, Pimp kicked up snow as he gingerbread man'd all the way to his car. Yet, Messiah stayed on clutch until the fella gathered his hoes and sped out the parking lot.*

*"It ain't ova, P!" He shouted as the car sped by.*

*"Tell him, daddy, uh uhh, it ain't over!" One of his hoes seconded, and Cakes burst into laughter. Messiah merely took another bite of his apple before turning and heading to his whip.*

*"Wait!" Cakes was caught off guard, but ran to catch up. Messiah didn't pay her no mind as he turned to ensure his ladies had done his bidding. He smirked. He'd had them pass out "candy" apples to as many hoes as they could, and seeing a few Pimps partaking of the delicacy, he fought not to laugh. And only after they'd made it back to him with empty bags, did his gander find Cakes. Tutts and Paradise slipped behind the wheels of their respective cars before Messiah addressed her.*

*"You got something for me?" He probed, and Cakes studied him for a quiet moment before slipping her hand into her coat. Yet, when she handed him an apple, he frowned. "Bitch," he spat, but paused when she slipped out the coat. It fell at her feet before she gripped the sides of her attire*

and when she yanked, the buttons unsnapped, and the cat suit tore away.

"Awww shit! This hoe done up and done it, P, and it's a sad day when a county boy out pimps a pimp like me!" Cried a pimp named Pretty Ricky.

"Uh uh, baby, respect the game, cause it's to be sold, and if you spur you ain't get chose, you need to change ya propaganda to get chose for a pose!" Stacy Dash, another pimp chimed. All eyes were glued to the spectacle, watching Messiah's jaw drop, cause before him, Cakes stood "literally" wearing money! Somehow, she'd pasted hundreds, fifties, and twenty dollars bills over month percent of her body; from her collar down! And spinning so Messiah could get a good gander, she paused with her back to him.

"Bitch lookin like a lick, huh, daddy?" She giggled before smirking at him from over her shoulder. And when she leaned forward, reached back, and spread her cheeks, Messiah shook his head in shock before bursting into laughter.

"Remember when I asked you if you trust your intuition?" He asked, and when Cakes nodded, he ran a finger down her crack. "Think quick when I'm talkin' slick, hoe, cause I drip sauce when I pop my shit. I'm opening the door to let you "in" cause your wearing ya "tuition"." He waved a hand at her efforts. "In tuition, love." He chuckled before nodding to his Benz. "Now get ya fine ass in, I know you cold."

"Uh uh, daddy, not this time." Cakes shook her head. I'on need no roaring fire nor a mink coat on this cold day, cause this money keeps me warm! But if you don't hurry up and get the rest of ya choosin fee, I may freeze into an ice sculpture!" She confused him, and Messiah's vision fell a bit lower, to find a string dangling from her twat. "Get it, baby, fresh out the womb," Cakes seduced, and when Messiah pulled the string, he was amazed as a magnum condom stuffed to capacity with rolls of money, slipped from her pussy. "Muah!" Cakes moaned with a bite of her bottom lip, and Messiah examined the condom. It was shipped like a ten inch *dick, and after Cakes corrected her posture, she turned to face him. "Negro, it took me hours and three hundred dollars to have someone help me so this!" She waved at her body. "Why it take you so long to come back and check for me?" She sassed, before placing a hand on her shapely hip. Every playa present that had solicited her whoring had to salute Messiah's "P"! And parlayed in the cut, either leaning or sitting atop their cars, a cluster of playas and hoes got eyefuls! Messiah playfully slapped her with the condom before returning the apple, and without hesitation, Cakes partook. It was official! And after waving toward the car, Messiah slapped her ass as she slipped in, but just as he went to follow.*

*"Texas," someone called, and glancing over his shoulder, he spotted Top Choice smirking. Though from that land, he was hip to Messiah's tale, and in fact; he was the only pimp on deck to have prevented his ladies from accepting Messiah's apples.*

*"Sup, P?" Messiah acknowledged.*

*The vet pimp folded his arms Ain't ya gonna clue 'em in to their mistakes before you serve 'em their fates? Tell these jive ass niggas why you gave their bitches the forbidden fruit." He chuckled, and laughed.*

*Messiah slipped into the backseat and closed the door. Top Choice, I'on know what you talmbout."*

*Pretty Ricky chuckled before biting into the candy apple. "This mu'fucka delicious! You shoulda gotten one, ya dig!" He smacked with apple juice glistening on his lips.*

*"Um hmm, you sho' right, daddy!" Sin, one of his freaks seconded before taking another bite of hers. Pretty Ricky froze mid-bite, nothing moving but his eyes as they shot to her.*

*"Hoe, who asked yo' opinion?"*

*"Daddy, I'm—"*

*"Give me this shit, bitch!" He snatched her apple before taking a massive bite, and after a mouthful, he stomped*

*down! "Matter fact, why you ain't somewhere getting paid off, hoe. I ain't gave you no days off!" He spat, and Top Choice shook his head before his attention captured Messiah's whip's Cadillac turn. And when the Benz eased to a stop alongside them, Messiah flashed a diamond studded smile. Not only had he put on for Texas, but as Cakes head bobbed in his lap, the sucking sound emitting from the backseat upped his clout.*

*"A "P" done broke luck, OG, and..." he addressed Top Choice. "The game ain't meant to be told, so I won't be the one to expose, but just like when the snake gave Eve the fruit, and after she ate, her eyes were open to the power of pussy and dick." He glanced to the bobbing head in his lap before returning his vision to the playa. "Every hoe that's eating my fruits will always remember my ism, so that cuts my work to knock 'em down to a minimum! And just how Eve ate first, then fed Adam." He glanced at Pretty Ricky, who held the apple midway to his mouth with an expression of utter horror on his face.*

*Top Choice burst into laughter as the Benz and Jag slid out the lot." The Apple is the serpent's fruit, and just as he snuck the first bitch that ever whored, so will that youngin sneak yours!" He cried laughing as Pretty Ricky and the other pimps who'd at the fruit, began to spit it all over the ground. But their ladies didn't spit a bit, and in fact, they had a taste for more. Yet, Messiah could've never fathomed what the game would do a week later.*

# Chapter 9

*A Week Later*

*Downtown's Government Center was a gladiator jungle, and only the strong survived! A place of captivity that brought the worst out of its captives. The jail was a mad house! And that's exactly where Sunjay found himself. He'd just sat down to eat the jailhouse chains the inmates dubbed chow! And gazing down at the dirty water that was supposed to be soup, he glowered. Tasteless, and with only three carrots floating in it, it was hardly eatable, and in spite of the half cooked potato, and over cooked corn bread, the only appealing thing on his tray was the chocolate frosting cake. He'd been trapped within that belly of the whale since Spinx and his unit of swine stormed his home and mysteriously found two bricks of raw, numerous calibers of guns, and a hundred bands of counterfeit money. The hubs was his; the rest was planted! Yet, the D.A just wanted him off the streets, so he knew screaming setup was useless! Shaking his head at the way his story was spinning, Sunjay was reaching for the piece of cake when...*

*"You gonna eat that, kuz?" An animal growled before the cake was snatched off his tray. Sunjay's eyes shot to the man just as he took a massive bite from it, and with crumbs and icing on his lips, big man smiled as he chewed. Six foot four, and weighing two eighty, C-Loc was one of the tank bullies, and even worse, he was crip crazy. Chuckles trickled throughout the day room as anticipation hovered in the air.*

*"Damn, kuz, yo' shit taste better than mine,"* C-Loc smacked before downing the rest of the cake. *Fear blossomed in Sunjay's eyes as he glanced around at all the murderous stares, he knew most of those boys rode for the blue team, and he had no wins. Slipping from his seat, he grabbed his tray and tried to give C-Loc the most disarming smile.*

*"I wasn't gonna eat it anyway, Bloo—I mean, homie,"* he corrected self, and dude smirked.

*"Yeah, glad you ain't let that word slip, kuz, cause as you can see, the tomato heads are—"* He waved at three men at the back table, obviously avoiding eye contact with them. *"Tamed",* C-Loc chuckled as Sunjay's eyes darkened. *"In fact, ain't you one of them 4 nine queen niggas? Heard y'all responsible for downing my loc, C-Bo."*

*"Naw."* Sunjay shook his head before trying to walk passed him. *"I'm the nigga that axed that rab ass nigga."*

*"Fuck you just s—"*

Before C-Loc could complete his question, Sunjay pivoted and cracked the tray on his face. Blood exploded from C-Loc's nose, and when he stumbled, Sunjay tossed the tray before stepping to his work. Overs, unders and hooks put dude on his little debbies, but the victory was short lived. Half the day room was on Sunjay's ass in seconds, and the three cowards at the back table should've aided him, because they got flipped too.

\*\*\*

*"I'm coming dammit, hold on,"* Pimpin growled at the impatience of whomever was pounding on his door. Yet, when he snatched it open, the tongue lashing he planned to give was D.O.A! His mouth fell open at the sight before him; Messiah stood before him in a wrinkled suit, nappy hair, complete with a five o'clock shadow.

"What," Pimpin Maxwell mumbled in shock. "The hell happened to you, young blood!" His vision fell to the suitcase his protégé carried.

Messiah dropped his head in shame. "I need a place to camp, Pimpin'. I should've never went to those dens of snakes! Oakland and Milwaukee is pure evil, and a "P" done lost my stable to game that's more able!"

Pimpin' shook his head in shame. He'd heard the tale of Oakland, and knew Milwaukee was a savage land for a slow pimp to try his hand.

"You know my doors are open, "P", but what about—"

"The spot in Desoto? Mannn." Messiah shook his head. "How I'mma pay the rent with no hoes, no dope, and no job, "P"? He splayed his arms like a bird's wings. "And though the game took me fast, a bonafied "P" takes it with class. I sold the house, so I need 'bout two weeks to get back on my tip toes."

Pimpin Maxwell nodded before stepping to the side so he could enter. "Ya room the same way ya left it, baby."

# Chapter 10

*Next Morning*

*Pimpin's mind had bothered him ever since Messiah had shown up, busted and disgusted the night before. It was just "something" about his tale that didn't sit right, and as Foxy chauffeured him through the city, he relaxed in the backseat of his Benz, nursing a cognac and cigar as he thought. He was so enraptured with his mental that he barely registered the car ease to a stop on the quiet street in Desoto, Texas.*

*"You don't believe him?" Foxy interrupted his peace, and his eyes lifted to behold hers in the rear view.*

*"The life I live forces me to see the worst in people." He smirked before taking a sip from his glass. Foxy lifted a brow, she'd helped raise Messiah.*

*"So, why'd you leave him there with the girls?" She was curious.*

*Pimpin' took a puff of his cigar. "Foxy, first, you know better than to question my decisions, and secondly, how long have you been with me?"*

*Foxy laughed, she'd been licked in since she was eighteen, and now at forty-three, she was just as beautiful as ever. "Boy, I been with ya ass since ya was chili pimpin' and sticking ya Johnson in more pussy than ya was selling."*

*Pimpin' chuckled before lifting his glass in toast, "So, ya old ass already know ole Maxwell knows the difference between a friend, and an enemy climbing down my chimney posing as Santa Claus?"*

*Foxy turned in her seat to glance at him from over her shoulder. "Old!" She spat. "Maxwell, I'm far from old, and if this is the new old." She cupped her breast. "Just remember, the older the violin, the sweeter the music, honey." They shared a laugh, but Foxy wasted no time getting back to it.*

*"So, you're saying Messiah is the enemy?" She lifted that brow again, and Pimpin' sucked smoke from his cigar. He knew she saw Messiah as a son, and loved him as much.*

*"No, love, not at all. What I'm sayin' is it takes savvy shit to be a savvy nigga, and that boy has taken too many Ls in life, not to crave a few Ws. He been gone for a year plus. That's four hunnid days of proper P's to prepare him for a lifetime of proper W's. And I can bet my last penny on it, that whichever W messiah has prepared for, it won't stand for without!" He chuckled before taking a sip from his glass. Foxy corrected her seating before her eyes drifted to the three bedroom home Messiah claimed to have sold. A red minivan was parked in the drive and an abandoned soccer ball lay in the yard.*

*"Which reverts back to my question," she whispered just as he front door to the house opened. Two white kids ran out; one young boy, hyper and excited, and the other, a teenage girl with headphones in her ears. "Why'd you leave a snake in the pigeon coup?" Foxy completed.*

*And seeing all he needed to see to confirm Messiah's story, Pimpin chuckled. "Foxy, a playa as myself doesn't lose sleep 'bout the next playa exercisin' his game on my hoes, cause if he can knock 'em, I've already forgot 'em, and will replace 'em before I chase 'em. Now, he tapped her head rest. "Would you be so kindly, and get me to some money?"*

\*\*\*

*The rays of the morning sun poured in through the window and bathed him, and when Messiah's eyes cracked open, he had to remember he was in his old room. As his mind came awake, he smirked before sitting up in the bed, yet, when spotting an intruder, he jumped in surprise.*

*"Boo." Candy laughed as she sashayed over to him with breakfast on a tray. Messiah gazed down at the omelet oozing cheese, onions and sour cream, complete with hash browns, turkey sausage, and a glass of pineapple juice.*

*He smirked. "What's this? My welcome home meal, or is this treatment of the house!" He smirked, recognizing intrigue in her gaze; it was in that exact room she'd taken his innocence. Candy studied him intently, unbeknownst to him and Pimpin' Maxwell, lady was in the know. Word spread in the streets, especially amongst freaks of how lit Messiah had his stable, and as she eyed him, regret was born. Messiah was so into his food, he didn't notice her gander, but when his vision lifted to capture it, his brow raised. Candy was gorgeous! Latte hued skin, long curly hair, and shaped like a bottle, lady was exotic! Chewing, Messiah's vision took in the soft pink jogging suit she wore; no shirt or bra beneath the midway zipper jacket, and obviously no panties beneath the soft material of her pants.*

*"Sup?" He inquired.*

*"I always knew you'd be the baddest mu'fucka to put his foot in a pair of Gators, I—"*

*She was saying before Messiah raised a palm to silence her. "Dig the slang in my campaign, hoe, if you believed, you would have never been knocked by Pimpin', so miss me with the extracurricular!" He spat with more spazz than intended, and it was then he realized he was still salty about it. Candy smiled sadly before making her way to the window. The view was made for a playa.*

*"Messiah, a woman is still a woman emotionally, no matter what she does with her body," she whispered. "When I chose Pimpin' over you, you were just a kid; a kid with nothing." Her realism massaged his ego, and Messiah stiffened.*

*"Bitch, I wasn't a kid when you gave me that pussy, huh?"*
*He capped.*

*Candy smirked, her reflection staring at him in the window. "Messiah, my pussy has had a price tag ever since me and my family came here from Puerto Rico, and realized that just cause this is the land of the free, doesn't mean you get nothing for free. She pointed out at the skyline. "This city causes a woman to make hard decisions, so"—she turned to face him before crossing her arms over her chest. "Me givin' you my vagina was ABCs compared to choosing between you and security, and if a man coming up, how you did can't respect that!" She shrugged, and Messiah cut into his omelet before sucking the piece from his fork. He glared, but real can't be disputed.*

*He ate before placing the tray to the side, and in his boxers, slipped out the bed. Candy's eyes fell to the print of his power as he made his way to her. Messiah turned her to face the window before slipping behind her and wrapping his arms around her waist. Pointing at the skyline, he gazed out at what his queen had prophesied to be his. "You see that?" He asked while allowing his hand to slip inside the unzipped part of her jacket, and as he massaged her left nipple, Candy bit her bottom lip.*

*"Umhm." She nodded.*

*"What you see, Candy?" He whispered as his dick surged to life.*

*Feeling him, Candy's middle saturated. It's the city," she whispered, and just as fast as he came to embrace her, Messiah slipped away.*

*Confused, Candy turned to face him. "Did I say something wrong?"*

*Messiah made his way to the door, and after closing it, made his way back to her. "Hoe, get on your knees!" He demanded, and after a moment's hesitation, Candy complied.*

Messiah slipped his dick through the slit in his boxers before gripping it by the base, and without warning, he slapped her across the forehead with it. *"What did you see?"* He reiterated, and Candy frowned.

*"Nigga, I said."*

Smack! Dick slapped face.

*"Naw, hoe, what you saw was mine ! And since you're lyin under oath, I hear by charge you with perjury! See, I saw it in your eyes, love. You regret ya sins, but let me ask you something."* Messiah traced her lips with his dick head. *"You hoe for free?"*

*"Wha"*—

Smack! Dick slapped face.

*"Stop doing t—"*

Smack!

*"Answer me!"* He demanded, and glaring up at him with her arms crossed, Candy knew it was now or never.

*"Never!"* She spat, and Messiah smirked before lowering his meat to her lips.

*"I'm proud. Now kiss him,"* he ordered, and just as he'd anticipated, Candy was ready and willing. Still glaring, she tilted her head and wrapped her lips around the head, and just as she was slowly taking him in, inch for inch, Messiah slipped himself free and...

Smack! Dick slapped face.

Candy shot to her feet, *"Nigga, I told you to—"*

*"Bitch, a whore can't tell me shit! You're a liar and that I don't desire."* Messiah shoved her away with disgust in his eyes. And stumbling, Candy barely kept her footing before her Puerto Rican blood overflowed, and she charged him.

*"Arrrrugh!"* She screamed, and fingers formed into claws, her intent was thwarted when Messiah suddenly side stepped her, and just as she was flying past, he kicked her in the ass.

*"Ahhh!" She cried when she crumbled beside the bed. "I ain't lied about nothinn'!" She whined, and Messiah strolled over to the window to gaze out at the trip.*

*"Hoe, you lied when you said you don't hoe for free! You're under another playa's management, but you putting ya mouth on me like I'mma pay you a fee. You callin "me" a trick, Candy?"*

*Candy pulled herself up and once she was beside him at the window, rubbing her sore ass, she glared at him. "Fuck you, Messiah!"*

*His eyes cut to her, and she rolled hers. "No, I don't think you're a trick!"*

*"So, you must have my fee?"*

*"Messiah, Pimpin' will kill us if—"*

*"Bitch." Messiah turned and grabbed her by her curls. "Let me drip on you before I pimp on you! You ever seen that flick, The Wizard of Oz?" The question caused her to frown, but she nodded nonetheless "Yes."*

*"Hoe, the word "oz" stands for one or two things, an "ounce", or a make believe place, and wasn't no dope being sold in that movie, so where Dorothy, the lion, tin man, and the scarecrow was headed was fake!" He growled.*

*"What about Toedoe?" She asked, and he smacked her. Not hard, just hard enough.*

*"Who? The dog?" Messiah chuckled. "Candy, what type of dog you ever seen that can't find his way home? Point is, Dorothy wasted all that time on the yellow brick road, only to find the Wizard don't even know magic...On top of that, the answer she sought the entire time, the silly bitch already had it!" He loosened his grip before leaning in for a kiss, and Candy's eyes drifted shut; lips puckering in anticipation. Yet, when his lips never met hers, her orbs snapped open to find him flashing her his diamond smile. "See, Candy, you're just like Dorothy, eyes wide shut, expecting shit you know can never be! Travelin' a yellow road, but never understanding the roads that color so you'll see." Messiah*

*glanced out at the skyline. "To see that you're on the wrong road that can never lead you home, love. After dealing with a nigga for a year, if there's nothing upgraded about you, he's the wrong choice." Messiah released her before heading to get dressed. "And if a Nigga doesn't prove he's worth keepin', he's provin' he's worth leavin', mama."*

*"What's going on in here?" Creamy burst into the room, fully expecting a sexual tryst. Yet, seeing Messiah slipping into his pants, and Candy fully dressed, she frowned.*

*"Where's the other hoes, Creamy?" Messiah inquired.*

*Suspicion bled into her eyes as she glanced from him to how Candy stood, staring out the window. "I don't believe that's none of—"*

*"Creamy—" Candy turned to face her. They were like sisters, and it was law that they were a team. Creamy's brow lifted, and Candy's vision found Messiah. She had a strange feeling about his tale of why he was there, and his game only confirmed her suspicions. A game nigga can never fall flat, cause his game won't go for that! She thought and a smirk eased onto her face. "Messiah ain't a child anymore, and I think it's more to his visit than being hoe broke. Am I right, Messiah?"*

*Messiah was dressed when he chuckled. "You hoes peep the slang in my campaign," he began.*

\*\*\*

*An Hour Later*

*♬ I done bled the block til my foot hurt the slab/ for better or for worse/ I put the good with the bad ♬*

*Gator Mane rumbled in the trunk of the Jag as the rims reflected off the asphalt. Blowing an Optimo stuffed with exotic, Messiah maneuvered the grain as he peeped the city from the windshield. Dallas Ft. Worth was a no flex zone, and with the madness of gang banging and hood plex, the*

*Trinity River was ripe with the odor of decaying bodies. Messiah's mental was a tornado as he contrived a chess move that would change his game, but just as he was slipping up Hampton in the west, his thoughts were put on a pause as a familiar car slid behind him and police lights danced in the grill.*

♫ *I done made a choice to never ever come last/ and I done told the whole world to kiss my damn ass* ♫

*Gator Mane spat as Messiah eased the whip into the parking lot of the Fina on Inwood, and glaring into the rear view, he watched Spinx exit his car. It took him no time to the car, yet, Messiah didn't lower his window nor lower the loud bass as he took a drag from his blunt. The detective finally got the point, and made his way to the passenger's side, before inviting himself in. He smiled big when noting Messiah's nonchalance for his authority, and only after the song had ended, did Messiah lower the volume. Exhaling a cloud toward the law, he nodded.*

*"What you want, Spinx?" He spat, knowing no one knew he was back in town. So, for Spinx to know, that meant someone was watching.*

*Spinx splayed his arms. "Damn, playa, that's how you greet an old friend? After so long?"*

*Messiah looked him up and down. "Miss me with the extracurricular, guy, and speak your piece." He got to the business while studying the bandage on the man's head.*

*"Sho' ya right, Pimp." The detective chuckled, before using his fingertips to trace his goatee. Bald headed, and as black as oil, he resembled a "hood" Shaft! "As you know, ya boy Sunjay is in some deep shit."*

*Messiah studied him. He'd got word about Sunjay's predicament, but knew there had to be some fuck shit amiss. Not even Sunjay was that reckless! Their main rule was, "Never trap where you sleep", so why start now? He thought, and filling his lungs with smoke, Messiah rested his head against the headrest. His eyes drifted shut as he mentally moved a piece on his chess board. "Yeah, I heard, but what you want from me. Spinx, I gave that life up when I departed.*

*"Yeah." Spinx nodded before extending his hand. "So I've heard, but let me hit that real quick."*

*Messiah's eyes shot open, and his mouth dropped at his request. "Wha—what?"*

*"Nigga, let me hit the dope." Spinx urged and Messiah obliged. Spinx hit the stick and its power attacked his lungs so viciously that he dropped it twice during a fit of coughing, before regaining his composure. Messiah laughed at the tears running down the man's face.*

*"That's that Cali, boy, you gotta respect it."*

*Spinx nodded, "Yeah, I see."*

*"What you want, Spinx?"*

*"Same shit everybody else does." He wiped his face before smiling knowingly. "My piece of the pie."*

*"I just told you I—"*

*"Yeah yeah, you're out, blah blah! But, "Pimp." The emphasis on the title spoke volumes. "I've heard hoe money is just like dope money, I need them back ends, Messiah."*

*Messiah nodded, still playing chess mentally. "Under on condition; a favor."*

*Spinx spread his arms. "We're like family, kid, I'm cool with one hand washing the other. What is it? You need some of these pimp niggas off the—"*

*"Naw, nothin like that." Messiah waved him off when he tried to pass the blunt back. "I'm hoe broke, Spinx, so I need some help getting back on my feet."*

*"This fucked the detectives head up, and he frowned. "So?"*

*"You still takin work off niggas and reselling it?" His question brought shock to Spinx face, but common knowledge of how he got down, gave him a confident smile.*

93

*"Maybe I know some crooked cops that does, but I'm sure they already have arrangements with others."* He chuckled.

*"I need about two birds, OG,"*

The smile melted away, and seriousness became the vibe. *"Let's say this can happen, how long will it take to get my—"*

*"A week."* Messiah cut him off, *I already have clientele, just need work."*

*"What about yo' old plugs?"* Spinx's curiosity was official.

Messiah pointed down to the wrinkle suit he wore. *"Can't talk shop with no loot. I have a hundred grand to my name. I'll give you thirty for the tax, thirty two for the work, and ten for the interest."* He knew numbers awoke the greed in mu'fuckas, and just as he thought, Spinx salivated at the thought of all the lucci.

*"One week, we can get it done in the jects."* He agreed before slipping out the car. He stumbled a bit from his high and Messiah didn't miss the act of him pocketing the extinguished blunt. He chuckled before pulling a wrinkled business card from his glove compartment. He had one more move before the grand finale. Checkmate!

***

When Justice pulled up to her family's home in Houston, it wasn't the fourteen acre property the beautiful four bedroom home sat on, nor her father that navigated his riding lawnmower that generated her smile. It was the two energetic boys racing toward that made her giggle.

*"Nene!"* KK, her six year old nephew shouted as she slipped from her Lexus.

*"Hey, Nene's baby!"* She greeted, just as he crashed into her, hugging her waist. His seven year old brother followed suit, and as she hugged them, she realized how much she missed them.

*"You come back home, about time, Nene!"* KK glared up at her with a child's evil eye.

*"Yeah, about time, Nene!"* Carsen echoed, and Justice laughed before roughing their heads. By this time, her old man had spotted her, and from an acre away, waved. Justice gave him a sad smile, but reciprocated the gesture.

*"Nene, you gonna take us swimming?"* KK asked, and she laughed.

*"Boy, yuh crazy, it's December; too cold for a swim yuh know."*

*"What about take us fishing?"* He was adamant, and Justice knew he and Carsen would suggest all day if she allowed.

Hugging them again, she kissed both boys atop their heads. *"Maybe later, let meh speak to grandpa for a second."* She dismissed them, but—

*"Nene, does fish get cold?"* KK asked.

*"I don't know, KK, we'll talk later."*

*"Well, I need a hundred dollars because we helped papa pick up allll the leaves in de yard."* He stuck out his hand.

Justice laughed. *"If it's we helped, why do you get the hundred?"*

*"Cause him didn't ask, duhh!"* The boy was hell!

\*\*\*

The visiting room at the Government Center was noisy and full, and when Sunjay popped in, anyone with eyes could see he was the poster child for ass whooping! A black eye, swollen lip, and a limp was the evident, but if he was ashamed, one couldn't tell from the way he swaggered into the room. Messiah shook his head with a smirk.

*"This boy!"* He mumbled, before Sunjay spotted him at the back table. Sunjay resembled Larenz Tate off Menace To Society, but instead of the dreads, his wavy hair was shagged

up, and as he made it to the table, Messiah wondered if it was his man's time to crap out with the game.

"What's brackin, Blood," Sunjay greeted as he took his seat. Messiah had already purchased his snacks and Sunjay wasted no time attacking them. Hot Cheetos, two Butterfingers, a Sprite, and giant iced honey bun. The boy was about his business!

Messiah laughed. Damn, nigga, slow down."

Sunjay sucked the sweetness from his fingers before opening his Sprite, "Bro, I'm hungry as a bitch! These hoes got me in the hole, and the food here ain't made for a gangsta!" He chuckled bitterly.

"Fuck happened to your face?"

Sunjay shrugged while chugging from his drink, and belching loudly. He was ever Sunjay! "Ain't shit, just had to get some straightnin' with the opp" Again, he shrugged. You know how it go."

Messiah nodded before leaning back in his seat. "Yeah, I can dig it, but riddle me this Batman, when the fuck you start keeping work at the house? That's rookie boy shit, Sunjay, and—"

His words trailed and a chill ran down his spine when murder bled into Sunjay's eyes.

"Siah, you're my brother, Blood, if anybody should know better, it's you. Nigga, never trap where you sleep, remember?" His truths were confirmation to Messiah's earlier thoughts.

Messiah crossed his ankle over his knee, not liking his deduction. "So?" He waved around the room.

Sunjay was digging into the bag of chips when he answered. "Spinx set me up."

Messiah figured as much.

"Why?" He asked.

"I busted his head."

Messiah's frown deepened. "Why, Sunjay? The law? Come on, Brodie, your too smart for—"

*Bam! The chair toppled over when Sunjay exploded from it.*

*"Nigga, fuck twelve!" He raged, and his next words flipped Messiah's world upside down. "I was gonna whack 'em, but God was with 'em, and if I ever get out this hoe, I'mma rock his stupid ass!"*

*"Nigga, fuck you talmbout? That boy—"*

*"Killed Lil Zetti, Messiah."*

*Messiah almost fell out his seat!*

***

*"So now ya know," JoJo confirmed as he and Justice strolled the land.*

*"But why yuh never tell meh, Pa?"*

*JoJo kept his eyes straight abased. "De dreams, daughter, are personal gifts, and a man is deserving of having a few personals, isn't he?" He smiled, and watching a flock of birds soar through the gray heavens. Justice nodded her agreement.*

*"Is it the reason we moved here?" Her vision drifted to him, and JoJo finally looked to her. They were too close for him to hide his guilt, and she had her answer without his verbal. She nodded. "Because of Messiah, right?"*

*JoJo's smile slipped away as he stopped in place, and though Justice took a few more steps, she too stopped before turning to face the first man she'd ever loved. Their eyes searched.*

*"He's no good fah yuh, Justice."*

*"Pa, that's not yuh decision."*

*"You're my baby, Justice, and—"*

*"No." She shook her head against it. "No dad, I'm yuh daughter, not yuh baby anymore." Her response severed an invisible umbilical cord, and the hurt flashed across JoJo's face. Tears wet Justice's eyes. She hated that look, but knew as a woman she had to draw a line.*

*"Yuh'll always be my baby girl, Justice."*

*"Dad."*

*"But."* JoJo held up a hand, before a sad smile eased onto his face. *"Let's make a deal?"*

*"Deal?"*

*"Yes."* He nodded before closing the distance between them, and cupping Justice's face. *"Yuh heart is precious, Justice, but precious hearts aren't treated as such when in the hands of undeserving people. Yet, yuh grown now, baby, and I'll stop my meddling until—"* He chuckled, and Justice lifted a brow.

*"Until?"*

*"Until undeserving people reveal to us that they're deserving."*

Justice laughed, but knew that's all she'd get from him. *"Deal, dad."*

***

*Hours Later*

The cue ball smacked into the triangle of others, scattering their colors in every direction. The back of Maxwell's gambling shack was smokey, and on his day, empty, save for Maxwell, Bear, and Messiah. Pimpin' bit down on his cigar while chalking his stick, and studying his next move. Messiah angled himself for it.

"You never told me you knew Detective Spinx," he spoke before leaning over the table and placing his fingers on the table, aimed for his shot.

Pimpin' Maxwell puffed a thick smoke ring. "Of course I know the fella. He's worked the streets of—"

"Stop bein' slick, P. You can catch a hoe from shore to ship, so I know you can catch a playa drift." Messiah sliced through the bullshit before sending the three ball into the corner pocket. Pimpin's eyes flickered to Bear, who shrugged, before drifting back to Messiah.

*"So tell me youngin, what's your sudden fascination with the infamous detective?"*

*"Naw, not sudden,"* Messiah mumbled while taking aim. *"Six ball, middle pocket."* He announced before his pool stick causes the exact reaction. Straightening, he chalked his stick, *"Dude been putting the squeeze on me and Sunjay, and now he done bammed bruh in some setup shit. Yet, that still doesn't answer my question."* His vision captured Pimpin'. OG chuckled before pulling the cigar from between his teeth.

*"Me and ole Spinx history goes back to the eighties, "P",  but I can't see how that concerns you?"*

Messiah's expression became pensive as his eyes fell to the pool table, but after a brief moment, he cast his bait. *"It doesn't, but I asked because I have a nice play I wanna run but I'mma need your assistance.*

*"Naw."* Pimpin' shook his head in rejection. *"I don't want nothin to do with that rotten—"*

*"You'll get dirty stacks to put in ya piggy bank."* Messiah cut him off, and the older playa smirked.

*"Well, on that note, let an ole playa hear ya plan."*

Messiah chuckled with a shake of his head before leaning down, preparing for his shot. *"All you have to do is—"*

\*\*\*

After leaving Maxwell's spot, Messiah was picked up at the end of the block in his Jag, and after slipping into the passenger's seat, he immediately went for the half smoked blunt he'd left in the ashtray, and after sparking it, his vision trailed to the driver's seat. Black studied him curiously. *"How'd it go?"*

*"It's a go."*

She laughed with a surprised expression. *"How'd you convince that sneaky mu'fucka, I know he took you through it!"*

*Messiah exhaled a cloud of smoke, "Mama, as you already know, he and Spinx got long history. And when he asked why I couldn't do it, I told him me and my people were gonna pose as the police and rob them."*

*Black Diamond nodded, and Messiah chuckled. "Besides, thirty stacks too pretty to pass at." His revelation gave his queen a good laugh as she eased the car away from the curb.*

*"You's a cold nigga, boy."*

# Chapter 11

*Next Morning*

The morning was brisk, and standing gazing out the floor to ceiling window in her office, Kate watched the sun rise over the city as she served her morning coffee. Though she was dressed the part of her profession, the red tinge beneath her lids and the messy bun, she'd whipped her hair into, were telltale signs of her lack of sleep. Stress! Ten million, just up and vanished! She shook her head in disgust; though her family was wealthy, that painting would cost them more than it's worth, merely to save face with the upper crust of society. She was a disappointment to them, the epitome of irresponsibility! Sighing, "Why me, Lord?" Kate whispered and received an answer.

The knock at the door was soft, and knowing it was Marge checking on her for the hundredth time, she rolled her eyes before taking a sip from her mug. "I'm okay, Marge."

"A package arrived." Marge stuck her head in.

"Leave it by the door, will ya?" Kate spoke without turning around, and she vaguely heard her receptionist rest the parcel on the seat before stepping behind her.

"It's gonna be okay, hon. You have to let God do his job," Marge encouraged, and with her back to her, a lone tear dripped down Kate's face.

"I'm such a disappointment, Marge, my father won't even speak to me," she cried.

"Aw, honey, don't say that!" Marge protested before turning Kate to face her. "You're not a disappointment, you're human, and ya know what?"

Marge always knew how to cheer her up. Kate gave a broken smile as she wiped her face.

"What's that?"

"You're precious, darling, and you're gonna get over this. We'll weather this storm together!"

"Oh, Marge!" Kate exclaimed as she hugged her tight. "Thank you!" She murmured as they separated.

Marge smiled, "What're friends for, hon? Now." she grinned mischievously. "I think someone wanted to cheer you up!" Nodding to the gift wrapped parcel she'd just placed on the desk, Marge wanted to be nosey, but the ringing of the phone on her desk reminded her of her job.

"I want all the juicy details," she spoke over her shoulder as she rushed out the room. Kate smiled before closing her door and making her way to her desk. And studying the birthday themed gift wrapped tubes, suspicion bled into her gaze as she sipped from her cup. Yet, she opened the card lying atop of it.

*Your special day is tomorrow, and "we" wanna be the first to wish you the best. By the time you read this, Milton will be long gone, and we'll be watching. Do not contact the authorities, or there will be consequences. Thank Milton for his soft heart.*

*We'll be in touch,*

*-Favors-*

It read; her pulse quickened as her eyes fell to the gift, and with trembling hands, she reached for it. After tearing the wrapping and twisting the top from the tube, her breath caught as she slipped the Michelangelo out, and...

*That was a year and two weeks ago, and now, as Kate parked her car down by the exact lake she'd fornicated with Messiah at, she wondered why she agreed to meet him. Yet, second guesses were useless. She realized as her eyes found*

*Messiah leaning against the Benz, looking dapper as ever. Suddenly, Kate's temperature shot through the roof! Just the sight of him, standing there as if he didn't have a care in the world, lit a fire in her. She hurried from her car, and in seconds made her way before him, and just when he cracked a smile, Kate slapped it clean away!*

*"How dare you!" She spat, and Messiah glared. He rubbed his jaw. "For?"*

*"That was for never returning my calls, and this is for what your slut sister did to my brother," she raged before going for another slap, but Messiah caught her wrist.*

*"Bitch, the first one was free, but the next one will cost ya teeth!" He growled, and after an intense stare off, Kate snatched her arm free.*

*"Don't touch me!" She screamed before crossing her arms aver her chest. "What do you want, huh? To give your friends another go at robbing me?"*

*"Bitch," Messiah spat before stepping closer. "You have one more time to be disrespectful, and I'mma handle that! If I robbed you, I'd be ten million dollars away from here, and what happened between your brother and my sister is between them!"*

*"Fuck you, Milton!"*

*Messiah chuckled before his eyes fell to her attire. The tan pants suit was chic, but the way the pearl necklace she wore dropped down into her ample cleavage made his dick jump. "Maybe later, but we have other shit to discuss at the moment."*

*She blushed under the power of his appraisement, "We have nothing to discuss, we—"*

*Messiah's arm snaking around her waist before snatching her to him murdered her rant. He was a hoe boss and was bred to see the carnal of the disguised. He'd fucked Kate both mentally and physically, and when a woman has relinquished her mind and body to a man in those aspects, she becomes the lock to his key, and he can always open her up.*

*"Let me go, you, you user!" Her pain said, but Messiah's lips against her neck made her body contradict the request.*

*"I've missed you," he whispered.*

*"I hate you—"*

*"I need you—"*

*"You used me!" She cried as her body snuffed out pain and awakened lust. His kisses reminded her of their past trysts, and...*

***

*Within a sprawling twelve thousand square foot home, nestled on private, 6.43 acres of Denton, Texas' land, six of the country's most top shelf pimps laxed in a massive room. Cushion chairs were situated in an arch and faced a roaring fire burning within a beautiful fire place. Ferrari Motti, from the Midwest, Beautiful; hailing from Chicago, Top Choice, Pimpin', Yellow Shoe, and Res Bone Tyrone, all nursed tumblers of Yac, as they counted votes on who'd win pimp of the year.*

*"The Playa's Ball" was birth from the movie, The Mack, and though Chicago use to host their own from the 70's into the early nineties, by the year of '93 it had fizzled out. Yet, since Beautiful had arrived in the metroplex, rich off the sweat from his hoe sex, he'd raved of respawning the flame. So, he'd called the meeting at his place, where he and his brethren tallied the votes they'd collected from the other pimps they'd asked. Taking a sip from his glass, he chuckled.*

*"Well, all eyes lifted to him, and he held up a list of names. "Before we speak on who the people deems fit, let's vote amongst self on which of us should get it."*

*"Well, playas, you know my "P" 1000 degree, and ain't a playa within the fifty states got a larger stable than me," Motti gloated. "I should receive that award, baby."*

*"Naw, daddy-o," Pimpin' disagreed. "You may have a larger stable, but dem there whores you got ain't exclusive work. Ya bottom hoe even gots a lil mustache, P!"*

*"Nigga, that's that French blood in that hoe. In France, hoes don't shave!" Motti defended, and Beautiful tilted his glass to him.*

*"That's exactly why you can't wear the crown this year, P. How it's gonna look with ya steppin' on them floors with ya bottom hoe upper lip trimmed better than yours," he capped as the laughter subsided, and he was voted out. And the same went for the rest, for the reasons that didn't compliment the season, until Pimpin' was sure nuff bet!*

*"Well." He lifted his glass in a toast. "That settles it, gents, I'll..."*

*"Now hold on Pimpin', we still gotta tally the people's choice, and the man from my tallies ain't even on deck." Motti's admission was followed by strange expressions, and reluctant nods. And when he passed the card hosting the name the streets were hailing, Beautiful chuckled before sipping from his glass.*

*"Well, I'll be a chili pimp with a funny link if mine don't say the same," he revealed the very name of his cards. And it was the exact result throughout the arch until four cards met Red Bone's mitt and he chuckled with a confirming nod. Pimpin' Maxwell, the ending of the rainbow, smiled arrogantly, for his own cards hailed "him" the victor.*

*"Like I said, Ps, the people knows bonafide pimpin', even if—" He was saying when the cards touched his hand, and when he flipped through the small stack, his jaw dropped. Why? Cause the name the people chosen was...*

\*\*\*

*"Mes—si—ahhhh!" Kate cried as he stood behind her doing his dance. From that lakes they'd departed, and within her office he'd gotten it started. With the door locked, it*

105

hadn't cost Messiah a drip of effort to pimp lady out her clothes and have her facing the large window; palms against the glass, back arched, and ass tooted for his movements. Gazing out at the Triple D from the fifteenth floor toward heaven, Kate's facial was captured within her moment of ecstasy as Messiah gave long slow strokes. Not because he was making love, but because he'd taken it back to a pimp's original kicks, and was eight inches deep within her asshole; leaving her pussy for the tricks. Holding her cheeks open, he watched his chocolate slip in and out of her vanilla, and if asked could a woman cum from her ass, he could answer honestly! The white froth slicking his dick was evidence, and as his pace began to quicken, Kate began to attempt to clench the glass as if it were the sheets on her bed.

"Ah—h—ohhh!" She cried.

"Whose bitch are you, Kate."

Messiah drove in until his pelvis met her ass crack.

"Your bi—tch, yoursss!" Ecstasy murdered the pain, causing her to scream recklessly, and the door handled jiggled before Marge pounded the door.

"Kate? Honey? Are you okay? Do I need to call security?" Concern was evident in her tone, but Kate's mouth formed an "o", pleasure her expression.

"No-ooo! I'm o-kkkay, Margie!" She managed.

"You sure?" Marge insisted, but Messiah reaching around and creating a Hurricane against her clit stole her verbal.

"Hhhhhuh," she swallowed a long whoosh of air.

"Kate?" The door knob jiggled again. "What's going on in there!" Marge demanded.

"One mom-ent, I'm cummmi-n-ggg!" Kate cried as her anus secreted her nectar. Messiah's fingers became a vortex against her clit and simultaneously, her rain fell while her exit wound creamed. Her body trembled, and he leaned back to watch his work, yet.

*"Kate? Are you doing the nasty with that—that black guy!"* Marge *exclaimed, aghast. And though Kate was speechless, Messiah popped his shit.*

*"No, Marge, not the nasty; this shit the fountain of youth, and if yo' old ass would have taken a few sips, you wouldn't be round here lookin' like you've drank a few gallons from the fountain of ancient!" He capped before slipping out of Kate's exit, and coating her ass with his release.*

\*\*\*

*"Well." Pimpin' sipped from his glass, before slipping from his seat. And after making his way before the fireplace, he tossed the cards inside, watching the flames erase their existence. The other men's glances were mirthful. They knew he hated to be beat. Pimpin' Maxwell turned his face to them.*

*"See, I'm all for Junior "P" accepting his accolades for his ism, but that trophy "can't" be his this season," he chuckled, and though the other men frowned in confusion, it was Yellow Shoe that spoke.*

*"And why's that, P? The gent earned his way." He tilted his glass toward Top Choice, who nodded his agreement. And Pimpin' downed the rest of his drink.*

*"Well, that may be absolute, but how can we crown a playa Pimp of the year when he done blew all his freaks?" He asked, and Red Bone slapped the arm of the chair.*

*"Goddammit, Maxwell, stop tryin' to jinx the man's game, and—"*

*"Negro, put some pimpin' on my name, and what I say is true, as sure as the sky is blue! Cat daddy is hoeless and livin' off my pimpin' til he regains his focus!" Pimpin' declared, and though four of the men stared at him in shock, suspicion bled in Top Choice's veins. Last he'd seen Messiah, he'd put on a spectacle in Milwaukee, so he couldn't fathom a playa so swift, doin' so much to cop, only to blow it all.*

*"Where ya g'tting' ya info, P?" He asked and Pimpin' Maxwell smiled connivingly, knowing the trophy was his.*

*Making his way to the exit, he spoke over his shoulder. "Nigga, I ain't ever met Joe from Cokamo, and gossip don't compliment pimpin'! I got this revelation from the very man's presentation when he showed up at a pimp's den, hoeless and lookin' soulless! Say he was knocked down there in that city you from," he chuckled before exiting, and maybe that's why he never noticed Top Choice's and Yellow Shoe's visions collide. They'd both witness Messiah's work, and the question dancing within their eyes was, who'd knocked him?*

***

*They'd redressed and Kate sat studying the business card Messiah had given her. "So you think this will really work?" She was skeptical. She'd called to check Sunjay's status only to find out his charges had been picked up by the Feds, and they themselves have been building a case on him. Messiah stood gazing out at the skyline, contemplating his last move of mental chess.*

*"Just call the man and do exactly what I asked of you, love. Let me do the thinking," he spoke over his shoulder, and after a moment's uncertainty, Kate did just that. Lifting the phone from its cradle, she dialed the number on the card and after a few rings, it was answered.*

*"Um, hi, Agent Barnes, this is Kate O'Riley." She informed, and though Messiah couldn't hear the response, Kate's verbal made him smile in triumph. "Yes, the lawyer, um, is that dinner proposal still open? I know a very handsome place we can rendezvous." She giggled, and when Messiah's eyes found her twirling a lock of her blond hair, he shook his head. Women!*

# Chapter 12

*Four Nights Later*
*6AM*
*Beneath the cover of the night and deep within the
trenches of Oak Cliff, a black Benz pulled into the Butta
Beans Apartments and eased toward the back. ♫ They smile
in yo face/ all the time tryna take yo place/ back stabbers/
what they do ♫ —The O'Jays vibe flowed through the
internal, and when the car eased to a stop beside the
industrial dumpster Foxy's eyes found Pimpin's reflection
from the rear view. The man's poise was playa as he eyed the
duffle bag stuffed with mula, and when his gaze lifted to find
her eyes capturing him, he smirked.*

*"Are you sure about this?" she asked, and when Pimpin's
eyes trailed to the Crown Victoria that pulled next to them, a
strange feeling eased into his gut.*

*The night seemed treacherous, and when Detective Spinx
slid from his car, followed by one of his dirty narc partners,
Pimpin Maxwell's vision returned to Foxy. "Even if I'm not,
forty large is too large not to be sure bout that!"*

\*\*\*

*In the frigid air of the night and standing not too far away
from where the business was being handled, a man down on
his luck and dressed in soiled clothes tilted a bottle wrapped
in a brown paper bag to his lips. The Thunder Bird burned*

*down his throat, and warmed his belly as a freezing wind caused the ends of the man's dirty coat to flap in the wind. Yet, oblivious to its chill, the bum ran the back of his hand across his mouth before glaring up at the moon, and it was to that full moon that he gave his blues. "See, Mrs. Moon, if the freaks come out at night, you gotta be the biggest freak of 'em all, and ya husband, the sun, doesn't know it, 'cause while he's sleep, you're on the creep! A low-down dirty shame how you love him but gives me company through the night. It's a low-down dirty game, how not even my closest friends has a heart for my plight.*

*"I done lost the house, the kids, and the dog, and my ole gal done left me for ole Jodie...now the kids and the dog act like they don't know me! And that ain't even the saddest blues of them all. Ya see, all I had left was my last two dollas that I vowed not to lose! But, Mrs. Moon, tell this ole bum what you would've done in my shoes? One for the bus fare, and one woulda been for the jukebox if I ain't need to cop me a bottle...*

*"But with these ole woes, I need something strong to swallow. See, I'm drownin' in these blues, and no drownin' man will ever know which drop of water drowned him...*

*"And if God didn't give a damn about him dyin', neither will the devil, nor the one that found 'em...*

*"Floatin' down that river Sam Cooke was born by..."*

\*\*\*

*When Pimpin slipped from the backseat, the smile Spinx had slipped away in confusion. "Maxwell Davenport, wha— what's good, old friend?" He stammered before he forced his smile to return.*

*Pimpin nodded his greeting as his eyes trailed to the stranger beside him, and seeing the suspicion within his appraisement, Spinx took initiative.*

*"This is my man, Thor, he's cool." He waved toward him before his vision drifted toward the backseat Pimpin slipped from.*

*"I'on like surprises," Pimpin stated, before glancing around suspiciously.*

*"You either, playa? Say it ain't so!" The sarcasm dripping from Spinx's tone drew Pimpin's attention back, and the image of the bald-headed detective heightened that strange feeling he'd earlier had. A black leather coat over a black turtle neck, Spinx wore was the poster child for crooked, and his snakish eyes seemed demonic. Freeing a cigarette from his pocket, he lit it and after exhaling a stream of smoke, he nodded toward the Benz. "Where's our boy?"*

*Pimpin shrugged before reaching into the car and retrieving the duffel bag. "Had other shit to do," he informed before tossing the bag at the men's feet.*

*Thor's eyes fell to it, but Spinx' stayed on Pimpin as he sucked from his cigarette. It glowed bright until the detective ended his assault and exhaled a cloud of smoke. Chuckling, he stepped toward Pimpin. "Now put ya hands behind ya back. You're under arrest for attempting to bribe an officer of the law." Pimpin tensed before spitting in the ground, cursing himself for not trusting his gut, but before dread could set in, Spinx burst into laughter. "Just fuckin' wit' ya, boy, lighten up!" He slapped the relieved man's arm.*

*Pimpin didn't share in the humor, and instead, lost patience. "We're gonna do business, or what, pig? Ya know ain't no love here."*

*Spinx chuckled with an agreeing nod. "Sho ya right, baby." He smiled sinisterly before tapping Thor's shoulder.*

*The white mama made his way to the back of the Crown Vic, and after retrieving a green backpack, he tossed it to Pimpin.*

*Caught off guard, he frowned. "What the fuck is this," he growled before unzipping it and frowning.*

*Spinx laughed. "Oh, ya ain't know you were doing a drug deal?" He laughed harder, and Pimpin was just about to return the dope, the part of the deal Messiah failed to mention, when the night came alive! Out of the darkness, dark figures emerged.*

*"Freeze!" Someone screamed, and shock registered on the three men's faces as Messiah checkmated the game from afar!*

\*\*\*

*The bum spun and did a Michael Jackson move before gripping his nuts with one hand and tilting the bottle to his lips with the other. And after having his fill, he bowled at the moon.*

*"Jim Crow still runs the show, and mama dearest done lost her damn mind since crack hit the hood...*

*"And for trying to make a measly dolla, the white man puts my brothaman in handcuffs and call it the better good.*

*"Enslave the slave, work 'em and he never get paid, until he screams 'I'mma be hood, Mr. Peckerwood.*

*"My daddy was a rolling stone, and my mama used to tell me it'll be days like this, but what she never told me was 'bout, when a nigga broke as a joke, love would have no ways like this! That these streets stink like this! That when the dog and my kids left me along wit' my ole gal, that I would find peace in a drink like this!" He screamed, before scratching his ass. "It's a low-down dirty shame how the game turns, and makes me wanna holla, 'cause no matter how many times niggas get burned, niggas just never learn!"*

\*\*\*

*Red and blue lights reflected on the walls from the numerous Fed and police cars. The natives of Butta Beans Apartments watched as Detective Spinx's story came to an end. Thor was dragged kicking and screaming to the back of the paddy wagon, and Pimpin Maxwell and Foxy were led to the back seats of separate cars. Pimpin's smile was genuine until it dawned on him that what Messiah said would be a hoax was actually real life! He shook his head in confusion as he watched Spinx get arrested.*

*"Detective Spinx, you are an embarrassment to the good officers of Dallas, and it's my pleasure to aid in bringing an end to your despicable ways!" The chief of police told the shamed detective as he was led to the back of the car.*

*The neighborhood had gathered to watch the spectacle, and suddenly, someone clapping transcended into the entire gathering applaud of the man's downfall. After Spinx was secured in the backseat of an unmarked car, he glared out at the crowd, and it was there that his mouth fell open in shock. Within the crowd's midst stood Murda, Sunjay— who'd been freed due to the play of Messiah— and clad in designer, with a black trench coat over a silk Versace shirt, stood the man of the hour. Messiah smiled, and Sunjay formed a mock gun with his fingers before disappearing into the crowd. Murda followed shortly after, and Messiah smirked arrogantly before saluting him and allowing fate to do the rest.*

# Chapter 13

*A week had passed and since then, on this Friday night, The 1996 Playas Ball was held in South Dallas at club Two Cousins between Pensen and Grand Avenue. The night was festive in the city as people from around the country came to parlay amongst playas. A red carpet was rolled from the door of the club to the curb, and though the line to get in was forever long, most knew they'd never make it in, and was cool with parking lot pimpin' to see the show. Cameras flashed as mu'fuckas struck poses with the elite, but when two 1983 cherry Cadillac Eldorados pulled to the curb, all eyes captured it. A tall, elegant man slipped from the driver's side, and dripped in a tailored, fire red two-piece with a black shirt beneath to hail the black reptiles on his feet, he flung his long, permed hair over his shoulder before flicking the top of his nose. Eldorado Red was a stone-cold pimp from Harlem and he was certified! With a snap of his fingers, the remaining doors opened on both cars and out poured six bimbos— three from each car— and all three wore red jackets and pumps, and though each woman was elite for a freak, what stood out was their nakedness from the waist down.*

"Bitch, I'm Eldorado Red. Been pimpin' since a hoe learnt to put extensions in her head, and Santa hooked reindeers to a sled. Either a hoe gone break bread or play dead, and a dead bitch ain't heard what I said, so I must be talkin' to a live hoe that can fuck for my bread!" *He waved toward his hoes, and as they strutted toward the club, the crowd ohh'd and awed, for upon the nude flesh of each woman's ass was air brushed Cadillac symbols.*

*Valets moved the cars, and after the pimp and his ladies had made their entrance, a cocaine hued stretch limo pulled to the curb. The flash of cameras lit up the night as the people snapped shots. The limo driver slipped out and raced to the back, and when he pulled the door open, four Ken the Barbie dolls exited; shirtless, with spiked collars and dog chains around their necks. With black tux pants and Cohans on their feet, each man was built like Greek Gods. Yet, it was when they turned in union, and knelt with their heads bowed and hands extended toward the backseat, that pimpin' took form. A jeweled, manicured hand reached out from the darkness, and the long red nails attached to it was affirmation that pipmin' comes in different forms. When the prostrated gents took the hand, out slipped a vision of seduction that generated sharp intakes of breath from the crowd, and gazing about from beneath long lashes, Madame Cat took in the scene. Cameras flashed; capturing the image of her holding the ends of the chains in a hip-hugging sequin dress that hosted a plunging neckline so deep that her breast threatened to spill out. The dress, coupled with the red pumps on her feet, complimented the devilish, red bull whip in her other hand and blew a kiss to her high yellow skin tone and dark eye shadow. Each man kissed her hand until she waved them off dismissively, and without having to be told, they rose to their feet and faced the entrance to the club.*

*Madame Cat smiled seductively at the crowd before blowing them a kiss. "The white man whipped and enslaved my people for four hundred years, and I don't fault them, so who can fault me for sex enslaving such exquisite pounds of flesh?" She giggled before giving a light crack at her whip and allowing the men to lead her in the club.*

\*\*\*

*The inside of the club was a movie! Champagne bottles, freaks popping their asses, playa's playin', tricks trickin', and gangstas getting their G on. Unlike the times before, this playas ball had opened the doors to all creatures beneath the moon! If one had the means, they could be on the scene, and that they did! Even Pimp Maxwell, fresh out the can, had his P turned to the max, and had a crease in his slacks. He and an entourage of playas parlayed, kickin' some P until the main event. At twelve that night, it would officially be Christmas, and each man was elated to still be upright in his gators! Some of their ladies were in their midst, but even without Santa screaming it: most of the others were somewhere winging him the extravaganza— ho ho hoin' with tricks! People danced around the stage that was to be used, yet, in that VIP, only playas and cons were allowed; and with their tables pushed together to form one, the vibe was groovy.*

*"I'm tellin' you, gents, Cleopatra was the first hoe to ever run slick con on John!" Red Bone Tyrone argued before waving a bottle of Don. "Julius Caesar had conquered every nemesis and had reached Africa to make Egypt a Roman colony. That boy never knew a seductress had been exiled and awaiting her chance to seduce her way back onto the throne. Smuggled into Alexandria, rolled up inside a carpet, the bitch had herself unfurled at that dictator's feet!" Red Bone slapped the table with a high pitch, pimpish laugh. "That white man ain't even seen no shit like that, and after puttin' that ole cat on him, the man gave the scheming bitch exactly what he'd arrived there for in the first place! The throne!"*

*"Cat daddy, you as wrong as a man in a thong!" Top Choice disagreed with a shake of his head. "The hardest bitch to ever piss from a split has to be the Virgin Mary! Not only did she seduce God to give her some dick, but even after she gave birth, she not only convinced her man Joseph to*

116

*stay, but she macked the world into believin' she's still a virgin!" He capped with three snaps of his fingers before poppin' the collar of his bright purple silk shirt. "The pimp God ain't God at all if he don't bless my game wit' a hoe the same!" he exclaimed, and the people laughed.*

*A table down, Pretty Ricky sat pretty, with his long hair cascading to his shoulders in thick Shirley Temples, and surrounded by four of his ladies, he sipped from a glass of spirits. And after the laughter subsided, the usual happened.*

*"What about Betty Boop, daddy? That was a bad bitch, too!" Sin, his ditzy hoe, spoke out of turn.*

*It seemed as if someone had frozen the room as all eyes shot to them in shock.*

*Pretty Ricky paused with his glass halfway to his lips as his eyes slowly trailed to the hoe. And without breaking eye contact, he acknowledged Lucy, another of his ladies. "Baby, hand me that bottle of champagne," he requested, and after she'd complied, Pretty Ricky shook the bottle as hard as he could. "Hoe, Betty Boop! The cartoon?" He growled, and Sin was too stupid to know the danger.*

*Sipping from her own glass, she waved him off. "Yass, daddy, that hoe was official! Bitch hoes in daisy dukes like—"*

*The top flew off the shook-up champagne bottle with a whoosh, and punched her in the right eye.*

*"Awww, nigga, my eye! You done blinded me! Ahhhh!" She screamed at the top of her lungs while getting a champagne shower. Sin flopped around in her seat, hand over her eye as she cried, but Pretty Ricky had no sympathy.*

*"Hoe, next time it'll be both; you'll be the first blind hoe to work a trick, and when asked how ya lost ya sight, you can tell 'em 'cause ya mouth was open for somethin' other than suckin' dick!" He jazzed before tilting the bottle to his lips.*

*Yellow Shoe chuckled as Sin's wife-n-laws helped her to the ladies room, and after he composed himself, his vision drifted to the table set up for—"Say, pimp friends, where's* the P Messiah?" His question was the reflection of other's curiosities, and naturally, all eyes found Pimpin.

He winced after tossing back a drink of clear, his mental was the devil's playground. He knew coincidences happened, but nativity had never suited his game. Naw, whatever went down with them pigs was calculating! And the Feds ain't lettin' nan nigga off after getting popped red handed, he thought with a sad shake of the head. "I done told y'all fellas, P hoe broke! And ain't no true playa showin' up to no pimp's day wit' his misplays on display, ya dig." He gave rationale, and before anyone could respond, the host of the shindig took the stage.

The music died down and a spotlight cast him beneath its game. "Ladies and gents, gangstas and whimps, and hoes and pimps, the time has finally come for that moment we've all been waiting for," beautiful announced to the roar of the crowd. Draped in a lime green, alligator skinned suit, complete with the matching kicks, and with his long hair dried, dyed, and laid to the side, the man bounced his shoulders dramatically before waving out at the gathering. "Now, we won't make this long, 'cause," he glanced at his Rollie, "in twenty minutes, it's officially Christmas, and I see many gifts, so I know somebody got somethin for a beautiful mu'fucka like me!" He dusted off his shoulders, and a slim, jazzy thang yelled toward the stage.

"I got a gift for yo beautiful ass, baby, and—"

"Hoe!" She was snatched back by her weave. "You tryin' to pay another P's pimpin'? I'll break ya mothafuckin'..." Her man was raging as he drug her off, and the room burst into laughter.

Beautiful flicked the tip of his nose. "Gotta keep ya eyes on this beautiful shit, especially round a beautiful bitch, ya dig!" He capped with a pimpish laugh. "But without further ado, let's make it do what it do! Y'all give a warm welcome to one of the hardest hoes to have ever strolled a stroll. Sassy," he intro'd.

*Sassy stepped onto the stage clad in a sheer royal mini dress with red Vikki Secrets that barely concealed all her secrets beneath it. Yet, over it was draped a royal blue, floor length mink. Hair and makeup slain, the chocolate hued buxom beauty smiled brightly before waving a small stack of reading cards at the crowd. The people's greeting was righteous— all knew of her infamy and respected the game. "Aiight, okay, I get it." She patted the air for calm. "Okay, I know I'm a bad bitch, but Beautiful, baby?" Her eyes found him standing to the side of the stage. "Hoes hoe, but a bitch like me ain't bed a trick since Moby Dick sprouted a dick. So, not too much on my last indecencies, okay, honey? You almost hurt my lil ole feelings," she playfully chided. Beautiful blew her a kiss, and returning her attention to the crowd, she held her smile. "And merry fuckin' Christmas to all the real ladies out there, who's not ashamed to be flat-backin' for a real niggas mackin'!" Her salutations were met with wild whistling, cheers, and "heyyys"! She laughed. "Okay, now, for the moment we've all been waitin' for." She gazed down at the first card and giggled with a shake of her head. "And as we all knew, this year's playa of the year award goes to, Pimpin Ma—" Before she could complete her sentence, commotion from the front of the club paused her.*

*Pimpin seized the moment to lean towards Foxy. "Baby, go find the girls and tell them to hurry they ass back to the table, so when the spotlight hits me, the world can see ain't a stable aliv, mo' able than mine!" He jived, and Foxy hurried off to do his bidding. Pimpin's eyes trailed to the commotion that had the crowd parting like the Red Sea and frowned when spotting three gorgeous felines struggling to wheel a dolly hosting two massive boxes lavishly wrapped in gift wrap. Yet, when it registered that the body suits, they wore weren't body suits at all but body paint, tricks and squares rushed to their aid.*

*The giant gifts were wheeled to the VIP, and only then did the three beauties allow their heels to carry them to the table reserved for their daddy. All three women were stark naked, except for black satin thongs, heels, and the blinding apples dangling from their necklaces. Yet, it was the oil black paint blanketing from their necks down, that created erotica. Nipples protruding, and their hair slayed, all three pulled out daddy's chair before standing behind it, and that's when Messiah made his entrance. As soon as Pimpin spotted Tutts his heart raced, yet, recognizing Paradise; knowing she was once Sassy's foundation, unveiled the fucked up feeling he'd been having since Messiah had shown up on his doorstep.*

*"Well." Yellow Shoe chuckled before lifting a bottle of Moët toward the approaching man. "If this what ya call hoe broke, I'd say you a slow poke that's fallen for the oldest trick of a playa's mojo!"*

*"Fuck you, sucka!" Pimpin spat with a sinking feeling in his stomach as he eyed his protégé suspiciously.*

*Messiah slipped through the crowd shirtless, diamonds heavy around the neck and wrist. And besides the white suit pants, crocodile belt with the matching shoes, it was the albino python draped over his shoulders that spoke his peace. Taking a bite from a green apple, the man entered the VIP and took the seat his ladies stood behind, and peeping the scene through the lenses of gold framed designer glasses, he peeped when Foxy, in a panic, rushed over to Pimpin.*

*"Pimpin, Pimpin, it's some shit in the game!" She spoke hurriedly, before offering a quick glare at Messiah.*

*"Hoe, what ya bumpin' 'bout? Slow down and spit it out!" Pimpin Maxwell demanded, and Foxy's next words were a playa's kryptonite.*

*"The girls, Pimpin, they've—"*

*"Defected, P," Messiah helped.*

*"Wha-What!" Pimpin stuttered, but his heart already knew.*

*Reclining in his seat, Messiah waved to an empty one beside him. "Come parlay wit' a boss, OG, and let me pour* you a sip from a pimp," he suggested before popping a bottle of the good shit, and filling two glasses.

Pimpin frowned within his hesitancy before sucking up his pride and joining his creation. The silence was so thick in the club, one could cut a slice for later, and Yellow Shoe and Top Choice shared a knowing look; the game had no love! Taking a seat, Pimpin crossed his ankle over his knee, real pimpish as he listened.

Messiah sipped before he pimped, "Back in the gap when you peeled me for them sluts, my heart was cracked. You put me out in the cold without a hand to hold, tellin' me to follow the yellow brick road, and—"

"Ah." Pimpin held up a finger before retrieving the second glass of Cris. "But I warned you that there was no such thing as the wizard, and the road was only yellow because it's creators knew it'll get dark in a playa's world, and he'd need to be able to see his way from it!"

Messiah chuckled. "I can dig it, daddy-o, but it took me to travel that road to understand that a colored road is only colored because its designers wants to lead you somewhere. But, following that mu'fucka only made me self-conscious. And guess what, P?"

Pimpin shrugged with a sad smile. "Don't leave a pimp in suspense, mack buddy."

"It took me leaving that road of the self-conscious, in order to find that those words were backwards—"

"Conscious self." Pimpin flipped the words and laughed. And after downing half his drink, he eyed his brainchild. "That play wit' me and ole Spinx?"

Messiah pointed over at the large gifts. "It's Christmas, baby. I had to treat myself." He chuckled before snapping his fingers, and his ladies rushed over to the giant gifts. The gift wrap tore away easily, and the strange boxes fell apart to reveal Creamy and Candy. Both women were identically body painted as his other ladies, and the twinkling apples *dangling from their necklaces made it official. The crowd went dumb.*

*"Aww shit! Junior P done knocked senior P, and senior P the one that gave him the P!" Someone shouted.*

*"Gave 'em the five P's, ya dig!" Red Bone chimed and Beautiful chuckled. "Proper. Pimpin'. Performs. Perfectly. No pressure!" He gave the five P's, and even Pimpin Maxwell had to smile when his former hoes stepped over to him and planted kisses on his cheek, before placing twin apples on the table before him. And after hipping him to their new management, they joined the others standing behind Messiah's chair.*

*"When Pimpin' begins, friendships end, daddy." Messiah read him his rights. "Yea, the play with Spinx was more for him than you, but I needed you out the way so I could knock these hoes properly. And after they cleared ya safe and paid me my fee, the last part of my play with them white folks was complete! For Spinx and his boys, you and Sunjay walked."*

*He laughed, and to his utter surprise, Pimpin Maxwell lost his ism!*

*"Nigga, cleared my safe?" He roared before exploding from his seat, and staring bullets at him. A multitude of playas rushed over and restrained him. It wasn't pretty when a playa blew his stable.*

*Messiah nodded his affirmation. "The entire two hunnid racks, and the jewels. The rest of ya ladies are currently outta pocket 'til I can get em in pocket." Tears in his eyes, Messiah chuckled. He'd finally gotten his lick back, and after he'd been crowned Pimp of the Year, he and his ladies made it a Christmas to remember!*

*** *

*She'd seen it all from afar and it blew her mind to see the cutthroat "ish" between Messiah and his mentor. Justice laughed bitterly before tossing her last drink back; she'd needed it.*

*** 

*The heavens were bruised; violet and soft pinks clashed as the sun made its way around. He was on his way to his car when he thought the liquor was playing a silly trick.*
*"Messiah, wait!"*
*A voice—that voice— that'd always had a spell on him. Messiah paused midstride and when his vision captured the red bone standing with her arms crossed over her ample breast, and framed by soft light of the sunrise, his mouth fell open. Justice was made for a playa! Her hair was braided, and each braid was two toned; fading from black to white at mid length. She'd slung it over her left shoulder as she stood with her right leg cocked at an angle to give just a peek of inner thigh, but it was the skintight, soccer ball checkered mini dress that hugged her thickness that made him fight against his ism. Sleeveless with a turtleneck, it was ideal for the knee-high checkered boots on her feet, and at five-four and weighing one fifty, mama was thick-thick.*
*"Well, say somethin', yuh go just stand dey looking dottish?" She smiled sheepishly, and as the sun rose to its perch, Messiah's heart reminded him why it had frozen so long ago.*
*His face became stone before he laid down the law.*
*"Maybe you should have said something before I ran out of something to say, 'cause I ain't gonna tussle with a bitch that ain't tryin' to aid my hustle, ya dig? You willin' to pay my pimpin', bitch?"*
*Justice's jaw fell. That wasn't the reception she'd anticipated. "Nigga—" Her face was a mixture of hurt and anger as she placed a hand on her hip. "Don fix yuh lips to eva disrespect meh, I—"*

*"Broke ya promise, hoe; that's what you did; and I ain't a pain freak for broken hearts. So if you ain't tal'm 'bout hoin', we ain't got no reason for convoin'. So, what's up, hoe? You wit' it or what?"*

Justice went rigid, and with her small hands balled into a fist at her side, she allowed him to see her pain. Her eyes became baptized, but Messiah's heart was more concrete than a mu'fucka that had stared into Medusa's eyes. Ignoring the lone tear dripping from her left eye, he turned and allowed his gators to carry him to the Benz where Tutts and Cakes stood waiting. He and Cakes slipped in, but Tutts eyed Justice with a smug expression on her face; Black Diamond had told her about the Trinidadian that had broken her son's heart, and seeing the girl's beauty up close stirred the first touch of jealousy Tutts had felt in a long time. Yet, Messiah's ism had pacified her.

"You're not his type no more, baby, but if you ever decide you wanna use what you got to get what you need—" She suggestively ran a hand over her private area. "Let me know and I'll talk to him."

"Bitch, get in the car!" Messiah demanded from the driver's seat, and Tutts blew Justice a kiss before complying.

As the Benz dipped out of the parking lot, Justice watched her first dream turn into ash like a vampire being exposed to the sun.

# Chapter 14

*A Week Later*

*Zetti's funeral had been held on a gray Sunday, but Messiah hadn't attended. Yet, he'd spend the piggy bank to ensure shorty's wings went out in style. Proud, he'd admired the view to as he strided behind his three felines; each woman before him had jiggle in their asses, and anyone with eyes could see their promiscuity without needing glasses. And while watching the sway of their work, Messiah hadn't realized they'd came to the hole in the earth until their struts halted. Gazing up, he peeped out the lenses of his Versaces, and smirked at the tall, slim beauty standing above a white casket resting on the cold ground. Beside it, two grave diggers stood, waiting to do what they were paid to do.*

*"Damn, nigga, what took ya ass so long? You tryin' to turn a bitch to a snow woman!" Black Diamond complained before Messiah pulled her in for a quick hug.*

*"My fault, mama, you know I be on P time, but 'preciate this." He nodded to the casket. He'd cashed out so that after Zetti's service, he could have his personal one with little man before he was lowered into the earth.*

*"You boys give us a moment, Jeff." Black spoke to one of the men and nodding, he and the other man turned to do just that.*

*"Just holler when you're ready, Black. We'll be over there, tending to another plot." He spoke as they departed.*

*When Messiah's eyes fell to the casket, his chest hurt. "Damn, Zetti," he mumbled. The breath of winter twirled through the cemetery, causing his ankle length, blood red cashmere suit to flutter. The white slacks and silk shirt offset it and fed attention to the red gators on his feet. Slipping a fifth of Hennessy from his pocket, he made his way over to the casket, and squatting down, he opened the top half; his eyes instantly saturated at the stiff form of Zetti. Cracking the seal on the bottle, he took a deep swing before resealing it, and resting the bottle inside the casket. "Ya know," he began, before freeing a gray Glock from his waist. And yanking one into the head, a tear slipped from his right eye as he gently laid the fire on Zetti's chest. "Just in case," he whispered with a shake of the head. "Lil bro, it's a cold reality when you're running wild through the jungle, looking for a hug from all the wrong mu'fuckas. The snake's embrace is too tight, and comes with a poisonous kiss. The lions don't know how to hug, plus, their claws too sharp! And they always use their teeth! The gorilla's love is too rough, and the tiger's only sense of a hug is followed by you becoming a meal." Messiah ran a hand over Zetti's fresh haircut, and when a drop of his eye-rain splashed against the gray suit the boy wore, Messiah smirked. "Yet, I taught you this, fam, and you still ran wild, expecting hugs from animals, just 'cause y'all were bred in the same jungle. Now look," he spat before waving toward the six foot grave a few feet away. "Who did you, Zetti? Huh? The lion, tiger, snake or gorilla!" Messiah asked before wiping his face. The women around him hurt because he hurt, but suddenly, the vibe changed. Messiah smirked. "Send me a sign, lil nigga, and I'mma handle that, but till then?" He chuckled as his vision drifted to Tutts, who smirked before turning to Cakes.*

*Both women wore skintight fuck me dresses, with quarter coats and heels. Yet, inspite of the chill, they aimed to please daddy. Taking her wife-n-law by the hand, Tutts pulled her closer, and within the chill of the day, their tongues began to dance. Cakes moaned as Tutts ran her hand down her back, over her cheeks, and paused just at where the hem of her dress stopped beneath the bottom of her ass. Black Diamond made her way over and handed Messiah a small tote bag, and gazing into it, he chuckled. A camera, film, and the x-rays of a set of pictures were inside, and he happily placed it in the casket before closing the lid on Zetti and his own secrets. Erecting himself, he smiled at the thought of Lil Zetti's adolescent lust for Tutts and Liberty.*

*"I told you, a real nigga gotta strive to keep his word, fam, and..." His vision drifted to the freak session Tutts and Cakes had pulled their dresses up to bunch around their waist, and pantiless, Cakes lay on her back upon the casket. Pantiless, Tutts climbed aboard in the sixty-nine position, and when their tongues began to please, Messiah chuckled. "I told you I'd let you get ya rocks off with my freaks." He waved towards his girls. Their licks, kisses, and moans were a symphony. "Rest easy, lil nigga, I just broke luck and got my lick back from my old friend, and—" The tap against his shoulder gave him pause as his vision trailed to his T-lady. Black Diamond nodded over her shoulder, and when he spotted Pimpin's Navigator, his mind went to the burner he'd just rested in the casket. When his eyes drifted back to Black Diamond's, she shook her head against the urges.*

*"Only during Pimpin does y'alls friendship pause, but never deny a man his just closure, 'cause without it, his bitterness will turn snakish," she hemmed, and with a nod, Messiah turned and made the trek to his idling SUV.*

*Yet, when the window rolled down, he was surprised to find not Pimpin, but his bottom; Foxy. She smiled a sad smile. "Get in, Messiah, I want to show you the next and last phase of the game," she whispered, and though suspicious, Foxy was like a second mother to him, so?*

\*\*\*

127

*Twenty Minutes Later*
*Spanish Point and Harvest Hill Apartments in North Dallas were nondescript and created with the lower class in mind, and in their rear, in apartment 225, Doll Face sat in a robe on a leather sectional. Crack cocaine had sucked the shine from her skin and made her once long hair brittle, but the strangest thing about crack and black women is that though it tarnishes so much of them, it somehow avoided stealing their asses and ideal of sex appeal. Though Doll Face had shrunken up, her ass was still plump, and on days such has this one, she was in tune with sensuality. Though the apartment was nice, and the furniture was new, it was a reminder that she was the side bitch. It was a reminder of why she'd fallen from glory in the first place.*

*Rick James' greatest hits played softly as Doll Face sat cross legged and smoked a cigarette, yet her eyes were fixated on the glass dick, pusher, and the thirty dollar piece of crack resting on the coffee table. Exhaling a stream of smoke, she shook her head bitterly as her body craved her addiction*

🎵 Remember when I use to/ looove them and leave them/ that's what I use to do/ use and abuse them 🎵 *Rick James sung and placing the cancer stick in the ashtray, Doll Face retrieved the objects of her fascination, and after going through the motions, she was just about to put flame to the pipe's tip, when the front door opened and in stepped Pimpin Maxwell.*

*They both froze, their eyes searching; him hating the view, her hating the hate in his eyes. Yet, after a moment's pause, pimp lost and locked the door before he slouched back and allowed his kids to drift close. Doll Face, pipe still between her lips, gave him the side eye as she awaited the usual rant of crack's destruction. See, Pimpin's love for her ran deep, and it was he who paid the rent on that apartment, and ensured she kept food in her belly. All on the low!*

♫ Then I laid eyes on you/ it was paaain, before pleasure/ that was my claim to fame ♫ — *Rick serenaded, and Pimpin mumbled the damnest thing. "Light that shit, Doll. Help a Pimp take his stress away."*

\*\*\*

*Parked mere yards away, Foxy and Messiah had seen ole Maxwell enter the apartment, and with a bitter shake of her head, Foxy sucked spirit from her cigarette. "So, that's what you were doing the entire time, huh? Playin' for those girls while me and Pimpin were clueless?" she whispered, and Messiah frowned at the riddle of why the hell would Pimpin be visiting his dopefiend ex?*

*Messiah's orbs drifted to her, and after a moment's appraisement, a knowing smirk creased his lips. "Foxy, you been like a second mother to me since the eighties, and you stood there that day when Pimpin popped me for my stable and taught me the most powerful gem known to the game of Pimpin."*

*Foxy's eyes were fixated on the apartment Maxwell had ventured into, but it was the way her irises clouded that revealed to Messiah she was recalling the faithful days, and after a drag from her square, she nodded. "When pipmin' begins, friendships end," she whispered over an exhale of smoke.*

*Messiah chuckled. "Yeah, ma, and that confirms my suspicions. See, when I knocked Candy and Creamy, I made sure they tried each hoe Pimpin had to see if they could put 'em under new management, so I know they tried you, too!" He chuckled. "Yet, not only did you decline, but you also never hipped Pimpin to my dealings. And at the ball, you acted as if it was all new to you. Why?" He smiled, but when a lone tear dripped down Foxy's pretty face, she was taken back! "Wha—" he began, but Foxy dropped a bomb powerful enough to top the first atomic bomb ever used in warfare; Hiroshima!*

*"Messiah, you knew Pimpin would look into ya story about being hoe broke, and selling that pretty house in Desoto, didn't you?" She smiled sadly when Messiah nodded his confirmation. "Yet, what you couldn't have known was me going back alone a few nights later and seeing Black Diamond and Tutts packing boxes onto a U-Haul truck." She laughed and Messiah stared in awe at her.*

*"You knew—"*

*"Yea, negro, ain't nobody sellin' no damn house that damn fast!" She dumped the ashes off the cigarette as they shared a laugh. And that's when her smile vanished and the bomb dropped. "Messiah, me and Pimpin have been married since I took him from his first love."*

*Messiah went rigid beside her. "What! Married? First—"*

*"Yes." Foxy nodded. "His first love, which is my older sister, Doll Face." She jabbed her cigarette toward the apartment. "The same bitch he put up in this apartment and thought I wouldn't find out."*

\*\*\*

*Doll Face was as high as a cloud as she pulled Pimpin's pants down to his ankles and took his flaccidness into her hands. And stepping to her duties, she licked and kissed him until she felt that familiar pulse beneath his flesh, and he was semi erect. Lady released him to retrieve her crack pile. Lighting its tip, she sucked a cloud into her lungs, and to Pimpin's utter amazement, when she exhaled the cloud onto his meat, it stretched to its maximum. Smiling seductively, she climbed to her feet, their eyes dancing.*

*"How that shit make you feel?" Pimpin's curiosity was a sin.*

*Doll Face's eyes were buck. "Like nothin' else matters in the world, baby."*

*"How many times it took you to get hooked?"*
*Doll Face smacked her lips with a roll of her eyes.*
*"Pimpin, you watch too many movies! Nigga, crack don't hook nobody! It's just so good, you want to keep smokin',"*
*she lied, and when Pimpin Maxwell's eyes went to the stem in her hand, Doll Face flipped his life upside down. Slipping out her robe, she wasted no time straddling him, and with their stares battling, she placed the demon between Pimpin's lips. No more words were exchanged as she lit its tip, and like a professional, Pimpin Maxwell filled his lungs! Doll Face, positioned him, and after impaled herself upon him, she rode that dick, but knew she could never ride him as hard as crack cocaine was doing!*

***

*Foxy chuckled bitterly. "I was young, beautiful and blinded by his game when Pimpin Maxwell got me pregnant, and even more blinded when he came to me one day, looking like a sad ass puppy. Ya shoulda seen him, Messiah. The man had tears in his eyes and everythang!" She laughed before flicking the finished cigarette out the window. "And when he gave me a spiel of how he'd fallen on hard times, and if I truly loved him, I'd do what he needed for me to do to help us keep our apartment." Foxy shook her head in shame. "That was the first time I'd ever turned a trick, and by the time I'd had our baby girl, I'd become the most sought-after hoe on this side of the Hoe Strolls-R-Us!" She giggled before glancing to him, and Messiah again, shook his head I disbelief.*
*"You and Pimpin have a lil girl?"*
*Foxy laughed before shaking her head. "No, Messiah, she's not a lil girl no mo'. In fact, my baby just graduated from UNT in Denton, where she lives with my sister. And—"*
*She paused to turn the key in the ignition. "The reason I never hipped Pimpin to ya lil play is for the same reason I*

*never confronted him about this." She waved toward the apartment before easing the truck into the drive. "A stomp down bitch honors her nigga and abides by the laws of the life they've creating together, Siah, and my man lives a life where he must be respected! Besides." She laughed bitterly. "You knockin' his ass for them nothin' ass hoes only leaves me, and I'm done selling pussy. Messiah, times are changing and we should too. Which leads me to the last lesson of the game you must learn." She eased the Navi out of its spot, leaving Pimpin to what neither her nor Messiah could fathom. Messiah respected her that much more for not being an average bitch and going to confront Pimpin. Foxy smiled as if she'd read his thoughts. "Never lie to a bitch about what ya do wit' ya dick! She's gonna have to respect it or check it, 'cause a real nigga gives it to 'em off the muscle! That's what makes a boss, baby, when you ain't gotta lie about what you do or how you do, 'cause you know even if you lose a hoe for being solid, you gonna knock for six mo' for that same reason!"*

# Chapter 15

*That night, after he'd gotten home, Messiah showered and retired to his room to relax, but when he entered, he throws in place at the side of the white rose, resting against his red comforter. His heart did something strange in spite of him, and plucking the token from its place, a sad smile touched his lips. He remembered, "This rose is a symbol of what I feel for you. It'll never die, and as long as you keep it safe, it will live forever!" He whispered what he'd written Justice so long ago.*

*"Did you mean it?"*

*Messiah turned to find his Queen standing in the threshold of the door, and though the ism in him refuted the truth, Black Diamond knew who he was beneath the armor. He reluctantly nodded. "Yeah, ma, but—"*

*"Let me tell you something, Messiah. It's a big difference between a natural love, and a taught one. Taught love is way more powerful because it's customized by you, for you. When love is natural, so are the mistakes that come with it, but—" She paused to make her way to him, and cupping his face, Queen smiled. "But when you teach a mu'fucka how to love you— specifically you— when they sin, you have the right to be fucked up about it."*

*"You knew she was back this entire time!" Messiah's brow rose as hurt bloomed within his gaze. "Why you ain't tell me, mama?"*

*Black ran a hand down the side of her baby's face. "Go ask her, baby, and turn your natural love for her into a taught one!"*

***

*Most of her things were packed, and the few that weren't, would be. The dim living room was silent as Justice stood gazing around her apartment. In a black SMU hoodie with the hood pulled over her curly hair, black leggings, and black Air Max, she was ready for the road. Boxes were stacked in every corner of the room and would be picked up and transferred to Houston the next day. Sighing heavily, Justice retrieved her purse before heading for the door; it was a three-hour drive to Houston, and she knew it would be the loneliest ride she'd ever taken. While rummaging through her purse for her keys, she simultaneously opened the door.*

*"It took me a minute to understand that just because we locked pinkies doesn't mean a promise is unbreakable." The sound of his voice caused her head to snap up in surprise. Messiah stood before her, all black from beanie, thermal shirt, Guess pants, to the K's on his feet. The only deviation from the dark tone of his fit was the gold herring bone necklace adorned with a huge diamond encrusted medallion that had "Oak Cliff Baby" inscribed across it in gold.*

*When the shock wore off, Justice rolled her eyes, and smacking her lips, she glared. "What yuh want, Messiah, huh? To recite more of yuh little nursery rhymes to me? Eh? What, yuh wanna see if yuh lil pimp words can sway meh into selling myself for—" She was ranting when Messiah took her fast. Before she could register it, he'd step into her space, pulled her close, and had his tongue in her mouth. Its tango had a sensuality so erotic that she moaned. Trapped in the moment, she reciprocated the yearning, but when her mind shoved her heart, it screamed: "Stupid bitch, you don't know him anymore!" With that, Justice gently pushed Messiah away. The separation of their lips smacked as she placed her hands against his chest. And shaking her head, a storm converged beneath her lids. "Naw, yuh can't play me and tink I's some weak bitch that yuh can run back to." Her Trinidadian tongue was thick.*

*"Can I come in?" Messiah ignited her, his vision trailing to the dim apartment.*

*"No," Justice declined before crossing her arms over her chest.*

*"Cool." Messiah nodded before nudging her out the doorway and entering in spite of.*

*"Boy!" Justice rolled her eyes before following him in and closing the door. She placed her back to it as she watched him.*

*Messiah smiled sadly as his eyes took in the boxes; the thought of almost missing her doing something to his chest. "You were just gonna mash without a word?" He chuckled bitterly with a shake of his head. "Again," he whispered as an afterthought, and for some reason, his eyes froze on her unpacked stereo and CD collection.*

*Justice shrugged, but the sadness of his tone bothered her. "You didn't seem to be worried a week ago, so—"*

*Messiah nodded before making his way to her CD collection, and after finding one he liked, he placed it into the stereo.*

*With her hands in the front pocket of her hoodie, Justice sighed. "Messiah, what's up? I have to go and—"*

*"I once heard some bullshit 'bout if you love somethin', let it go; and if it comes back, it was real?" He spoke over his shoulder before pressing play. And just as Freddy Jackson's Old Time Sake filled the room, Messiah turned to face her. The only light source in the room came from the few lights Justice kept plugged in, and within their glow, Messiah gazed at her. "I've never believed that shit, ma. Why would a mu'fucka have to let go of love just to test its authenticity?*

*What if it is the real deal, but letting it go is what makes it never return, 'cause it hurt so bad when you let it walk away?" Messiah's eyes were searching as he made his way to her.*

*"What yuh sayin', Sias?"*

*"I'm sayin'," he whispered before taking her hand and wrapping an arm around her waist. And when he began to slow dance to the song, though she rolled her eyes, Justice smiled. "Heyyy, girrrl, long time no see," he sang along with Freddy. "Do you have a lil time, to spend...wit'...me? I wanna know, what's been goin' on." He grinded against her with a suave nastiness. "In ya life! Talk to me baby! Your hair—" He pushed the hood back on her hoodie before pulling the scrunchy off her ponytail; watching as her thick hair tumbled down. "The perfume you wear, brings back memories, ohhh of you and me! So much, has happened in my life...since we parted! What about you? But since I got myself together, I know just what I want...and right now, I know that it's youuuu! Rock with me tonight! For old time sake" He sung, and saw it when he cracked through the jury he caused her.*

*Justice's eyes watered as she studied him, but what she couldn't have anticipated was the brokenness reflecting from his gaze.*

*"You didn't come back, mama, and that shit twisted my heart backwards," he admitted.*

*"I'm back now," she whispered as their eyes danced. Shadowed by the darkness, and surrounded by boxes, fate was born.*

*With a sly smirk, Messiah used his thumbs to wipe the rain from her eyes. "Yeah but not with what you promised to hold for me. I ain't lil Messiah no more, Jus. I'm an animal with no heart."*

*"Cupid gave me your heart a long time ago, big head, and I'm no longer little Justice either, ya know?" She countered with amusement in her eyes.*

*Messiah chuckled with a shake of his head. "Cupid lies, Justice, just like everybody else, but—" He studied her; so used to closing his heart to a woman that opening it to one seemed to be an enigma. Yet, if only for that moment, he retired his pimpin'. His vision took in how time had loved her.*

*"Yeah, maybe. But, negro, yuh was talkin' real salty the other day when yuh was wit' yuh lil hoes dem, but now yuh tryin' to romance me. What happened to all that tough mess yuh was ah kickin'?" Justice giggled, and to her astonishment, Messiah's hand slapped her face with so much power her head spun.*

*"Bitch, you gonna either break bread or fake dead, 'cause pimpin' is the only thing I'm kickin', unless my gators have to find yo ass for slippin'!" Messiah stomped down.*

*"Messiah? Are you okay?" Justice's voice jarred him back to reality to find her studying him peculiarly.*

*"Huh?" He asked, and it was then it dawned on him that he'd let his imagination get the best of him, and him slapping lady was all in his head! He laughed—hard! She frowned.*

*"What the—" Justice was mumbling when Messiah's laughter faded and he pulled her to him and his tongue reclaimed hers.*

\*\*\*

*The night was frigid, the sky starless and dark as the Jag pulled into a cheap motel off St. Augustine and I75. Paradise pulled into a parking space before scrunching her nose at the rachetness of the establishment. "Girl, you sure this the addy?" She glanced to where Tutts sat pretty in the passenger's seat.*

*Tutts glanced out at the ran down buildings and though she frowned suspiciously, she nodded. "Yeah, this where Cakes said the date would be; room 230."*

*Paradise smacked her lips. She disliked Messiah's new regimen. His girls no longer walked the blade, and instead, was booked by phone book with payment going directly to Messiah. He'd even made Black Diamond and Cakes his public relations team, who travelled around with pics and bios on each of his girls, and all one would have to do was pick and schedule their fantasies.*

*"Shiiish." Paradise blew through her teeth. "Who the hell you meeting? A corner boy?" She spat, and Tutts burst into laughter.*

*"Nigga name Klayco!" She laughed harder when horror was born in Paradise's expression.*

*"Uh-uh, bitch." Paraside shook her head before shifting the car back into drive. "Messiah will just have to—"*

*"Paradise, chill." Tutts giggled before touching Paradise's arm to pause her. "Girl, whoever he is, he paid! He has to be "somebody" if he can fuck off five grand for a night!" Her rationale was sound.*

*"Well," Paradise gave her a skept look, but when Tutts pulled her skirt up to reveal the .22 holstered to her thigh, her wife-n-law at eased. She'd totally forgotten it was one of Messiah's new creeds; all his girls must be armed. Reluctantly nodding, Paradise reached over and hugged her girl. "Ok, I guess!" They laughed as Tutts hugged her back.*

*"Girrrl, you turning into the mother hen, stop trippin," she whispered before slipping out the car into the cold of night. She waved before making her way towards a night of fornication.*

\*\*\*

*Standing naked before each other for the first time was a fantasy turned reality. Messiah's uncountable time standing newborn before a woman, and Justice's second time before a man. His dick saluted at the vision before him; her heart paced at the sight before her. Justice was juicy; titties, thighs, ass, and her Bermuda Triangle.*

*Messiah's mouth watered. "Come here, Justice."*

*Obeying, she stepped before him and though butterflies spread their wings in her stomach, placing her hands on her shapely hips, Justice gave him a sexy smirk. "I told you I ain't that little girl anymore, I'm—" She used a finger to trail from her collarbone, down the middle of her chest, and down to where God split her. "—all woman now." She smiled as Messiah pulled her close before gripping her ass cheeks with one hand.*

*After partaking of her lips, he sucked her neck, kissed her collarbone, and licked his way down to her right nipple; all the while, his free hand created a beautiful song between her legs. Cocking her left leg to give him better access, Justice's lips formed an "o" as pleasure awakened.*

*"Si-ahh," she moaned, never knowing pleasure could sing such a song.*

*Messiah suckled her nipple so hard his jaws caved, and Justice moaned pleasurable pain. His lips smacked when he released her flesh. And navigating her around stacked boxes, and over to where he aspired to slay her, Messiah sat her on the arm of the couch. Reigning over her, he stroked his thickness as Justice's eyes captured him. Precum oozed from him as his vision fell to the fullness of her breast. Her chocolate nipples saluted him and when he beheld how fat that pussy was, for the first time within his years of thuggin', Messiah became curious of the taste of the forbidden fruit.*

*"All woman, huh?" He chuckled, and when Justice bit her bottom lip, leaned back, planted her hands on the couch cushion, and Lambo door'd her legs, Messiah knew he'd test her claim.*

*Justice felt sensual. Powerful! "Can you tell!" She smirked as both their eyes fell between her legs.*

\*\*\*

*When Tutts made it to the room, she found a note taped to the door. "Be back in a moment; needed ice for the champagne. Make yourself comfortable and I'll return shortly," it read, and that she did.*

\*\*\*

*The verbal was nonexistent as Messiah stood up in that pussy. Justice's face was a mask of ugly sexiness as she balanced on her hands and legs in a giant V. Messiah danced his strokes, and in some freak shit he grabbed her ankle and pulled her foot to his mouth. Sucking her toes, he used his free hand to massage her clit and it did it to her.*

*"Uhhhh," she inhaled sharply as Messiah's pace quickened.*

*His dick dripped with her juices as it slid in and out of her. "Watch it, baby. Watch this dick go in and out this pussy," Messiah growled before wrapping his lips back around her big toe.*

*Justice's eyes obeyed, and her fuck face deepened. She never experienced good dick, and the sex talk fed the freak in her she wasn't truly secure about. Yet, pulling out until her lips were only hugging the head of him, and giving it to her with short, rapid pumps before unexpectedly driving in until her pussy lips kissed his pelvis, Messiah called to the wild in her. "Ohh, shii-it!" She cried.*

*Messiah suckled her toes until spit dripped from the sides of his mouth, and turning his animal up, he slipped from inside her. Pulling her up and turning her around, Messiah placed her right knee on the arm of the couch before bending her over into a hiking position. Her juices dropped from his nature as he ran it between the crack of her ass.*

*Justice shivered, hands planted on the cushion with her ass cheeks tooted up. She felt when he spread her cheeks, but when the thick head of his masculinity pressed against her exit wound, she jumped in surprise. Her head whipped back so she could glare at him. "Boy—"*

*"Shiiiish!" Messiah shushed her, and slowly slid his dick a bit lower until it knocked at the doors of her virtue.*

*"Mmmm," Justice moaned, biting her bottom lip as Messiah's girth split her.*

*He stroked in until her femininity kissed his nuts before slipping out and holding Justice's left cheek open. Running his slick dick over her asshole, he chuckled when she tensed. "Trust me," was his whisper before applying pressure. The tip of his head pushed against her exit wound just enough to crack her open before he pulled away and ran dick-deep into her vagina.*

*"Ooooh, bo-boy!" Justice cried from the unexpected, and gripping her waist with one hand, and gripping the back of her neck with the other, Messiah showed his work! The sound of his nuts slapping against her flesh intermingled with their love song. "Ah! Ahh, Si-ahhh!" Justice purred, but Messiah's response was quickening his pace. Justice's cheeks jiggled from his pound game, and Messiah was mesmerized by the vision of his dick disappearing in and out her nature. Justice's juices turned him white.*

*"Damn," he growled as that pleasure demon surged from his nuts, and when Justice's hand slipped between her legs, the sight beckoned to Messiah's finish. "This-pussy-fat-tt-as a-bitch!" He gritted while stroking quicker.*

*Justice's fingers were a cyclone against her clit. "Ba-byyy! Get-it-zad-dyyy!" She cried as her eyes rolled, and her lips formed an 'o'.*

*Messiah sweated as he watched her juices froth on his dick like a thick lotion. "Shit!" He growled, and that's when—*

\*\*\*

*Tutts was in a bad way! And as she sat naked with one wrist handcuffed to the headboard, she could only shake her head at how she'd come to that conclusion. She'd entered the room to find it dim, the only light source being ten flickering flames dancing atop candles. The queen-sized bed was freshly made with white rose petal littered upon it, and she was so enchanted with the romance that she never registered the presence slip behind her. The click of the door closing made her jump, but when she turned around, a damp cloth was placed over her nose and mouth. Everything went black, and when she regained consciousness, she found herself handcuffed with Pimpin Maxwell sitting beside her and aiming a pistol at her. Confused, she'd watched him slip a metal object from the pocket of his rumpled suit coat before staring down upon it as if it were the cure to aids. And it was then that she realized how glossy his orbs were.*

"Pimpin—"

"You know," *Pimpin cut her off, his eyes lifting to her.* "Back in the late eighties when niggas traded the needle for the pipe, I assumed shit would be better because in my head..." *He tapped his temple with the crack pipe and smirked.* "Nothin' could be worse than that boy!" *He chuckled bitterly with a sad shake of his head.*

*Tutts treaded lightly, knowing that when one is under the influence and dangerous, her best bet was to keep him talking.* "And is it?" *she asked, attempting to still her quaking body.*

*Wrong question! Pimpin smirked wickedly.* "Try it and see." *He extended the metal to her.*

"Wha-I-I don't—" *Tutts stammered, her expression horrified.*

"Bitch!" *Pimpin roared.* "You can either get higher than the angels or die and join them mu'fuckas! Either way, I gotta get my lick back—"

"Lick back?" *Tutts was lost until it dawned on her. Her face fell.* "Messiah?" *She whispered and Pimpin chuckled.*

\*\*\*

*Within the dimness of the living room, Messiah and Justice lay on a pallet; bodies sweaty and her wrapped within his arms, back to his chest. "Messiah," she whispered.*

*"Sup," he mumbled.*

*Justice turned to face him, smiling to find his head resting on his forearm and his eyes closed. "Do you remember way back when we were kids, and I asked you what you wanted to be when you grew up?"*

*Messiah's kids cracked open as his vision captured her. "Yeah."*

*"You said—"*

*"I'mma be a boss." He smirked as his eyes fell from her face and fell to her full breast.*

*Justice giggled. "How'd that turn out for you?"*

*Messiah's dick hardened at the sight of her chocolate nipples, and licking his lips, he slid down until he was face to face with them. "Perfectly," he mumbled before sucking her right one between his lips.*

*"Mmmm," Justice moaned. "Don't start nothin' you can't finish."*

*When her flesh slipped free, a wet popping sound emitted, and rolling her over onto her stomach, Messiah used his knees to kick her legs apart. "Keep your body on the ground but toot that ass up just a lil," he demanded, and resting her face in the crook of her arm, with her knees spread as far apart as they could go, Justice obeyed.*

*"Hssss!" She sucked a sharp breath through her teeth when he slid in.*

*Messiah lifted into a push up position and began to stroke that pussy. Deep...long strokes. "Let's see if I can put that ass to sleep."*

*Justice's face balled up in ecstasy. "O-okay!"*

# Chapter 16

*Present Time: 14 Years Later*
*Sunday—9AM*

The vibration of his phone jarred him awake and disoriented. Messiah's lids cracked open. Lifting his head from the back of the chair, it took him a moment to recall falling asleep as Coffe read to him from the black book. Frowning, his vision trailed to find the book resting on the seat beside him, but the only remanence of Coffe's presence with a soft lingering of her fragrance. Pulling his phone from his pocket and opening the text message, his eyes turned dark: *Last chance to save her player! Anymore games with my money, and your wife dies! You'll receive the time and place soon. Don't be late, Pimp!* The text read.

"The Lord knows what he's doing, Sunjay, just believe—" Messiah's eyes shot up to the sound of Ms. Betty's southern voice. She stood over Sunjay's bed, with Dream standing beside her. Yet, it was as if both ladies were invisible to Sunjay as he glared up at the ceiling.

"Fuck you ain't just take me out, nigga, huh? It's 'cause you ain't no different than nan other hoe ass nigga! You do fuck shit just 'cause you can!" Sunjay spat, and it took Messiah a moment to understand he was talking to God.

Messiah shook his head at the irony; first Zetti got paralyzed for the life Sunjay glamorized to him, and now the teacher was being spanked for it. Slipping from his seat and stretching, Messiah made his way bedside, just in time to capture a lone tear drip down Sunjay's face.

"*Who gave you* the right to rule, nigga? *Errybody* has a superior, pussy boy, who's yours? Huh? Whose God over you?" Sunjay spewed, not giving his mans even a glance.

"Sunny!" Ms. Betty demanded, and though Sunjay became a silent storm, his eyes never strayed from their focal point.

Large wet spots stained the pillowcase where his tears were captured, and when Ms. Betty ran a hand down the side of his face, her own eye thunderstorm converged. Messiah observed her in wonder; her long gray hair was pulled back into a tight bun, and though in her late seventies, Queen could pass for late forties. Dressed in her Sunday's best, and clutching her Bible to her side, she'd forsaken church to be there for her baby. Dream hugged herself as she cried, and though Messiah was enveloped with their pain, he couldn't understand why they weren't "celebrating" Sunjay's survival rather than harping over him being shot?

Ms. Betty ran a hand over Sunjay's head. "Baby, I's always told ya; a hard head makes a soft—"

"Fuck that!" Sunjay shouted. "And fuck God too, Granny! Fuck Heaven, and fuck living!" He spazzed.

Ms. Betty jumped in surprise. Covering her mouth to muffle the sob that raced up her throat as she watched Sunjay glare down at his feet…willing them to move, but they ignored him.

Tears ran steady down his dark face. "Why they won't move, Granny? Huh?" He demanded, and Ms. Betty shook her head in pity, reminded of Zetti's duplicate condition. Suddenly the machines Sunjay were hooked up to began to beep hysterically, and in moments medical staff filled the room in a panic.

"What's going on?" An Asian woman, the doctor on call, asked as her staff tended to Sunjay, and then her eyes drifted to the monitor of one of the machines. "Oh my!" She gaped at the reading of Sunjay's blood pressure.

The heart monitor began to go crazy as the man lost his marbles, and jabbing a finger toward the Bible his grandmother held, spittle flew from his mouth as he screamed at the top of his lungs. "Lies! That's all that book tells! All God has ever given us! Lies, Granny! The nigga don't give a damn about me or you!" He raged as the nurses tried to calm him.

The doctor rushed over to his family with sympathy in her eyes. "I'm sorry, but you'll have to leave until we can—"

"I'm…not…goin'…nowhere!" Dream gritted, and though her orbs were a rainstorm, the finality radiating from them was evidence of her claim. Yet, Ms. Betty's soft touch eased the tension.

"Walk with me, chile. Let's get some breakfast and let these people do their jobs," she offered, and when Dream's wet eyes met hers, she nodded assuring.

"We'll come back." Her eyes dropped as they trailed to Sunjay; though four people fought to keep him still, the man was inconsolable.

"Lies, Granny, all dem prayers you've prayed, and God ain't do shit! He ain't real; can't be!" He cried before pushing a thin lady away, and punching a male nurse in the lip. And just as two securities stormed the room; Messiah had enough!

"Watch out, mane!" He growled as he paused a nurse aside and made his way beside his mans. "Sunjay!" He shouted.

As if he'd flipped a switch, silence ensued. Everybody froze as Sunjay's tantrum died a slow death, and with slow streams zig zagging down his face, he fell back against his pillow before setting his vision on Messiah. Sunjay's brokenness titled his heart and Messiah's eyes satiated. Sunjay's voice cracked with each word. "They say I'll never walk again, bro. I'll never step again, Blood."

Messiah's mouth opened and closed, but no words escaped.

Sunjay chuckled bitterly. "I'm a stepper, Siah. Without my legs, I'm a dead man."

Even before he said it, Messiah was shaking his head; rejecting it. "Naw, brotha. I'm my brotha's keeper and—"

"I'm talkin' 'bout my spirit, Messiah. My spirit is DOA, bleed, and I wish my physical woulda went wit' it. On me!" Sunjay professed before his eyelids drooped and though he was still speaking, his words became slurred.

Messiah's eyes shot up to find a nurse releasing the IV line running to Sunjay's veins; their eyes met, and the nurse gave a meek shrug.

"It'll help him rest."

"Messiah," Sunjay mumbled groggily, and Messiah's eyes fell to him. "Get me outta here before dem people show up," were Sunjay's last words before he fell into a deep unconsciousness.

It took Messiah a moment to realize he was speaking of the police, and that's when something strange dawned on him. *Fuck that boy Murda been at,* he thought.

***

"Amen, Pastor, have some church in this place!" A woman in the front pew shouted, while fanning herself.

First Missionary Church was packed to capacity, and Pastor Matthews, formerly known as Blow, had used every Penny of his stash away money to have it built in the slums of West Dallas, and as he stood behind the pulpit, he used a silk handkerchief to dab his perspiring face. Pulling the microphone from the cradle, the man continued his testimony as the choir hummed a low melody. "Boy, let me tell ya! Ya see, I stood over that man with the power of life and death in my hands, while his beautiful wife begged for

147

his life! Yet, see, I was like Saul before he became Paul!" He shouted, taking a step from behind the pulpit.

The church wasn't mega, but it was large, and within that two-hundred-person congregation, Black Diamond sat in her Sunday's best. Though she hated him for what he'd done to her family, she had to admit that the man was a prodigy before a church.

Dapper in a three-piece, latte hued suit, with matching Stacy Adams and tie, the pastor paced the stage before spinning dramatically to face the congregation. "Even after I chose to spare that man's life, God—" he stomped his foot "—I say Goddd!" He stared fiercely before giving a sad shake of his head. "Y'all ain't hearing me this mornin'!"

"You better tell it, pastor!" A woman shouted.

"Give that testimony! Let the Lawd speak, brotha!" A gent seconded, and the pastor chuckled.

"God had other plans," he whispered into the mic. "That man died in his wife's arms because of my ungodly decisions, and though I was saved from that injustice, God chose an entirely different way to get my attention." His eyes watered. "Sentenced to prison and struck blind by sin, I couldn't see, until I found myself in a dark hole in my life, cryin' out for salvation! And y'all know what?"

"Tell it, pastor!" Someone cried.

The minister gave a spiritual expression as if he was about to reveal the secrets of the ages, and in a whisper, he preached, "Lord, help me!" He cleared his throat. "*Nothin'* happened yall! So, I began to cry like a baby; Lord Jesus, cover me in ya blood, and release me," Pastor Matthews whispered again, and he could see the crowd studying him; they weren't quite understanding while he was *whispering.* He chuckled. "Lawwd have mercy," said he, and walking to the edge of the stage, he took a seat. "Nothin' happened y'all, until finally, broken in that cold cell; I fell to my knees and cried with all my *heart!"* He confessed, and as the pianist began to play *Mansion, Robe and a Crown*, the pastor made his point. "I know it's plenty of y'all out there that's been *whispering* ya words to God. Somebody out there done left their job, and no matter how hard you try, ain't nobody tryna hire you." He waved to the congregation. "It's somebody out there that has a broken heart and has lost to love. There's somebody in this place that has the weight of the world on their shoulders and feel as if you'll crumble any minute! Well, I'm here to tell ya brothas and sistas that it's *not* that God isn't listening, it's just, you're not telling him loud enough! You have to speak diligently! *Heart* talk!"

"Hallelujah!" A woman at the back of the church shot from her seat, tossed her hands up, and with her eyes closed, began to speak in tongues.

"Speak powerfully!" The pastor shouted. "'Cause I'm here to tell ya, that if you want God to hear you, *you better talk to him loud enough that he can!*" He shouted before knocking a fist to his chest. "And there's no louder voice than that of one spoken from the heart!"

"Amen! AsphJehovahsssssnismalah!" The woman cried in tongues, her eyes rolling to the back of her head.

Black Diamond smirked before clapping her hands in praise.

"Church!"

***

The sun was at its zinc, but the brisk wind of the day was a welcomed addition. Exiting the hospital, Messiah texted feverishly, but pausing to glance up, he was appreciative to find his Bentley valeted out front. Slipping into the backseat and closing the door behind him, he tossed the black book beside him. He and Paradise's eyes met in the rear view.

"You stink!" She made a face, and Messiah chuckled.

"I—" he began, but stopped when his sense of smell was assaulted by a foul odor. Growing, he lifted his arms and smelt his pits. *Not me, but,* he thought, pausing because the smell was too close for it to not be him. And that's when it hit him. Patting his pockets, he felt the gift Keisha had had her shooter to give him before he'd departed. He'd totally forgotten it, and when he reached into his pocket, his frown deepened. *Fuck?* He wondered. His pocket was damp and sticky, and after extracting the package, the smell emitting from it made Paradise gag.

"The fuck?" She spat before hurriedly lowering the window, but it was the severed finger peeking through the gift wrap that held Messiah's attention.

It wasn't the fact that he was holding someone's finger that held him captive, but more of him *knowing who the finger belonged to!* "Paradise?" He whispered, his mind becoming a chess board.

"What, Messiah? Throw whatever that is out; dang!" She griped with her head out the window.

Ignoring her, Messiah stared down at the tattooed finger with the word *loyalty* tattooed around it. "You still fuckin the Jamaican like I told you to? He probed.

"Off and on, but what—"

"He still doesn't know you're one of mine, so hit him up and tell him to meet you at ya spot in an hour," he demanded before returning to he and Coffe's texts.

\*\*\*

Not too far away, *ex* detective Spinx sat behind the wheel of an unmarked car, chewing on his signature toothpick as he observed. His eyes were murderous as he watched Messiah in the backseat of that luxury truck, with a bad bitch behind the wheel. Chuckling bitterly, he wondered how the man seemed to get one up on him, and as he sat there within his envy, his mind ricocheted him back to one of those times long ago, when he experienced the special talent of the fella.

*After being setup by Messiah the day meant for the money exchange, Spinx had been tossed in a cold cell. Yet, with a smirk on his face, he knew he'd be granted immunity after the DA got his hands on the dirt he held in his lock box at home. He hadn't been in custody five minutes before he'd went to singing! He had dirt on many dirty officers, and film capturing Messiah and gang in acts of heinous activity was the icing on the cake! So, he'd lain in that hard bunk with a satisfied smile, but after hours turned to days, and days into weeks, his stomach dropped. He'd stricken a deal with the district attorney, and couldn't believe the sucka would make him wait! Yet, as he entertained the thought, he heard the jingling of keys, and he sat up with a smug smirk. 'Bout time, he'd thought, but making his way to the door to find a jailer extending a folded piece of paper to him caused his smile to waned.*

*"Fuck this is?" He growled, and the guard shrugged indifferently.*

*"Came from the higher ups," he said before turning and making his exit.*

*With suspicion in his eyes, Spinx unfolded the paper and read:*

*"You made a fool of not only the department of DPD, but now of the attorney's office with your trickery and false allegations. Upon your request, we had your home searched for this mysterious lock box you claimed held the crimes of the century, and you know what we found? Inside said box was a half a kilo of pure heroine! So, for you thumbing your nose at the great citizens of Dallas, I'm honored to aid in putting you away for the rest of your natural life!"*

Mad laughter jarred Spinx from the memory, and when he realized it was his own, he laughed harder. Yes—Messiah had gotten one up on him, but Spinx starved to get his lick back!

# Chapter 17

*A Week Later*
*1AM*

🎵 *I'm on some other shit/ I'm dressed in all black/I'm with my niggas nem, and all us strapped/we on that killer shit, somebody gettin whacked/ you know I mean bizness, when I'm in all black* 🎵 —

Plies' anthem filled the living room as the clicking of clips snapping into place fed the vibe. Kush smoke was potent in the air as fifteen shooters, draped in all-black, blew their brains back as they piped up. ARs, AKs, SKs, FNs, Kel Techs; a shooters desires was on deck, but it was what lay across Sunjay's lap that helped Messiah's interest.

"A grenade launcher, Sunjay?" He asked, his eyes glued to the weapon.

Sunjay, a day out the hospital, smirked before massaging the side of the RPG. Sitting around the dining room table, three pairs of eyes fell to it.

"Nigga been waiting to use that bitch since he copped it from them H-town boys." Murda chuckled over lungs filled with smoke. Attempting to pass the bling to Sunjay, he shrugged indifferently when his mams spat on the floor of the bando before glaring menacingly at him. Murda smirked; the beanie he wore, down to the Timbs on his feet were demon black. Yet, the strange device that lay on the table before them contradicted his appeal.

Messiah eyed it contemptuously; a bitter reminder of a resurrected op. Sitting on the arm of a warm couch, his hand tightened on the grip of a beautiful street sweeper with a scope on its top, and an extending jutting from its ass, while his other hand held the phone he texted on. Lifting it, he smirked at the screen

—: *See you left the kid*
*Coffe: Boy hush! You were snoring! Lol!*
—: *I'm trying to see you*
*Coffe: At the hospital?*
—: *Am I not good enough for your spot?*
*Coffe: My house?*
—: *Tonight*
*Coffe: K...*

She'd sent the addy after a moment, and only minutes after, a more heinous text rolled in.

—: *It's time playa! Tonight! No more games or your wife dies! The counterfeit bills were a nice touch, but for getting slick, I want the entire grip! BTW, throw that finger away, it's disgusting!* The text was followed with the address, a warning to come alone, and a promise of they'll be watching.

Messiah shook his head in shame. It had all been in his face out the gate, but emotions blind a man's critical thinking, and causes him to miss the banana peel in the street until he's slipped and busted his ass!

"You think she's still breathing?" Sunjay's question brought Messiah's gaze up to meet his before it drifted to the duffle bag bulging with the ransom.

"Justice my soul, nigga. If she stopped breathin', I'd know," he whispered, before his eyes found Murda. "So, Spinx back at it, huh?" He chuckled when Sunjay growled.

"Fuck that bitch boy shake that forty years they gave 'em?" he spat, before he too glared at Murda. "And fuck you end up wit' dude, Blood?"

Murda smirked, and though he *yearned* to *man down* Messiah, he knew the man had the mind to spin a web that had the power to free him from the clutches of those crooked pigs. So, he'd told them the business and left the rest to fate. "You think this shit will work?" He lifted a brow to Messiah, and dude stood and admired the pole he clutched.

"If it don't—" he shrugged "—trust ya gun, nigga!"

Murda slipped from his seat before retrieving the wire. "That's easy. I been doin' that shit since the jungle gym."

\*\*\*

*Ten Minutes Later*

*The night was black as Messiah slid into the passenger side of a gray Ford Explorer, and as soon as he'd gotten comfortable, Murda passed him a blunt.*

*"So." He exhaled a cloud of tainted smoke. "What's our two-step?"*

*Messiah hit the stick, it's cherry glowing bright within the darkness of the truck. "Shid, I'mma pay this lucci to get my Queen back, and I'm leavin' Dallas behind." He spoke over a lung full of gas.*

*Murda nodded as he reclined in his seat and gazed out at the night. "What's the ticket for her return?"*

*"A ticket?"*

*"A M?" Murda clarified, a stupefied look on his face.*

*Messiah chuckled. "Yeah, nigga, a million in cold cash; enough loot to change a man's life." He nodded before returning the dope and pushing the door open. "Bruh, you can't show up to this play, Messiah. This nigga ain't gonna let you just walk away to live happily ever after."*

*Messiah paused midway out the truck and glanced back at dude. "You got a better idea!"*

*Murda sucked the soul from the blunt before resting his head against the headrest and closing his eyes, and only when his lungs felt as if they'd explode did he leverage the stream of smoke he'd incarcerated. "Let me go instead." His offer was a chess move, and both men's eyes fell to the console where Spinx's wire was capturing the entire convo!*

\*\*\*

Law 15
Crush Your Enemy Totally
*If one ember is left alight, no matter how dimly it smolders, a fire will eventually break out! More is lost through stepping halfway than through total annihilation: The enemy will recover, and will seek revenge. Crush him, not only in body, but in spirit!*
    Robert Greene—48 Laws Of Power

\*\*\*

Inside the church was dim, the only illumination being that of the flickering flames dancing atop numerous candles inside the sanctuary. Their scent was heavy on the air, and within the vastness of the empty room, up the aisle running between the multitude of pine benches, a man knelt at the alter, resting his burdens at the feet of a nine-foot cross, baring the weight of a crucified metal Jesus.

"Lord, for I sinned against the blood, and been the instrument of Satan my entire life, I fear that my repentance isn't enough to wash away the iniquity. Forgive me, Father." Eyes closed, Pastor Matthews prayed in a whisper. Head bowed, the shadows of the flickering flames reflected over his dark face as he bared his soul. Bare foot, the man wore a green dress shirt with white slacks, yet, as he bared his spirit, he felt naked. "Purge my slate, Father, for the good book says ask and I shall receive, search and—" The kiss of a barrel to the back of his head silenced him. A chill breeze wafted through the air causing the dance of the candles flames to sway sideways, and when reverend's lids cracked open, with a soft smirk, his vision lifted to behold the agony etched into the face of the copper Jesus that hung before him. He'd left the doors unlocked to the church and invited any with woes to come rest their worries upon the Lord.

"Hello, Pastor, I've come for confessional." The intruder had a soft voice. "The confession of *your* sins," they whispered.

***

The room was filled with shadows. Dark, except for the pale light of the moon climbing in through the bare window beside the queen-sized canopy bed, the ambiance in the room was carnal.

"Yes—yasss!" Keisha cried, naked…body shining with sweat as she rocked her hips.

"Uhhhh-shiiiih!" Her lover cried as *she* rotated her own hips. She was a gorgeous pecan hued freak, and in a scissors position, her and Keisha grinded their essence against each other's, the friction driving both wild.

"Faster!" Keisha growled, her face a mask of determination. Dreads wild about her pretty face, she bit her lip as her partner needed the command.

"Kiiisha!" The girl cried while working her hips while gripping Keisha's extended leg for leverage. Their kittens warred, slick with juice as climax reared its beautiful head.

"Ohhh, myyyy," Keisha cried, her eyes rolling. The speed of their gyrations was at its limit, their clits swollen, throbbed.

"Cum-inggg!" The girl cried, mouth agape.

"You-toooo?" Keisha purred, reaching the top of her mountain, and just as she leaped from it, three explosions erupted. Hers, her lover's and the one that had nothing to do with ecstasy.

***

Beneath the cover of night, the black Ford Excursion had pulled outside the gate of the estate, just as the dark sky began to cry. Soft drops of rain fell as the gate keeper, a slim dread head carrying a powerful assault rifle stepped out beneath the awning of the guard house. "Wah gwan, Star," he greeted the driver, just as a second Jamaican stepped out clutching a choppy with a drum attached.

"Who dere, rude boi?" He nodded to the truck, just as Messiah hopped out the driver's seat and hurried to them. Recognizing him, the first dread glared, refusing to let him under the shelter out the rain. "Wah him fun boi wan, huh?"

Messiah's smile was meant to be disarming, but those men merely glared. A flash of lighting struck across the heavens, briefly illuminating them. "I need to tap in with Keisha, homie," Messiah requested, now glaring as the rain splashed down over his bald head.

The two men smirked, and Messiah knew they enjoyed seeing the abuse the rain inflicted on his clothes.

"Naw, ya ah na see she here, yea, de rude gyal ah fa busy." The leader declined, and his man's chuckled.

Messiah gritted his teeth as he nodded as if coming to some type of decision, and as if beckoning him back to the warmth of the truck, his phone rung where he'd left it on the passenger's seat. All eyes shot to it, and Messiah smirked wickedly at them before back pedaling toward the truck. "You boys respect the night, so it'll let you see the day." He bid farewell, and the first dread spat at the ground in response. Messiah slipped into the confines of the truck and they watched him reverse out of the drive.

"Him boi deserves death, Star," the first Jamaican spat before turning and making his way back into the small guard house.

His brethren followed, and though he hated Messiah, it was merely because of JonJa's feelings. "Why, Star, wah him ah do to us brethren?" He inquired.

His brethren gave him a look that screamed: *stupid question!* "Jah, ah crazy, Star?" He laughed before plopping down in his seat and resting his gun across his lap. A few years older than the other, the man propped his feet on a unturned box they used as a makeshift table and after interlocking his fingers behind his head, the dread allowed his eyes to drift closed. "Da mon is ah killin' the boss lady's cat, and—"

"Mon—"

"Oh, ya doh believe—"

"Mon!"

It was the horror in his friend's tone that caused the dread's eyes to fly open. "Wha—" he was saying when his orbs flew to the TV monitors the other man's eyes were stuck on. "De bumba clot tinks like mad mon!" He raged before leaping to his feet and snatching up his gun. And though he rushed out into the rain to dance with the devil, the reaper was two steps ahead.

*Vroom!* The powerful engine roared as the massive truck sped at suicidal speed and crashed into the gate; *Blam!* The mad crunch of metal against the metal was profound as the ten-foot gate crashed in. *Tttuuuu! Tttuuuu!* The dreads let their weapons breathe; flames leaping from the barrels of them. Yettheir roars cursed the shooters, fore they never heard the reaper's footsteps until it was too late. The younger dread caught movement out his peripheral, and a quick glance over his shoulder almost made him piss himself. His face balled up in rage as he attempted to spin his arm, but standing two deep in the rain; Messiah and his demon had the ups. Their sticks created a symphony as the fire leaping from their barrels illuminated the demonic expressions on their faces. The two Jamaicans were cut down, and when the fire ended, a streak of lightning struck against the heavens like a camera's flash. Rain fell and slid down Messiah's bald head as he and his mans walked over the corpses, and a wicked smirk touched his lips at the sounds of war ahead.

He'd slid through with four killers; three of which were engaging the Jamaicans homicidaly! And though he knew death was in the air, he only had one thing on his top...*Justice!*

\*\*\*

"I'm going to rise now, sista, and turn to face you," Reverend Matthews whispered, his eyes still upon the fixture of Christ hanging upon the wall. Taking the intruder's silence as consent, the man climbed to his feet, and slowly turned to face fate. As soon as their eyes met, Faye smiled, and the pastor nodded with a sad smirk of his own. "What took you so long, Eddie Ruth?" He asked.

Black Diamond gave him an expression of curiosity. "You act as if you've been expecting me."

The man chuckled. "One whose loved wrong for so long should know that no matter how much living right he's doing, the laws of wrong will feel betrayed and look for him in the streets of right." He shrugged before crossing his arms over his chest.

Black smiled, her aim of the .357 steady as she nodded her agreement.

The preacher studied her. "I owe you so much, Ruth, and I'm sorr—"

"Shut up!" Black demanded, her facial becoming a mask of agony. Tears welled in her eyes. "I've waited so long for this; you *stole* so much, Mr. *Blow,* and ain't no amount of sorries you can give that'll mend my heart on revenge," she hissed.

Blow studied her. In a black dress that barely clung to her frail frame, black gloves, and black pumps, she'd dressed for a *funeral!* Then his eyes captured the gun, and the irony brought a short laughter from him; it was the same caliber he'd used to kill her late husband. "Revenge makes the heart bitter, my lady, and bitterness allows the devil to—"

"Fuck the devil, nigga! And fuck your sermon!" Spittle leapt from her lips with the proclamation, but staring at her, the pastor saw his sins.

His own eyes watered at the surge of regrets that overwhelmed him. He lifted his palms in a calming motion. "Okay, Ruth, I *see* your pain and for it, I won't fight destiny, but all men sentenced to death deserves their last words; right?" He proposed and Black sniveled but shrugging her indifference. Reverend Matthews exhaled a hard breath. "A man can live with a million regrets, Eddie Ruth, and still be able to stare himself in the mirror, but it's *always* that *one* regret he can't say I'm sorry for that bows him." His left eye began to leak. "A man that smiles in the light, but cries in the dark is a man God is talkin' to, but sometimes pride makes him deaf to the conversation, and begins to talk to his soul instead of his heart," he whispered before spreading his arms wide like the soar of an eagle. "A broken man isn't an unfixable man, it just takes someone to *wanna* fix him. I accept my fate, 'cause God has forgiven me, but without your forgiveness, Ruth, I'll still regret, even in death." A sigh escaped him, and beneath the glow of dancing candlelight, rivers fell from Black's eyes. The slight shake of the gun revealed the effect his words had on her, and empowered by the spirit, Reverend Matthews took slow steps until he stood before her. Their wet eyes searched each other's as he placed his hand atop of the gun and tenderly pushed it away.

A sob wrecked Black's body when the man's arms wrapped around her in a tight hug.

"I'm sorry, Ruth, I—"

*Boom! Boom!* The explosion made him choke on his words as his eyes grew wide. Slowly, he released her with a mixture of pain and surprise in his gaze as he stepped back, and glanced down at the holes the slugs punched through his shirt. "Huuuhh." He sucked in a sharp breath as his eyes lifted to the smoking gun in Black's clutch.

"God in the New Testament is too weak! I praise the one of the Old Testament who didn't believe in turning the other cheek." She smiled, wiping the tears from her face with her free hand.

Blood poured from the man's stomach as he stumbled before grabbing the side of a pew for balance. His chest was tight as he gasped for air, but he knew it was a feeble attempt. Their eyes danced before the preacher stumbled to the front pew and fell into it crookedly. His eyes shot up to the crucified Jesus as he began pawing at his stomach while gasping for air.

Black Diamond made her way over and retrieved a candle, before taking a seat beside him. Resting the gun in her lap, she reached into her bra and came out with her trusty crack pipe and glancing down at it. "This'll be my divorce from this shit," she vowed before placing the glass dick to her lips, and using the candle, she lit its tip.

The man formally known as Blow took his last breath as Black allowed the last cloud of crack smoke into her lungs.

By the time Messiah and the gang had entered the mansion, bodies littered the front lawn; one of his, and eight Jamaicans. Inside the massive home was dark, and as Messiah's remaining four men spread out inside, he stood in the doorway; a scar of lightning illuminating him just as thunder rolled in the distance. Rain dripping from his bald head, he held the street sweeper down by his leg as he observed. His eyes adjusting to the darkness, it was only familiarity that allowed him to see beyond the many stone fixtures, hanging vines from the many ivory plants, and many other designs of art the Jamaican had used to turn his home into a small piece of his homeland. Large columns ran floor to ceiling, more of decoration than needed, and in the far corner of the massive living room, a six-foot-long stone statue chiseled into the likes of a crouching, roaring lion stood, seemingly; challenging him. Not far away, Messiah spotted one of his shooters on the hunt, but pausing to admire a tiny jungle of hanging vines, and it cost him!

*BOCA!* A shot rang out, and dude's melon shot a soft spray of his thoughts into the air. Messiah spun back outside, back to the side of the door frame, but not before seeing a blur of Keisha on the second floor.

"One down, bumba clot!" Keisha screamed from somewhere over the banister.

"Where my wife at, bitch? You think this shit a game, huh?" Messiah shouted over the cry of rain.

"Jah bitch wife, hmmm? Jah ah come here and disrespect mi home, and tink mi ah give him boy him gal?" Keisha screamed with a wicked giggle before—*BOCA! BOCA!* Shots sung, followed by the sound of a body dropping.

*Fuck? Fuck is this hoe, the terminator?* Messiah thought.

"Say, Blood, she shootin' from up top, but she's too fast for—" *BOCA!* Fire silenced the foolish man who'd spoken and revealed his location.

Glaring out at the pouring rain, Messiah knew he was now in the jungle with only two more predators on his side of the food chain, and if the lion couldn't protect his *pride*, within the *pride's* eyes, he didn't deserve them! Growling, he spun into the doorway, weapon aimed at the second floor. *BOOM!* He yanked back on the grip of the gauge, and fire leapt a foot long from the barrel. Diverting his aim, he again yanked on the grip. *Boom!* With each explosion, that dragon breathed fire, and a shell ejected from the side of the gun. *Boom!* "Bitch" *Boom!* "Fuck is!" *Boom!* "My wife!" He roared, diverting his aim with each shot.

*BOCA! BOCA!* Return fire sounded, and as slugs flew inches from his noggin, Messiah spun, placing his back to one of the many columns. Yet when a bullet punched into it and knocked a chunk free, Messiah sprinted for the massive statue. *BOCA! BOCA! BOCA!* Slugs sought him, but diving over the back of the crouching monument saved the bar. The bullets knocked chunks from the hind of the statue, and to his relief, to the left of his duck off, a stick talked. *Cattttah!* One of his shooters had appeared, the fire of his AR briefly illuminating the madness in his eyes as he sprayed the second floor. Yet, Messiah cursed when the jungle strangled his self-preservation. The sound of screeching tires sliding across wet pavement echoed from outside, followed by the swearing of *numerous* shooters—all with Jamaican dialects.

From somewhere above, Keisha's laughter was gleeful. "Jah ah dead mon, ya know," she swore and Messiah could hear the demon in her tone.

Messiah deflated in defeat, he knew he'd come face to face with the reaper, and the fella didn't believe in freebies. With nothing else to lose, he was in the midst of going out with a bang when a cold kiss of steel touched the side of his head. He never heard her on the lurk, as when his vision lifted to capture the naked woman aiming a burner at his top, he spat at her feet.

"Cute," she whispered before *BOCA!* Lights out!

# Chapter 18

The rain had slowed to a patter, its drops falling soft against the windshield of the SUV as the second half of Messiah's plan unfolded. Taking deep pulls from a Kush stick, Murda pulled the truck up to a ten foot high fence with an aged sign threatening *Beware of Dog!* Hitting the horn twice, he exhaled a stream of smoke before rubbing a hand over his bald head, cursing Messiah for making him shave his long hair off. The plan was for him to double as Messiah, and then being the same height, with the exact hue of dark skin, the chess move had promise. Messiah was counting on the decoy play to kill two birds with one stone, and as someone approached on the other side of the gate, Murda prayed Messiah's game was as raw as it's always been.

The thick chain that secured the gate was pulled free, and only when the man rolled the gate open did Murda notice two deadly Doberman Pinschers barring their teeth within the illumination of the headlights. He eased the window down when the gatekeeper approached— features hidden beneath the oversized rain jacket. The only feature Murda distinguished was the man was Caucasian, with a weather-beaten face sheltered under the hood of the slicker.

"They're around back; drive straight for a half mile, and ya can't miss 'em," he grumbled.

"*Them?*" Murda lifted a brow.

The man chuckled. "Yeah, about five, all with guns they must've gotten from a military friend; I reckon."

"Military friends?"

The man nodded before glancing back toward the darkness of the junkyard. "Yeah, the type that can knock the motor out a car." His vision recaptured Murda's just as a clap of thunder rolled across the heavens. "I don't want to imagine what they can do to a mere man."

\*\*\*

Just a quarter mile down the road, eight men in black FBI tactical gear were geared up to go. Two bureau SUVs blended with the night, and in the lead one, Spinx sat peeping the scene through night vision binoculars. A wicked smirk touched his lips as he watched Murda enter the property. *A million benjies. I can't believe Messiah trust his team with that much! Well...he'll learn tonight,* he thought as he glanced to the man in the passenger's seat. "You ready?"

McHenry, the ex-federal agent who'd supplied the agency's paraphernalia, nodded before slipping the clip into the AR-15. Spinx glanced into the rear view, eyes capturing the two shooters in the backseat. Eight men; four of Murda's men, and three of his, made up their counterfeit FBI group, and they all salivated at the thought of their piece of the pie. Yet Spinx and McHenry had crooked designs, and knew they'd be the only two walking out alive.

\*\*\*

Blood splattered the side of Messiah's face as lady crumbled to the floor, and followed by a flash of lightning, four rude boys rushed the room and spread out with deadly intent. Infrared lasers flashed from their sticks as they waved the guns back and forth; on the lurk for their target.

The lights flicked on, and Keisha appeared at the top of the stairs. Naked, save for a pair of J's on her feet, lady clutched a smoking pistol with a seductive smirk on her face. "Jah can't win, Measiah, doh be mad mon," she said.

"Maybe not, but *somebody* going wit' me; that's *law!*" Messiah signed it in stone, and two of the rastas swung their weapons toward the statue, on the ledge of firing when Keisha reached the bottom of the stairs and lifted a hand to pause them.

They eyed her perplexedly as she tiptoed in a wide circle around the huge monument, tool aimed only to find— *nothing!* Though the lady she'd just smoked lay DOA at her feet, Messiah had vanished. Keisha's heartbeat quickened as her eyes fell to the puddle of blood that pooled around the body, and that's where she spotted the bloody footprints leading to—

"I ask again, Keisha. Fuck my bitch at?" Messiah spun from around the corner leading to the west wing of the estate.

Keisha smirked, turned on by the vision of him aiming the monstrous rifle at her, and her nipples hardened as she lowered her own weapon. "Him boo opened me gift." She chuckled with a confirming nod as she studied his posture.

Her two gunmen rushed forward, both taking aim. "Him fun boi die fa de blood of mi brethren!" One growled, his shirt dreads wild.

"Don't!" Keisha spat, and both henchmen's glare found her.

The second shooter spat at the floor in disgust. "Back in the yard, de woman don—"

*BOCA!* Before he could complete his statement, a slug pushed his forehead back. His brother flinched as the man fell sideways. All eyes shot to Keisha, and though the smile never left her face, the demon reflecting from her eyes thirsted for more blood. Time froze until sounds of a tussle broke the tension, and the attention was diverted to the other Jamaicans dragging Messiah's last goon into the room. His mask had been snatched away, and the hideous cuts and swelling of his face spoke to the hospitality he'd received.

Relieved of his weapon, dude was held captive by a muscular Jamaican with long dreads cascading from his head. Yet, rather than a gun, the man held a wickedly shaped machete to his victim's throat.

Keisha returned her vision to Messiah and took a step forward, her movement sensual. "Ya wah him, wife, huh?" She smirked. "Surrender ya gun fi dem, and mi take ya to her."

Murder twinkled in Messiah's eyes. "Bitch, if you value breathin', you better recognize a monster when you see one!" He gritted through clenched teeth.

"Monsters, Messiah." Keisha giggled. Then suddenly her face became placid as still water. "Tonka!" She demanded, and confused, Messiah's grip on his weapon firmed as he studied her.

That's when a strange sound filled the air. Messiah's eyes drifted over Keisha's shoulder to find his man's fighting to get free of the Jamaican's grasp. The viscous blade cut into his flesh like a shark fin through water, dark blood bursting free like the milk of a cracked coconut. Eyes wide in terror, dude desperately grasped at the blade, only to have it slice through his fingers just as his murderer grasped his chin and held his head back. And with a maliciousness born to the heartless, the rude boy yanked the blade with so much force that it severed three of his victim's fingers before slicing deep into his victim's throat. The blade slipped clean through before the Jamaican pushed the dying man away, watching as he grasped at the gorge in his neck and choked on his own blood.

"Monsters?" Keisha's whisper recaptured Messiah's attention. "Only scare children, mon, mi scare de monster." She smiled wickedly before nodding at Messiah's weapon. "Ya gun, rude boy?" She eyed him, and knowing it was his only option, Messiah tossed it. Keisha turned and headed for the door. "Come, mi take him mon to him wife."

Messiah shivered from the brutality, but just behind his repulsion, lust smiled. Keisha's ass cheeks swallowed the thong, and juggled as she led him to what he most desired.

***

The truck pulled to a stop in the midst of the organized junk. Numerous rusted old cars were stacked to a giant's height, along with piles of scrap metal and other miscellaneous debris piled sky high created strange lanes and alleys throughout the property. And standing in the middle of one of such lanes stood four men, their dark clothes allowing them to camouflage with the night as they brandished the types of fire power that could cut a man to shreds.

"Cut the lights, playa, you fuckin' up the peace," one of the men demanded, and Murda allowed a moment to pass before he did so.

The sudden darkness could only help the ploy, and as he slid out the truck, he unconsciously slipped the burna off his hip. A chuckle from the darkness let him know the move wasn't as conspicuous as he'd thought and making his way in front of the truck, he took his last drag from the blunt before tossing its end to the wet ground. Beneath pale moonlight and soft rain, he exhaled a cloud of smoke before pulling the hood of his coat over his head. "I don't see my wife," he acknowledged, and even beneath the veil of darkness he could feel Messiah's twin studying him. About fifteen feet separated them, and though Messiah had warned him to keep his distance, Murda had a vague feeling that the man was playing his own game of chess.

"I don't see my money either," he responded, before turning his face up to the rain. "You know who I am now, huh?" His voice rode on a soft wind as he refocused his attention on Murda.

Murda had no time. "Nigga, fuck my wife at? I ain't here on no friendly shit," he spat, and noticed the profiles of the men before him bristle.

The leader stood slightly apart from his dudes and even within the darkness Murda noted his smile. "Step closer," he demanded, and when Murda didn't move, three barrels leveled on him; red beams dancing over his form. "Nigga, as you said, ain't no friendly shit, so I ain't repeating myself." The resolution in his tone left little room for debate, and reluctantly, Murda closed a bit of the distance. And just as a roll of thunder shook the heavens, Murda's guy told him he'd been lured from the truck for devious reasons.

"You're not Messiah, playboy," someone hissed from behind him, and just as the butt of the gun slammed against the side of his head, Murda remembered the gatekeeper telling him there had been *five* shooters awaiting him. Everything went black as he fell to his knees.

***

They'd wound up in the woods surrounding the backyard; about eighty paces in, and within a clearing of the thick undergrowth, and dense plant life, they came to a weathered tree with a shovel propped against it. The thick canopy of tree leaves had protected most of the earth from the rain, and even without the light emitting from the flashlight one of the three Jamaican men held, Messiah would've noticed the freshly overturned earth. *A grave!* His mind screamed and his heart cracked.

"Keisha." His voice was strained as he shook his head against what his eyes was telling his heart. "Quit playin' games, mane, where's my—"

"Tonka!" Keisha called to the big Jamaican, and when his dark eyes captured her, she nodded to the shovel. Without a word, he handed her his sharp knife and began unearthing whatever had been buried. "She *had* to die, Measiah, she'd betrayed you," Keisha murmured.

"Kii-sha," Messiah grit, his eyes clouded as he watched the shovel dig into the soil over and over again. "You didn't kill my—"

"Did ya know mi and de gyal were lovers?" Keisha cut him off, her eyes transfixed upon the grave.

"You lyin', bitch!" Messiah spat, before taking a step closer to her.

Keisha smirked. "Jam miss her pum pum, huh, baby, was it better dan mine!" She taunted just as the grave digger's exhumation ended.

The grave wasn't but four feet deep, and he'd only removed the top half, but it was enough. A scar of lightning cut across the sky and beneath its glow, Messiah's mouth fell open in a silent scream at what he saw. Buried with her eyes open, and soft earth caked against her rotting flesh, she still wore the exact clothes she'd worn the last time they'd fornicated. Messiah's heart cracked as heaven's tears began to drip just a bit harder, and falling to his knees, he dug his fingers into the moist dirt as he gasped for the breath the sight had stolen. "Wh-Why you kill her, Keisha," he sputtered.

Thunder roared in the distance as Keisha smiled in contempt. "Jah hurt fa she, but—"

Messiah's chuckle blossomed into a mad laughter and froze her mid-speech. "Jealousy." He laughed, slamming a fist against the earth. "The same evil that made you kill your own pops!" He spat before crawling over to the corpse of the woman he'd known his entire life, and sliding his hand down her face, he closed her eyelids. "You liked Gator for power, bitch, you knew he'd planned to pass the family to JonJa, and you felt he didn't deserve it! You've always been jealous of their relationship and—"

"Shut up!" Keisha's roar was punctuated by throwing the deadly knife at him.

Messiah's eyes grew wide in horror as in slow motion the blade flipped blade over handle in the air, and just when its blade twinkled under another flash of lightning, it stabbed the earth, just inches from him.

Keisha breathed erratically as if she fought for a breath, and as rain splashed upon her chocolate flesh and rolled down her body, she hugged herself. "No, Messiah, he *never* planned to give the reins to JonJa. Him know JonJa is a snake batty boi." Her voice was almost sad as she gazed down at the corpse. "He planned to give the family to *you!* And if—"

"So you killed him!" Messiah raged, and even her own men stared at Keisha in utter shock. Keisha stared down at Messiah, her eyes dark.

"Yes."

"Hate!" Messiah roared before slamming a fist against the earth, and as if Heaven had become one with his anguish, thunder roared. "Jealousy!" He growled, and lightning flashed. "Treason!" He shouted, and the skies opened up into a mad rain. And when Messiah's glare lifted to her, Keisha saw something flash within his irises, yet, before she could register it, the reaper appeared. His massive arm slipped around her neck swiftly before contracting like a hug of an anaconda.

Keisha's eyes were wild as she scratched at his forearms, gasping for air as he lifted her two feet off the ground. At six-four and weighing two hundred and sixty pounds of ripping muscle, JonJa's strength was monsterous! Rain soaked his dreads and poured down the mask of pure hatred his face displayed. His lips were inches from Keisha's ear as he squeezed her spirit out her body. "Death," he hissed, his eyes focused on Messiah. "*After* dishonor!" He growled, and beneath a flash of lightning, Messiah stumbled to his feet as Keisha's eyes plead for help. Yet she would never know that it was Messiah who'd devised the entire plot on her life.

After he'd had Paradise contact JonJa and reveal he'd been sleeping with the enemy, he offered the Jamaican not only the reigns to the family, but also Keisha's confession. Messiah's theatrics were merely to keep Keisha's attention on him as fate slipped from the woods, and as JonJa's men slipped from the shadows, Messiah gave the dead woman in the grave one last look before walking away.

***

The rain was heavy, and on his knees on the ledge of being executed, Murda began to laugh. The man behind him; holding the tool to his top, frowned. "Don't worry, my nigga. My twin brother will join you shortly." He smirked. The hood had been snatched from Murda's head to reveal the gash on his dome. Blood leaked, yet, as he gazed through the shower of warm rain, he knew revenge was at his fingertips. "Now," he hissed.

The man behind him chuckled. "In a hurry to di—" he was saying when a loud crash sounded in the distance paused him.

The sounds of sirens filled the night and the flashing police lights created chaos! His four men raced forward and laid fire at the oncoming officials, and though it dawned on him that he'd been setup, the money was the only denominator! Without delay, he turned and ran for the truck, and flinging the door open, he salivated at the sight of the duffel bag on the passenger's seat. Snatching it up, he never glanced back to see the conclusion of things, he merely fled into the shelter of darkness.

***

Five men less, Messiah eased the Excursion off the estate and out the ruined gate. Though smoke rose from the hood of it, the truck was more than competent of getting him home. Yet, on the long back road leading to the estate,

Messiah pulled alongside a stolen white van that idled in the rain.

The driver's side window rolled down and a man with skin as dark as midnight nodded to him. "You good?" His voice was a grumble.

Messiah's eyes were haunted, sorrow a dance within his gaze. "Shit crazy, but I'm on all ten." He shrugged before allowing his eyes to trail down the length of the van. At that moment, the phone on the passenger's seat rung, and retrieving it, Messiah smirked connivingly. "Sup?" He answered.

"De diamonds, mon, Jah say ya ah have dem. When con we meet to conclude our business?" JonJa spoke.

"Give me ten minutes and meet me at the front of the estate. I have them *now.*" Messiah's reply was met by the call ending. He merely glanced out at the driver of the van, and the man chuckled before the van eased away, heading for the ruined gate of the property. As Messiah headed for the last phase of his chess game, he wondered if Murda was still breathing.

\*\*\*

The downpour had ebbed, and beneath the cover of twilight, Junior, Messiah's twin, got away with the bag! Splashing in dark puddles of water as he ran down an aisle created by crashed old cars stacked sky high on either side of him, his head was on swivel for *anyone* attempting to get in the way of him and his ticket. Burna in hand and the heavy bag slung over his shoulder, the man was desperate for an escape, even if it took getting blood on the money!

\*\*\*

The two SUVs had spun into the junkyard at a dangerous speed for the weather, and as bullets knocked sparks from the frame of the lead one, Spinx played a suicidal game of chicken with them.

"What the hell are you doing, Spinx? You're gonna get us killed!" screamed McHenry, scrunched down in the passenger's seat.

A wicked smirk curved Spinx's lips as he glared at the four men gunning at them, and captured within the headlights, he watched the determined expression on the shooter's faces melt into shock! *Ping! Ping! Ping!* High powered bullets cracked through the truck's surface. And just as one punched the windshield; flying a hair over Spinx's bald head, two of the shooters dove out the way, one was trampled beneath the truck, and the fourth was flipped into the air before he crashed through the windshield...face first! The truck skidded to a halt, kicking up splashes of mud in the process.

"What the fuck was that! Have you lost you—" McHenry was saying, but *Boom!* The P.89 Spinx fired surprised his partner mid-speech as a splatter of blood and brain matter splashed across his pale face. And by the time McHenry's vision found the smoking hole in the temple of the man stuck inside the windshield, Spinx had jumped out the truck and gave chase to a fleeing Murda. The man never glanced back to see the fire fight that ensued, therefore, he was blindfolded by the treachery of his own team.

\*\*\*

Breathless, Junior slowed his sprint, panting as he searched frantically for a place to hide, hating he could flee with the check. He'd ran so deep into the chaos of the junk, that he'd reached the end of the property, and it was there, rounding a mountainous pile of scrap metal that the butt of the gun slammed into his face. Blood exploded from his face as everything went black.

\*\*\*

The sky had ceased its cry, and its black hue gave way to the storm gray of twilight. The driver of the van had slipped out and helped Sunjay out and into his wheelchair, before rolling it about thirty feet from the ruined gate of the Jamaicans' domain. Sunjay, draped in all black, stay within the chair, positioning the Grenade launcher on his shoulder. In the distance, the headlights of the Jeep Wrangler could be seen.

"You ready?" His accomplice asked, and Sunjay nodded while sighting the surprisingly light weapon.

The Jeep was almost upon them when the ringing of a phone filled the night; the slight static revealing the device was on speakerphone. The man behind him held the phone next to Sunjay's mouth just as it was answered.

"Speak," JonJa's gruff voice filled the night.

"Shooting a man in the back is a coward move. A real steppa gets close and personal." Sunjay smirked as he watched the Jeep close the gap.

"Who him boy talkin' like rude boy?" JonJa chuckled. "Dis Sunjay? Jah live? Mi have—" he was saying before the headlights captured the nightmare outside the windshield. Four deep in the Jeep, JonJa rode passenger with two rude boys piled up in the backseat, and when the Jeep pulled to a slow stop in the middle of the road, JonJa's eyes shot to the driver, smiling arrogantly. "Wah gwan, brethren?" He inquired, but it was the horror reflecting in the man's eyes as he gripped the steering wheel with both hands that snatched JonJa's gaze in the direction he stared. His eyes went wild in shock.

"Got my lick back." Sunjay chuckled into the phone and in a mad attempt of ducking final destiny, the Jeep erupted in chaos.

Fear filled the Jeep as the two in the back went to aim their weapons.

"Shit, mon!" The driver cried before stomping down on the gas pedal. The tires squealed as they fought for traction on the wet pavement; smoke rising from their fight.

"Go! Go, mon!" JonJa cried while reaching for the door handle.

Sunjay's smile was wicked, his twelve gold teeth twinkling as his finger tapped the trigger. The grenade exploded from the mouth of the launcher with fire and smoke waving from its ass as it sought its target. JonJa's mouth fell open as he flung the door open and attempted to dive from the speeding Jeep; but even as he leapt—*KABOOOM!* The grenade lifted the Jeep into the air and swallowed it into flames, and airborne, JonJa ignited.

*** 

Coming to, Junior found himself on his hands and knees in dirty water. Vaguely, he felt the bag of money being snatched from his shoulder, just as his gun was slipped away. Whoozy, he was down bad.

"'Preciate this, homie." The voice wasn't the same he'd heard earlier, and when the fuzz cleared, he looked up to find a smiling Spinx taking aim at his chest.

"Fuck are you?" Junior spat, blood leaking from the split on the bridge of his nose.

Spinx kicked him in the face, snapping his head back. "The law of the land, baby, and you're being charged with—" *BOCA!*

A gun clapped, and Junior flinched as blood sprayed the air. Yet, not his!

Shock spread across Spinx's face as his eyes fell to his stomach where the bullet made its exit. Pushing the FBI jacket open, he touched a finger to the hole just above his navel, and lifting his fingers, he studied his fingertips until— *BOCA!* His shoulder exploded, and the slug spun him in a half circle. "Arrrgh!" He growled, and clutching his stomach, he stumbled a little bit before coming face to face with fate.

A swirl of smoke snaked from the barrel of Murda's burner as he aimed.

Shock was a brief intermission between their showdown as shock melted on Spinx's face. "Nigga?" He coughed, and as the heavens turned a brighter shade of gray, Murda saw the spray of blood that flew from his lips. "You shot the-the law!" Spinx's shout was strained as he began to breathe heavy. "You're under arrest for ass-u-lt on-on—"

*BOCA!* Murda fired with a step forward. Spinx's body jerked as fear bloomed in his gaze. *BOCA!* Murda squeezed for the third time, and blood exploded from the ex-detective's chest. Spinx rocked on his feet, blood leaking from his hips, and as the dawn of a new day brought a purplish pink horizon, the sound of rapid gunfire sounded in the distance.

Murda chuckled, knowing his men had hit Spinx's people with the triple cross. "Checkmate, Blood, I'm sure we'll link again." Murda's smile was demonic, and with a last attempt at preservation, Spinx went to aim, but—*BOCA! BOCA!* The tool burped in Murda's clutch, bringing the mission to its end. Spinx crumbled to the soil, and only then did Murda's heart began to pound. A flock of birds swept overhead, and his eyes falling to the spot Junior had just lain, Murda found—*nothing!* Messiah's twin had vanished.

# Chapter 19

In fresh clothes and in the backseat of his Bentley truck, Messiah gazed out at the three bedroom, pale yellow house in Desoto, Texas. Smirking with a glass of yak midway to his lips, he knew Coffe's crib was where his web would end. "Paradise?" he called, and their eyes met in the rearview. He smirked. "You know why Freddy Kruger is the worst boogeyman ever created?"

"Freddy Kruger, Messiah, really?" Paradise laughed.

Studying the side of her face, Messiah smirked; lady was gorgeous! "Humor me," he whispered before taking a sip of Remy.

Paradise's creamy skin was flawless, and her hair pulled up into a Chinese bun, with her edges laid wavy, she tempted the strength of a playa! Patting the side of her head as if it itched, she obliged, "'Cause he had knives for hands?" She giggled.

Messiah downed his drink. "Naw, bitch, *most all* boogey men murdered with knives!" He shook his head. "Freddy was the worse 'cause he only came when a mu'fucka fell asleep!" He chuckled. "There's no escaping an enemy that's summoned only when your eyes closed, Paradise, and a dream is merely uncontrolled thoughts that allows a conscious mu'fucka to use you as a puppet. That's why the only way people defeated by Freddy was by going to sleep *with a plan!* Having someone there to wake them before Freddy could show the difference between a dream and a

178

nightmare." Messiah pushed the door open, but paused with one foot still in the truck. "What makes a lioness so dangerous, Paradise?" He asked, but slid out the whip before she could answer. "Tell me later, after I kill this hoe for her sins." He laughed at the shock expression on her face.

"Wha-What?" She sputtered, but the door slamming was her only response!

\*\*\*

"Baby, I have to go to work. Mama will be here in twenty minutes though. Do you need anything before I leave?" Dream asked.

Sunjay had been home for thirty minutes, and after Queen had helped bathe him and get him to bed, Sunjay lay there, frowning up at the ceiling as it had offended him. Ever since he'd awaken in that hospital room with his two-step fucked up, Sunjay's sanity tethered on the ledge of a steep cliff. Ignoring her, he allowed his eye to droop close, and Dream sucked her teeth in disgust.

Dressed in her Williams Chicken uniform, and tying her hair into a tight ponytail, she glared at him. "Look, dude, this little, *oh woe is me* trip you're on has to stop! Nigga, you knew the cons of the streets *before* you had to suffer for them, so stick ya damn chest out and be a man!" She spat, and when Sunjay didn't so much glance at her, Dream rolled her eyes. She loved him and knew his pride was cracked from being crippled, but—*Damn, the nigga still has life! I'm not going anywhere; ugh! Niggas never grateful!* She thought before shaking her head in pity. Leaning down to kiss his cheek, Dream had to fight to not break down in tears. Sunjay was threatening to rob their union of the things she loved about him. "I'll see you when I get off, kay?" She asked, and Sunjay's eyes cracked open in a glare.

"Fuck you, bitch, you not going to work; you goin' to get some dick! Just keep it real; I know I can't"—*Whap!*

Dreams palm meeting his face slapped the words back down his throat. Glaring, with tears baptizing her vision, she jabbed a finger at him. "Sunjay." She roughly wiped her eyes. "You won't disrespect me; that's what we're *not* doing! *When* I need some dick, *bitch,* I'll have yours or—" She held up her right hand and wiggled her fingers. "I'll use these." Dream rolled her eyes again before stomping over and snatching her purse off the dresser. "Get ya life, Sunjay. I'll see you later," she spat before making her exit.

Sunjay glared up at the ceiling, a lone tear dripping from his left eye. "*You* did this to me, nigga, and when we meet, we're gonna handle that!" He growled before reaching under his pillow and slipping forty from beneath it.

As Dream pulled out the driveway and onto the street, she was so emo that even Murda registered the distress in her posture as their cars zoomed passed each other. Dream was so busy texting that she didn't even glance up to see him wave a greeting. Murda chuckled. *Dick deprived!* He shook his head as he pulled into the driveway.

***

"Messiah?" Coffe exclaimed, a shocked expression on her face.

Messiah smirked. Standing in the doorway, though she wore a silk robe that hugged her slim-thick curves to perfection, it was the alarm dancing in her eyes that told Messiah all he needed to know. "In the flesh, mama." He chuckled as her vision beheld the image of his playerism. White silk Sace button down, turtle green tailored slacks, with white suede Versace loafers on his feet, Messiah ran a hand over the soft fabric of his shirt. "You look surprised." He smirked *knowingly.*

"I-uh-I, no," Coffe sputtered before patting the messy bun her hair was pulled up into. "Not surprised, just a bit disappointed." The shock had worn off and was replaced with a cure glare.

"Oh?" Messiah lifted a brow. *Bitch is a natural,* he thought with a smirk.

"Yes, you were supposed to be here hours ago, Messiah. I don't like being stood up." She pouted.

Messiah chuckled, he'd always had a thing for game bitches, and at that moment, Coffe's web of deception was making his dick hard. And without further ado, he did the unexpected! Stepping into her space, he pulled her to him. The surprise on her face was priceless as he pushed her back into the house and kicked the door closed behind them. His tongue created a sensual dance in her mouth, and though she'd tensed, his hands exploring her body's geography made her surrender. Messiah'd pulled the sash holding the robe closed and falling open, it exposed her feminine landscape. C-cups with jutting nipples surrounded by large tan areoles, sat up perky. Her flat stomach led to a slim trail of pubes below her navel that trailed to a diamond shaped fuzz trimmed pretty around pouring pussy lips.

"Messiah?" Her voice was raw with passion when their lips parted.

Pushing the silk fabric from her shoulders, Messiah watched as it fell in a pool at her feet. "Jazzy," he whispered, admiring her.

Coffe bit her bottom lip seductively and Messiah twisted her and led her to the couch, moistening her garden. Sitting her on the couch centered in the middle of the living room, he sat her down before pushing her legs back so far her knees touched her breast. "Keep 'em there," he demanded.

"Pussy wide open," Coffe moaned as Messiah placed soft kisses against her inner thighs, and in some freak shit, she squeezed her right nipple. Lids drifting closed, her lips parted. "Ohhh!" She cried, and just when Messiah's soft lips kissed her pelvis, he pushed his finger inside of her. Her back arched, but confusion sixty nined with intrigue within her expression; what she thought to be a finger was too cold to be. And when her eyes shot open to behold the evil reflecting from Messiah's gaze, Coffe almost screamed, but—

"Don't," was Messiah's demand, and it was her eyes that revealed the truth of her disobedience. Messiah never slowed down fucking her with what he had gripped in his hand. He smirked when her eyes fell to the long barrel of the .50 caliber disappearing in and out of her essence. Her juices glistened on the nickel plated steel, and when her eyes lifted to behold his, terror seized her. "You didn't expect me to make it, huh?" He chuckled, finger tight around the trigger.

"Wha-What? What are you talking a—"

"The surprised look on ya face when you saw me," Messiah cut her off. "You didn't expect me, 'cause you thought I'd be at that junkyard meeting *our* brother." Messiah laughed when shock registered on her face.

"I-I don't know what you're talking about. Brother? I-ahhh," she cried when Messiah began to work the barrel in and out a bit quicker.

"Of course you do, Coffe, it took me a minute to figure it out, but when you read a particular part of that *black book,* it hit me like a train." His laughter was wicked as he nodded. "Your eyes…the same hue as your fathers, and your skin?" He eased the barrel so deep that she flinched, and her pussy lips kissed the knuckle he'd wrapped around the trigger. "Latte." He licked his lips. "Almost red, like your mother's." His eyes lifted from her feminist and captured hers. "A beautiful combination of Pimpin Maxwell and his bottom hoe, *Foxy!*" He smirked when Coffe tensed, her eyes clouding.

"I *hate* you!" She spat.

"Bitch, I'm so immune to hate, I sometimes confuse it with admiration. Now." Messiah turned the gun sideways. "Either you're gonna tell me where my wife is, or I'm 'bout to give you the fastest hysterectomy known to life!" He spat.

\*\*\*

He knocked multiple times and even rung the doorbell before slipping his burna off his hip and trying the knob. *Unlocked!* Suspicion bled into Murda's eyes as he crept into the crib, not knowing what to expect. "Sunjay?" He called, head on a swivel as he clutched the tool. Living room clear, he made his way slowly down the hall leading to the master bedroom. "Jay, if you in this bitch, you betta speak up before—" he was saying before swinging the tool into the room and finding Sunjay laying in bed, back propped up by a stack of pillows. "Nigga, fuck you ain't—" Murda frowned as his eyes fell to the gun in his man's hand. "Sunjay?" He treaded, noting the tears of a gangsta dripping from Sunjay's face.

Sunjay smirked before his baptizing eyes lifted to his guy. "I tried to do it, but that shit takes more nuts than I thought." He chuckled bitterly as Murda tucked his own weapon.

"Tried to do what, Blood? What's brackin', Bleed?" Murda was lost, confusion his expression.

Again, Sunjay chuckled. "Tried to off myself, Blood."

"Fuck? Nigga, *why* would you try some shit li—"

"Look at me!" Sunjay's outburst was malicious as his bloodshots told his tale. Jabbing the gun down towards his legs, Sunjay sat up and began to rock, grunting as his upper half jerked in a strange movement. "See, slime, you see why I *need* to end it; huh!" Spittle flew from his mouth with his rage, and the confusion on Murda's face melted into a sad realization. Sunjay was trying to will his legs to move. No matter how hard he tried, his body failed him. Suddenly he became as still as a statue before deflating and falling back against the pillows. Eyes drifting closed, twin rivers dripped from beneath his lids. "Can't even use my dick, Blood, I'll never have kids," he croaked. "Never step again," he whispered.

Murda was speechless, fatigue from the crazy night clashing with the broken melody of his man's heart crack. "Blood." He ran a hand over his bald head, sighing heavily. "You can't fold just 'cause you gotta adjust. Real niggas don't fold! Only way we expire is if the op one ups us, and tonight we proved we *always* get our licks back!" He declared.

Sunjay's eyes cracked open, and drowning in their own pools, he stared down at his feet. "Here, dawg." He extended the tool to Murda, and the man wasted no time stepping over and attempting to relieve him of the fire, but just as his fingers wrapped around the steel, Sunjay lashed out and took ahold of his wrist.

It happened so fast, Murda froze. "Fam, what the—"

"I need a favor, Bleed." Half twisted in the bed as he held the man's wrist for dear life, Sunjay's eyes were wild.

Murda tried to yank away, but Sunjay's grip was official. "Sunjay—"

"A favor. You all I got, nigga!" Sunjay growled, and the finality in his tone caused Murda to still. Studying Sunjay, a chill ran down Murda's spine, and only when he saw he'd gotten his attention, did Sunjay release him and the gun. Falling back against the pillows, he allowed his eyes to fall back closed. "I need *you* to do it, dawg."

"Fuck outta here." Murda laughed, he couldn't help it. "Nigga, I ain't gonna—"

"Yes." Sunjay's eyes shot open to behold him. "You will."

Chuckling with a shake of the head, Murda ejected the clip from the bottom of the .40. "Blood, get you some rest. You talkin crazy."

It was Sunjay's turn to laugh. "Yeah, that's what ya twin thought before *I* flipped 'em." He spat, using his fingers to form a gun and mockingly pulling the trigger. "Pow! Pow!" He mouthed, and Murda pushed the clip back into place.

"Fuck you just say, Bleed?" His heart turned black.

\*\*\*

"You've always had it better than me and Junior," Coffe whispered, glaring to where Messiah stood, wiping her juices from the barrel of the tool with his shirt.

"Fuck is Junior? And *everythang* I got *I* got it out the mud!" He spat.

Coffe slipped her robe back on, but as if she were cold, she hugged herself. "Junior is *our* brother, and you may have gotten it out the mud, but it was by burying *our* father neck deep in it, and by default, made me and—"

"Bitch—" Messiah seethed, taking aim at her top. "Fuck ya life story! Fuck my wife at!" He growled.

Coffe shook her head with a sad smile. "I'll only tell you if you tell me how you figured it out."

Messiah chuckled, menacingly, but humored her nonetheless. "Back in the gap, Foxy told me your *first* name, but when you read the scene from the black book, *you*, left it out."

Coffe laughed bitterly. "You noticed."

Messiah nodded. "Google is official, so I merely inserted Ariel with the Lawson name on the name tag you always wear, and?" He shrugged.

Coffe nodded, respecting his mind. "And how you knew not to meet Junior last night?"

"Easy." Messiah smirked. "As soon as I texted you for your addy, his text came right in behind it, and it confirmed what I'd realized at the hospital."

"That was?"

"That if I tried to get too close to you, Junior would get nervous." He chuckled. "But *why* though? How'd y'all get on my trail? Find out where I rest my head?"

Coffe shrugged. "I didn't know of Junior until about four years ago. He'd come down from Houston at a time me and my mother was struggling. I was merely an intern at the hospital and when he offered to make life better for me and my moms…" She shrugged. "We watched you, and if I'm to be honest, Junior was a bit jealous of your success. Seeing how you lived in that big house, your drip official as you were chauffeured through the city in that foreign." She shook her head sadly. When a conniving smirk eased onto her face, Messiah frowned. Coffe's sudden confidence confused him as she slid off the couch, allowing her robe to flutter open. She was a masterpiece, and massaging her nipples, her eyes fell hall mast.

Messiah laughed in disbelief. "Bitch, you're my sister!" He shook his head in disgust.

"No, I'm not, Messiah, and even so, we've already shared intimacy."

It was then, even before a soft breeze blew through the room that Messiah smirked. "You didn't answer my question."

Confusion interrupted her seduction as Coffe frowned. "What question?"

"How'd y'all find out where I rest my head? My number?" He asked, and that's when a cold kiss of steel touched the back of his head.

"That's where I come in." Her sultry made Messiah smirk; he'd already figured it out. "You told me betrayal is suicide," lady whispered.

"Have you figured the answer, yet? What makes a lioness so dangerous?" He asked, and felt her shrug behind him.

"Tell me, daddy," she purred sinisterly.

Messiah eyed Coffe, but his words were for the woman behind him. "'Cause she's the closest one to the lion. She hunts for him, fucks for him, and feeds him, but as soon as a stronger nigga test her King's *pride,* and he shows he's too weak to protect it, the lioness will submit to new reign." He chuckled. "Like you, *lioness."* Messiah shook his head, tired of the game. "Yet, *why?* Why switch sides when I never failed my pride? Fuck you get in the bed with the enemy, *Paradise?"*

Paradise smiled sadly before stepping to the side of him, gun trained. "I loved you, fucked you, sold my soul for you, and even if you copped, locked, or blew other hoes, I stayed strong as ya bottom, but when this bitch Justice came?" She shook her head, blinking tears away. "You changed! Said fuck the woman that sacrificed for you and used the hard earned money we'd helped you get to build an empire for another bitch! So?" She shrugged. "When I met Junior, it wasn't hard to fall for him. He's *you*, just without the fancy words." She chuckled before planting the barrel against his temple. "Drop the gun, Messiah, or I'll kill you."

"The ransom note; it was you." Messiah grit, ignoring her.

Paradise nodded. "Kicked myself in the ass too. Thought you'd figured it out." She smirked.

"Where's Justice?"

Paradise shook her head. "Pitiful! You're about to die and all you care about is sweet…little…Justice!" She spat, digging the gun into his head. "Justice." She laughed in disgust. "We planned to just get the money and kill her."

"What changed your mind!" Messiah was curious, and Paradise smiled.

"The diamonds, Messiah. While fucking JonJa, he told me who he thought stole them. "So—" Before she could finish, a strange expression blossomed onto Messiah's face and Coffe screamed.

"Paradise!"

*Boca!* Blood shot in the air and Messiah tumbled from the impact.

***

"It was a nice play. You was never 'posed to get touched, but when you lied to us about Bam's whereabouts, I knew if I stretched him, I'd have to go through you."

187

"The nigga with the red flag around his face," Murda spat, remembering the night the reaper had snatched his twin's and G-lady's souls. "It was you."

Sunjay shook his head. "Naw, Blood, *I* loved you too much to draw blood. That was *Messiah* with the flag on his face, and Lil Zetti the other nigga."

"Fuck? Why blood try to—"

"We knew, Murda." Sunjay shook his head with a chuckle as confession blossomed across Murda's face. "We couldn't figure it out at first, dawg, but it made sense when we thought about it. Fuck Spinx kept hittin' our spots? In parts of the city no one knew but *us!*" He smirked, and resolution awakened in Murda's expression. Smirking sadly, his eyes fell to the metal in his clutch.

"They had me dead to the wrong one night, and just when I was being placed into the backseat of the squad car, here comes this nigga Spinx!" Murda spat as if the name was vile. "Wit' just a few whispered words to them pigs, the cuffs came off and in exchange for a lil info, I'd walk free from being popped with four and a baby; locked up!"

Sunja nodded. "And a one-time thang turned to Spinx hittin' our spots and breakin' *you* off, and that made being a rat even easier for you."

"You and Messiah were always puttin' y'all nuts in niggas' faces," Murda began, but then his face contorted in thought. "Fuck that!" His teeth clinched as his vision lifted to lick with Sunjay's. "That means, all this time I've plotted to down Messiah, I had the wrong target, it was *you* who smoked Bam." He seethed.

Sunjay smiled sinisterly. "*And* his BM, *and* his seed by default—"

"Nigga, you killed my G-lady! Pussy!"

"May they rest in *piss!*" Sunjay chuckled, and even before fire leapt from the barrel, he saw Murda's finger twitch. *Boom!* The first slug opened Sunjay's chest, and when he clutched at the opening—*Boom!* The second bullet stole his soul as brain matter shot out the other side of his head, where the slug made its exit. He went with a smile on his face.

\*\*\*

The impact of Paradise slamming into him knocked him off balance, but as she crumbled to the floor, Messiah pivoted to regain his footing.

"Ahhh!" Coffe screamed, her hands flying to her mouth in horror.

Messiah's eyes lifted from Paradise's dead form and beheld a beautiful sista that held a smoking gun. "Fuck are you?" He eyed her suspiciously. Bow legged, mocha skin, and thick in the hips and thighs, lady was gorgeous! Yet, Messiah noticed the trembling of her hands as she stared down in shock at what she'd just done. *First kill,* Messiah summarized, and lady didn't snap from her stupor until she felt him gently uncurling her fingers from around the tool. Releasing it, she smiled at him when his eyes narrowed as he studied her. "I feel as if I'm 'pose to know you!"

*Marcella* smirked. *Yes, you should, nigga. I'm your sister you and mama forgot about!* She thought but shrugged before nodding toward Coffee. "Maybe, maybe not, but reunions can wait. I think she has something you want."

Messiah studied her a moment before nodding and stepping over to Coffe, and without warning—*Boom!* Shot her in the foot. The .50 jerked as Coffe crumbled to the floor.

"Please!" She cried, clutching the gaping wound.

Messiah glared murderously. "You'll bleed out if you don't tend to that soon, so I suggest you tell me the bidness."

"You'll only kill me," Coffe cried, whimpering in anguish. "This was never my plan. They just wanted the diamonds."

"Bitch, save the explanation. Where's my wife?" Messiah raged, tired of the games, and losing it, he kicked Coffe so hard, her head snapped back; a splatter of blood shooting from her nose.

"Ahaaah!" She cried, fighting to keep conscious.

But Messiah was seeing red, the passed month finally catching up with him. *Fuck it, baby may be dead anyway!* His thoughts became homicidal as he stepped forward, leveling the fire at Coffe's top just as she was shaking off the stars.

Yet, just before he squeezed, Marcella's soft hand gently pushed the gun down. "Let me talk to her please?" She offered and his eyes trailing from her to the softly crying Coffe, he nodded. Marcella stepped around him and over to Coffe before kneeling before her. "Listen, honey, it's over. I don't know what's going on, but *any* man that'll spill as much blood over *one woman* as he has, means she's too dead to lose. Only Helen of Troy caused more chaos, and you being a nurse?" She nods down to Coffe's bleeding foot; blood poured from it alarmingly. "You know you can't afford to wait too much longer." Rubbing a hand down the side of Coffe's face, "Tell him what he wants to know," she plead, and with tears running down her face, Coffe nodded.

"Okay, okay, I need my phone."

***

*Mesquite, Texas— Twenty Minutes Later*

"Fuck!" Junior spat, fighting the impulse to snap the phone. Staring down at its screen in disgust, he concluded the worst.

"They're still not answering?" Foxy lifted a brow and Junior studied her. In her late forties, lady was curved as a violin and as sexy as sun.

Shaking his head, Junior's vision reclaimed the screen. "Neither of 'em." He replied. He'd been calling both Coffe and Paradise for the past thirty minutes only to be forwarded.

When his eyes lifted to capture Foxy, she noted the uncertainty. "You think he figured it out? Think he kil—"

"Better not have." Foxy deaded the idea, and Junior's eyes fell to the .38 special resting in her lap. "For your sake, he better not have,"she hissed, eyes narrowed. Their eyes tango'd until the ringing of Foxy's phone made them both flinch. Retrieving it from the coffee table, she exhaled in relief when she saw her daughter's number flash across the screen. "Baby, you ok!" She answered just as her and Junior's vision clashed.

Chuckling on the other end of the phone sent her heart into her stomach. "Long time, Foxy lady. Shame our reunion has to be under diabolical conditions." Messiah greeted.

"Messiah, is Ariel well?"

Chuckling, "Foxy, you taught me to be a gentleman, right?"

After a pause, "And you have been?" Foxy inquired.

"Outside of a lil blood payment."

Tears came to Foxy's eyes. "Are they—"

"One still breathin, the other expired."

"Which—"

"The MVP is still amongst the living; for the moment."

"You want your wife?"

"Stupid question."

Foxy laughed nervously. "Okay, how we gonna do this!"

"My brother around?"

Junior became animated, waving "no" while shaking his head.

Foxy smirked. "Not at the moment, but—" The sound of the door bell startled her and she flinched. "Messiah?" She murmured as Junior slipped his tool off his hip and slipped to the back of the house.

"Are you lying to me, Foxy?" Messiah's smile could be heard through the phone. The bell rang twice. "If you don't want your daughter to bleed to death, ya may wanna get the door, ma." Messiah chuckled before ending the call, and Foxy rushed from her seat.

Making it to the door, she nervously glanced back to ensure Junior was out of sight before hiding the pistol behind her back. She cracked the door to find Marcella smirking, extending a phone to her. Confused, she reluctantly took it. "Hello?"

"Ma," Coffe rasped. "Please give him his wife. I'm dying."

Foxy's hand trembled. "Whe-Where are you, baby? I—"

"Deception is only thirty percent of the game." The voice didn't come from the phone, and spinning to find Messiah behind her; the phone slipped from her hand in shock.

"Ho-How'd—"

"You know better than to leave windows unlocked." Messiah chuckled, aiming the fifty.

A breeze wafting through the house reminded Foxy of the girl standing in the threshold, but when she glanced over her shoulder, the lady was gone. Foxy smirked before recapturing Messiah in her sights. "You've *been* here, watching?" She chuckled when he nodded. "We taught you well, Messiah."

"Indeed." He smirked.

Foxy shrugged. "So, what's next?"

"There's only *one* conclusion for touching one of mine."

Foxy nodded. "You've always had some devil lurking beneath all that pimpin'."

"You were special to me. how's it come to this?" Messiah nodded at the .38 she held down by her leg.

"Wasn't my plan." She shrugged.

Messiah smirked. "The evil twins?" He concluded, and the swift wind behind him made him pivot, just as Junior snuck behind him; swinging the butt of his gun at Messiah's head. Inches from his noggin, Messiah heard the whoosh as the strike passed his ear, and with all his might, he threw an elbow towards where he assumed the man's face would be—

*crunch!* He'd hit dice. Blood shot from Juniors nose as his head snapped back, but luck last only so long with gangsta's—*Boom!* Fired blindly, and Messiah stumbled back, shock registering on his face. Glancing at his shoulder he noted the blood escaping him, but self preservation was law! *Boom!* The big Desert Eagle roared, damn near snapping his wrist with its recoil.

Junior was hit in the side and slammed against the wall from the slug's power. Both men growled, clutching their wounds, but Messiah was out numbered.

"Where's my daughter, Messiah!" Foxy asked, before planting the barrel of the .38 to the back of his head.

Junior chuckled sinisterly. "Big bad Messiah," he rasped through the pain.

"Shut up, Junior."

"Naw." Junior shook his head, his and Messiah's stare down murderous. "This nigga has always thought he was better than me! It wasn't good enough for you to have mama choose you over me, but you just had to turn pops into a dopefiend! You ruined my life, nigga, and now I'm gonna get my licks back!" He spewed, clutching his wound as he stumbled forward.

Something dark bled into Messiah's eyes. "Never die alone, Pimp!" He spat.

Seeing the future, Foxy stepped to intervene, but fate can't be deterred. "Messiah," she called.

"Fuck you, nigga," Junior roared.

"Let's go!" Messiah shouted, and simultaneously, both men's pistols lifted and fired.

Junior's neck exploded, blood spraying the air, just as Messiah doubled over from them the slug punching through his stomach. Crumbling to the floor, he rolled over onto his back, staring up at the ceiling as he fought to catch a breath. It felt like fire was cooking his insides, and he knew he'd die there. His heart pounded too fast, and as his vision dimmed around the edges a sequence of events happened in union. The twin brother he'd never known of fell face first, dead...

"Messiah-Messiah, baby?" The voice he'd killed, conned, and longed to hear since the day it's possessor had been snatched from its life, called to him. The moment seemed surreal when she raced into the house, dressed in nothing but a singly shirt and shorts, and fell to her knees beside him. Hair wild, and dark rings under her eyes, Justice had lost at least seventy per her usual hundred and fifty-five pounds of thickness. Yet, his Trinidadian was still his pride.

Marcella entered after, she'd found Justice exactly where Coffe had said; locked in a cellar someone converted into a small room.

"Where's my daughter!" Foxy demanded, and Marcella's glare found her, still clutching the smoking gun *she'd* used to shoot Junior in the neck.

Nodding down at the phone, Marcella shook her head in pity. "Ask her."

Lost in the chaos, she'd forgotten the phone, and dropping the gun, she hurriedly rushed over to retrieve the discarded device. "Ariel? Hello? Baby?"

"I'm okay, mom," Coffe sniveled, having heard it all. Yet, their moment was disturbed.

"No! Yuh won die on meh, Messiah, hol on baby!" Justice cried, cradling his head in her lap. Glancing back at them, her eyes wet. "Don't dry stand around, bitch, call the ambulance!" She screamed to Foxy. Messiah's touch brought her attention back to him, and her eyes overflowed to find him extending his pinky.

"Promise me love is real?" He gasped, his eyes leaking tears. Justice nodded vigorously, and as soon as their pinkies intertwined; something special happened.

\*\*\*

*The night was black in Oak Cliff, Texas, and blinking in confusion, Justice found herself back outside her house, where she'd climbed out the window. It was the year of 1987, and she remembered her father had told her they'd be moving.*

*"What's you just say?" Messiah asked her, and Justice's mouth fell open in shock.*

*They were eleven years old again! His adolescent face studied her, and her eyes watered as she remembered. "Messiah, I tried to stay. I don't want to go, but my dad..." She broke down as he pulled her into his embrace. "He said I didn't know what love is, but I do, Messiah; we're love! Ain't this love?" She cried, and Messiah released her and stepped back.*

*"I don't know if love is real, Justice, but I want it to be," he said before glancing up to the heavens before returning his gaze to her and extending his pinky. "Promise that you'll come back, Justice? If love is real, pinky promise me that you'll wait for me—that you'll be mine forever!" He pled.*

*Justice nodded before lifting her pinky to seal the deal.*

\*\*\*

*Twenty Minutes Later*

*Skrrrt!* The car slid to a halt outside the doors of Parkland's Emergency Room, and Marcella jumped out the drivers seat, hysterical. "Helllp! We need help! Someone's been shot!" She screamed, and in moments the car was surrounded by medical personnel.

Messiah was pulled from the backseat, followed by Justice crawling out, covered in his blood. After placing him on a gurney, they wasted no time hurrying him into the hospital, but it was a slim chance he'd live long enough to make it to surgery.

# Chapter 20

"Slick assed Messiah, look at cha."

Her voice woke him, and when his eyes cracked open, Messiah frowned in confusion. He was bewildered; his last memory being his go with Junior, but after his eyes adjusted to the dimness of the room, he summarized his situation.

"Umph um umph." Someone beside his bed drew his attention, and when his blurred vision trailed to them, his eyes grew the size of bull nuts!

"Sss." He tried, but his throat was as raw as freshly cut beef!

The woman chuckled as she smirked down at him. Shaking her head, sadly, she retrieved the pitcher of water someone had left on the table beside him and leaning, she tilted it towards Messiah's lips. The pain medicine the hospital had him on made him sluggish, and— "Poor baby, ya must be thirsty. Drink up," she offered as she began to pour.

Water splashed against Messiah's face, with some going up his nose and choking him. In an effort at shouting for help, his lips parted in a silent scream, only to be choked by the water. His attacker didn't cease her assault until the pitcher was empty, its contents soaking Messiah and his pillow. He gasped for air as the pitcher was replaced, and only when his coughing fit ceased was he able to mumble her name. "Sassy!" He spat, glaring up at her, but too weak to do much more.

Prissy in a tan mini dress and peep toes, Sassy'd grown her hair and had it pulled up into a chic bun. Yet, it was the silk cloth bag she held that spoke volumes. Whatever was inside it, writhed languidly. "Long time, baby." She smirked. "I've waited for years to see you again, and maybe even get some of this good dick you have." She reached down to grope him through the blanket. "There it is!" She smiled before giving him a squeeze. "But?" Her hand slipped away, and she wiped it in her dress. "I've found you in no condition to perform." She giggled. And suddenly her laughter ceased, and something evil bled into her irises. "So, I'll just do something that's gonna bring me to orgasm quicker than you penis ever can." She smirked before waving her hand toward the other side of the bed, and when Messiah's eyes drifted there, he had to rapidly blink to ensure he was seeing what stood above him.

Cakes, Candy, and six other hoes he'd once had under his management before he'd blew them for the sake of love, stood smiling down at him.

"I'm here to serve you yo papers, daddy, and a taste of revenge long overdue." Sassy whispered, and as if on cue, each woman, save for Cakes, stepped over and planted kisses on his cheek before placing green apples on his chest.

Before he knew, a pile of six of the fruit rested there, before one rolled down to his stomach before tumbling to the floor. As if this was Cakes's cue, she stepped forward and roughly took Messiah's left wrist. He tried to yank it back, but the medicine made his attempts feeble, and before he knew it, his was cuffed to the tail of the bed.

"Help!" He croaked, his voice coming out in a harsh whisper. When his other wrist was cuffed, he sucked in a deep breath. "Helllp!" He cried, thrashing his feet.

Cakes glared at him in contempt. "I gave you my all, and in return, you left me in the hands of another one who abused me until—" Her chest heaved rapidly as if it were hyperventilating until her eyes found Sassy. The older woman smiled reassuringly, and Cakes regained her composure. "Sassy rescued me, and has shown me how blind I was of your game, and so we devised the ultimate get back." She giggled, and Sassy stepped forward.

"This is for Paradise. Oh." She stepped around to the foot of his bed, and resting the bag at his feet, pulled lose the string holding it closer. "And for my *nephew* Junior." She shook her head. "I warned *my brother* about you, but no, Pimpin Maxwell didn't listen!" She spat, laughing at the shocked expression on Messiah's face. "Surprised?" She giggled pityingly. "Yass, honey, Maxwell Davenport is my baby brother, and—" she was saying when a vicious hissing emitted from the bag, and in a blur, the black head of an inland taipan shot forth. The most venomous snake, the serpents head lifted, it's tongue in and out it's mouth at flickering speed. The scent of the apples, coupled with Messiah's fear permeating the air beckoned the reptile and it slithered forward. "A beautiful species, Messiah," Sassy whispered as her girls filed out the room. "It's venom is enough to kill a hundred and twenty five people," she whispered before blowing him a kiss. "Your calling card was the apple, right? For the forbidden fruit?" She giggled. "Now you have the serpent, but you'll die knowing a bitch knocked you for your Eves," Sassy bloated before slipping out the room.

Within the dimness, Messiah sat as still as a statue as he watched horrified as the serpent lifted, and curiously eyeing the apples atop Messiah's chest rise and fall with his tamed head breathing, the snake watched.

Messiah was terrified, and as if the game wanted to dangle hope tauntingly before him, the door opened to the room, and a nurse entered. Eyes down as she studied her chart, she was oblivious until—

"Hel-p, ple-ase," Messiah murmured, causing lady's eyes to snap up in alarm, and taking in the scene, things took on a slow-motion quality as her lungs filled with air. "No,"

Messiah pled, seeing her reaction. "Don't," he tried, but woman's mouth opened in horror.

"Ahhhhhhh!" She screamed at the top of her lungs. The snake's mouth shot open in a menacing hiss; it's curving fangs twinkling, before it struck!

"Oh my God, what's wrong with you!" He registered the voice, but Messiah was behind being consoled as he thrashed around in the hospital bed.

Shooting up in a sitting position, he flailed his arms wildly. "Nooo! No! Don't!" He cried.

"Doctor! Hellp! Someone help!" Someone screamed, and vaguely, Messiah heard the door to his room fling open, and just as Messiah's eyes cracked open, Doctor Sung and his nurse rushed into the room. Messiah's eyes were wild as he slapped at his chest.

"Mr. Ridge-Mr. Ridge," Doctor Sung cautioned after making his way over to him. "Take it easy before you reopen your wound."

Messiah's eyes swept the room, sunshine poured into the window, and all was well. Suddenly, as if all energy was zapped from him, he fell back against the pillow, exhausted. His eyes drifted shut as the physician checked his vitals and the wound to his stomach.

"Everything seems fine, just calm down." He spoke gently before smiling at Justice.

She stood beside her husband's bed with a concerned expression on her face. "Is he okay?"

The doctor nodded. "As much as can be. As I told you, this is a miracle. The bullet punctured his abdomen cavity, but didn't touch any of his vital organs upon its exit out his left side. He's a very lucky man," he acknowledged before nodding to his nurse and heading for the door. "He just needs plenty of rest and love." He smiled, and after their exit, Messiah's heavy lids cracked open to behold his heart.

"Hey, baby." Justice smiled down at him. "Huh scared me." She giggled, and Messiah's eyes trailed from her, and took in the room. *It was all a dream!* He nodded as he noticed all the flowers, balloons, and get well cards surrounding his bed. Seeing his curiosity, Justice smirked. "Everyone wishes you well, even some people I'm very interested in learning your acquaintance with." Her eyes narrowed at him, and even within his fatigue, Messiah knew she spoke of women. He tried to chuckle, and his throat burned. Noting it, Justice hurriedly poured him a glass of water from the pitcher beside his bed, and the notion ricocheted him back to the nightmare.

Messiah flinched as she extended the glass to him, and when Justice frowned in confusion, he reminded himself it was all a dream, and accepted the drink. After taking a sip, he glanced at her. "How long have I been out?"

"Three days."

Messiah frowned. "Three days?"

Justice nodded and reaching over to set the glass on the table beside the bed, Messiah froze. "Papi?" Justice asked, perplexed. The glass tumbled from Messiah's hand, and his heartbeat quickened. "Messiah?" Justice was confused, as her vision trailed to what had snatched such a reaction from her man. And it was there, beside the pitcher of water that she'd spotted six green apples in a pile, with a rubber snake encircling them. "What! You want an apple?" Justice asked, puzzlement etched over her facial, but Messiah was rendered speechless as he tried to tame the gallop of his racing heart.

# Epilogue

*Three Weeks Later*
Sitting on the back porch of his home, Messiah was one with the day. The morning air was soft; carrying the warmth of the coming summer, and the sun was just making his way back from across the world. It's pinkish hue revealed it's own sluggishness, and Messiah exhaled a stream of white widow smoke as he watched its rise. Since being discharged from the hospital, healing had been a fight, both physically and mentally. He'd come home to the tragic news of losing two of the closest people to him—Sunjay, suicide? Taking the blunt to the face, Messiah battled the tears welling in his eyes. They said Sunjay had blown his brains out, but Messiah knew better; Sunjay was stiff, but would never have the balls to off himself. Gazing up at the sun, Messiah allowed the dro to burn his chest before liberating it.

*Damn, Mama?* His heart melted. Black Diamond had been found, heart expired on he front pew of a church? Messiah shook his head in confusion. *Why would you be at a church? Who was the dude they said you smoked?* His mental was a jigsaw puzzle he couldn't figure out, *until—* As a light clicked on inside his head, Messiah's eyes shot to the black book beside him on the porch. And as a heavy tear fell from his right eye as he burst into laughter— *Blow!* He remembered the entry his mother had inscribed of the man coming home, and Messiah laughed a bit harder—cried a bit more, when it dawned on him that his queen had gotten her memory back, and had simply played everyone! The world would never know! Lost in his moment, Messiah didn't hear Justice step out onto the deck-like porch until she'd taken a seat beside him.

"Good morning, Pa?" She smiled, until she spotted the rivers running down his face. "Baby?" She murmured as her eyes fell to the black book resting beside him. She hurt for him; the loss of his mother and his main man was heavy, yet, as his woman, she knew that the only reprieve she could give was being his peace while he was in pieces. So, pulling her knees up to her chest, she hugged them as her eyes drifted to the sun. Their backyard was massive, and surrounded by a multitude of trees, and the way the sun shone down, it put her in the mind of a meadow. Their own garden of Eden.

Messiah smashed the end of the blunt against the deck, sniveling as he regained his composure. His eyes found Justice and he knew he'd trade it all for her. Hair hidden beneath a multicolored scarf, and dressed casually in tee and sweatpants, she'd been up packing the last of their things. They were leaving Dallas behind, and even in her *around the way girl* clothes, Messiah knew he had a bad bitch.

"It's okay to not be okay, Messiah." Her eyes trailed to his.

"But it's not okay to keep secrets from the nigga that'll go to war wit' the devil behind you." He smirked, and though Justice frowned in confusion, a chill ran down her spine.

"Excuse me?" Her brow rose, and Messiah laughed.

"Justice Ridge, I've been thuggin' wit' you since we were nine, and you were in and outta the hospital 'cause of ya asthma." His face became placid, but his eyes told the tale. "Quit playin' wit' me, ma."

Justice's head picked up speed. "Yuh done crack yuh head oh wah? Talk don't accuse!" Her Trinidadian tongue became thick as she narrowed her eyes at him.

Messiah nodded. "It didn't mean much when I read it, but then I wondered *how* my T-lady knew what went on in that apartment where you and Sunjay were the only one's present." He chuckled before retrieving the book and opening it to the year 1996. Handing it to her, he gazed out at his property as she read:

*"My fault." Sunjay apologized once he was through throwing up. He let a leg dangle out the door as he slumped back in his seat, and wiping his mouth, he chuckled. "Shit all fucked up, Jus, now that Messiah out the picture. Gator's bitch ass tryin' to tax on the work. I'd be wrong if I stung 'em for them stones though." He laughed, but Justice was lost in the sauce.*

*"Stones?" She frowned. "Stung him! Hell yuh talkin', Sunjay, yuh drunk, boy? Get on out my car before yuh gal comes out here trippin'."*

*Sunjay laughed. "Yeah, I fucks wit' ya wheels, sis, it's smooooth!" He drug the word, the liquor on his ass. "And the stones? I'm tal'm 'bout the bag of diamonds Gator keeps in his wife's golden urn in his den. Them hoes worth some M's, and his old ass just got 'em in his dead bitch's ashes like the kid won't take em down."*

After reading, Justice sat the book down between them, and without a word, climbed to her feet and retreated into the house.

*Why would she keep secrets?* Messiah wondered as his heart cracked. His thoughts boarded insecurities as he wondered if Sunjay and Justice embraced treachery. Justice re-emerged and reclaimed her seat beside him, and seeing the knife she held, he spread his arms as if giving her a clear shot. "Sup? You 'bout to stab—"

"Shut yuh lips, Messiah, yuh talkin crazy—dottish ass!" She spat, giving him a look of belief. "Stupid!" She shook her head before pulling the book back into her lap, and flipping it spine up, she began to cut.

"Fuck you doin'!" Messiah spazzed, reaching for the book, but when Justice posed as if she'd stab him, he withdrew his hands like a scolded child.

"Yuh fucked Porsha," Justice spoke before returning her attention to her task.

Messiah's heart turned backwards. "Wha-I," he tried, but Justice ignored him as she cut the spine of the book open.

"Then yuh put yuh dick in the crazy bitch Keisha. You even kept up with yuh little hoe squad behind my back." Her revelations came out so neutral, that if Messiah's eyes hadn't lifted from observing the knife cutting through the book, he wouldn't have known she was crying.

"Ma, I—"

"Committed treason." Justice nodded to herself.

Messiah wanted to lie to rescue her from her pain, but knew lies were betrayal in their self, so nodding, "Treason, baby, I fucked up. Yeah, I cut them, but—"

"Porsha drugged you."

"What!" Messiah spat. He'd known *something* strange fed his carnal that night, but could never imagine Porsha's mischief. "I tripped out, Justice, and I won't add lies to betrayal. Neither bitch meant shit to me, and—"

"Why niggas always say that!" Justice wigged, pausing in her cut to glare at him. "Like, damn, Messiah, if you fuck up, admit that shit and accept what comes with it, but save the *she didn't mean shit* spiel, 'cause if you gamble all your love for something that doesn't mean shit to you, what that say 'bout yuh? Hmmm?" Her truths rocked him, and for a moment, Messiah was speechless.

Exhaling heavily before rubbing a hand over his bald head, he gazed up at the sky. "You're right, ma, but neither female much matters no more."

"Wha-What?" Justice needed clarification.

"Keisha killed *Porsha,* Justice, and burried her in the woods behind her house." His revelation stole a sob from his wife. Justice wanted to whoop Porsha's ass, but not see her dead!

"I—" She shook her head in disbelief. "I didn't see it."

Messiah's eyes trailed to her. "Your *visions?*" He summarized, and Justice nodded. "You gonna leave me, Jus?" Messiah was broken.

Justice didn't answer for a long moment, but—"Messiah, I'm *full* grown. Even without my visions, I'd known yuh gave *my* dick away. I knew when we reunited that the life yuh lived was too powerful for you to just up and leave."

"Is that what you and Sunjay—" Messiah grit his teeth, unable to verbalize the possibility.

Justice studied him peculiarly. "Me and Sunjay *what?*"

"Y'all—"

"Shut the hell up, nigga, before yuh speak blasphemy and have to sleep in the cot for *years!*" She glared before passing him the book. "Me and Sunjay have never crossed any lines, and I'm a solid bitch, dude. I won't fuck anotha nigga just 'cause you can't control yuh dick! My pussy is where my legacy comes from; our seed! I'm protective of it! I'd rather just leave if I can't forgive your sins." She stared at him, watching him push the flap back on the book. "Yuh mother bought the book so *she* could hide her um—"

"Dope?" Messiah whispered, staring in awe at the strange cubby hole cut into the spine of the book.

Justice nodded. "The book is called *a safe.* They're found at *head shops* everywhere. I was gonna leave you, Messiah, just pack a few things for me and Karma, and leave," she revealed just as Messiah dug a red velvet bag out the book. Yet, he froze, his eyes piercing her.

"But?"

"But I didn't have leave type money, and that's when—"

"You remembered what Sunjay told you." Messiah chuckled as he unfurled the small bag, and opened his palm beneath it.

Justice's smile was bitter. "On one of the days you and I visited Gator, and y'all retreated to the back to discuss business, I stole them out that urn, and knew no one would be the wiser." She smirked, and Messiah nodded as he tilted the bag, and watched four flawless diamonds tumble into his palm.

"Why didn't you leave?" His vision trailed from the glistening stones and captured her. "Once you had leave money? And *how* the fuck you knew 'bout the *safe* in—"He froze mid-sentence, his jaw dropping as self realization slapped him—*Mama knew!* He thought as Justice smiled; nodding to confirm the suspicion in his eyes.

"Messiah, your mother is very persuasive, and once she read me the parts of your story I was absent for, it was the question she asked me that made me stay with you."

Messiah's face balled up in frustration. "Quit riddling me, ma, and tell me the haps." He shook his head before his vision fell to the cold stones in his hands. "There's been enough secrets; what type of question could make a woman forgive the one who'd cracked her heart?"

Justice rose from her seat and dusted the back of her pants. "Let's get this over with so we can get our daughter. We've been away from her long enough, and I'm sure she'd drive mama Leah crazy!" She shook her head with a smile, but Messiah bristled as his patience wore thin. Noting it, the smile slipped from Justice's face and she crossed her arms over her bosom. *"The question was: If the beauty would have faulted the beast for being a beast, would her story have become so great that people still speak about it ages later? And if a woman can find fault in a son of a dopefiend becoming a street nigga, why would he be better off without her?"* She revealed before glancing down at the book.

Messiah frowned. "And that was strong enough to make you stay?"

"Naw." Justice shook her head with a sad smile. "But my love for you is." Her eyes found his. "That and *the answer* she wrote in her last entry to you." She giggled when Messiah's eyes shot to the book. Shaking her head, Justice leaned down, cupped his face, and made him look up at her. "Thank you for coming for me, Pa." She kissed his forehead before erecting, and scrunching her nose. "I never trusted that nigga, Siah. I knew he had snake in him. And you know what else!" She snaked her neck, attitude on full. "Sunjay *had* to know."

Perplexity was Messiah's expression as he studied her. "Huh? Fuck you tal'm 'bout, Justice? Sunjay knew what?"

"About Murda, Pa." It was Justice's turn to frown. Her eyes searched his as he sat the book down and scrambled to his feet.

"What 'bout Murda, Justice, elaborate!" He spat, his heart ponding.

"Messiah?" Justice's face went slack, her eyes dark. "Murda is dead...right!" She probed.

"Fuck? Dead? Why would he be dead? Sayyy...lady, you 'bout to fry me! What's the business, Justice, and I won't—"

"Oh my God, Messiah!" Justice cried, before placing both hands on her head as if she'd yank out her hair. "Murda! I-I thought you'd figured him out and that's how you found where I was!"

Messiah clenched his teeth, murder bleeding into his gaze. "*Paradise* and Coffe is how I found you."

"Paradise?" Justice frowned.

"Yeah, her and Junior were fuckin' and—"

"No!" Justice spat, before her arms crossed. She began to pace. "No...No," she moaned. "Yes, Junior and Paradise did their parts, but it was Murda and Junior that snatched up me and Karma, Messiah. Though Junior was the one who spoke, Ms. Rosa only opened the door because she recognized *Murda,* and when she welcomed him, *he* shot her in the face!" Messiah's blood boiled, and when Justice paused to study him, "They wanted the diamonds, Messiah, and it's only *one* person who could've mentioned *me* within their disappearance!"

Messiah's head shook in disbelief. *"Sunjay!"* He spat.

\*\*\*

*Eleventh Ave—New York City*

A pearl white Escalade eased to the curb, the twenty-inch Forgies it squatted on gleaming beneath the sunshine. Eleventh Avenue in the big apple has always been a haven for pimps, playas, and hustlers, and if one couldn't get a mint out of a whore's pussy upon that strip of land, they just wasn't meant for the life! This reality was well acknowledged by the playa behind the wheel, and pulling the cinnamon toothpick from between his lips, his vision trailed to the Jezebel occupying his passenger's seat. A petite, vanilla skinned dime that could've been a double for Toni Braxton in younger years, say pretty, and feeling his gaze upon her, she smirked. Thighs bulging, stretching the fabric of her dress, she was jazzy.

"You ready, daddy?" She purred.

The vet behind the wheel chuckled before glancing over his shoulder at the four felines in his backseat. Candy, Creamy, Juicy and a freak named Kelly, all smiled seductively. See, while Messiah was wrapped in the turbulence of his life, Pimpin was busy getting his *P* back! Not only had he knocked Messiah for the rest of his stable, but he'd also snuck into his old friend, Bear's, cave and kidnapped the heart of his bottom bitch. *Doll Face!*

"You hoes are the ones the game chose to get me back in my gators!" He jazzed, turning to glance out at the *opportunities* offered by the city that never sleeps. "I coulda knocked a *square* hoe, but a square hoe can't empower my *circle,* so you bitches get out here and hit all four corners of this street like a *rectangle* until my money forms a *triangle* that points like an arrow straight to my pockets," he jazzed, and like troops, the backseat emptied, his whores marching for the money.

"Damn, *Pimpin Maxwell,* it makes my pussy throb when you pop that shit!" Doll Face purred, fanning herself with a seductive smile.

Pimpin Maxwell's vision took inventory of her image. Bear had laced the bitch in furs, jewels, designer, and kept her hair and nails on fleek, and in return, she'd robbed him blind, and paid homage to Pimpin. Bear's jewels, clothes, the loot in his safe, and even the Escalade Pimpin and Doll currently laxed within were spoils gifted to Maxwell from the hands of the game, and he smirked before wiping down the Bill Cosby Coogi sweater that complimented the lime green slacks and gators on his feet.

"Oh yeah?" He wanted to know.

"Yasss, baby." Doll smiled seductively before reaching over and rubbing a manicured hand over his thigh.

Pimpin chuckled. "Good, hoe, that means a trick ain't gotta work too hard to slip inside before he pays you for ya time! So, rather than sitting on that pretty kitten, fuck you sittin' here tryin' to play *me* like I'm jive, instead of out there breakin' ya heels to get me my nickels and dimes?" He spat before slapping her hand away and nodding out at the activity of Eleventh Ave.

"Nigga!" Doll Face gaped, astonished. And crossing her arms over her breast as she glared at him, Pimpin admired the short bob her hair had been cut into. "I ain't sold pussy in years! Negro, I just took down one of Dallas' top D boys for you, and you got the audacity to come for *me?* Uh-uh." She smacked her glossed lips.

Pimpin studied her a moment before his expression softened, and nodding his agreement, he smirked. "Baby Doll, forgive my barbarianism. Hard habits are hard to break." He shook his head sadly. "You know I love you and appreciate all ya sacrifices, right?" Doll Face tried to keep her glare, but Pimpin reaching over to rub the back of his hand down the side of her face. "Right, Doll?"

Doll Face's expression softened. "Yes, Maxwell, but if we're doin' this, we're doing it *together!*" She declared, and before she knew it, Pimpin's hand was between her legs, beneath her panties, and creating magic! Doll Face bit her bottom lip, spreading her legs to give him better access, but Pimpin pulled his hand away. "Wh-Why you stop!" Doll Face demanded, but hearing the locks engage on the truck, she smirked mischievously.

"Take that shit off!" Pimpin nodded at her dress.

"Pimpin!" She giggled.

"Doll, we're behind the five percent tint, nobody worried 'bout us. Take…that…shit off! Then climb over here so an old playa can get his Johnson wet."

Doll Face ran her tongue over her lips. Pimpin was bringing the freak out of her, and shrugging away her apprehension, she took the dress by its shoulder straps, and slipped them off her shoulders. And shimmying the nylon material down her body, she slipped out of it. Braless, she massaged her nipples. "Like what you see, daddy?" She seduced, and Pimpin licked his lips before going for his belt buckle. *She thought!*

Yet, it happened so fast that she didn't even have time to look confused. Pimpin had upped a pretty .44 bulldog and took aim at her pretty face. "Get out, hoe!" He seethed. "And don't touch that dress."

"Wha-What?" Doll sputtered.

"Now, Doll Face, you know I ain't into repetition, don't make me ask again, or imma send that pretty face through that window," he vowed, and Doll saw the evil in his gaze. "Get out!" He hissed, and when he disengaged the locks, she complied.

Slipping out into the sunshine of the rotten apple in nothing but a white thong and heels, Doll Face was furious!

"Now close my door, hoe!" Pimpin spat.

Doll Face slammed the door before crossing her arms over her naked breast. "I hate yo ass, Pimpin!" Doll spewed.

Pimpin returned his burna before easing the window down.

"Damn, shorty, let me holla!"

"Yo, B, he put shorty out the truck down bad!" The block came to life.

Pimpin chuckled as Doll Face glared. "Hoe, being a kept hoe was last week, but today is a new day for a freak! Rather lame, creep, or a playa wit' a million benjies, you gonna hoe up and pay this pimpin!" He broke the hoe, and giving him the finger, Doll Face turned on her heels and stormed off. Pimpin Maxwell had reclaimed his grace, and with a flick of the tip of his nose, he knew *nothing* would ever again get in the way of his management of prostitution—purse first and ass last, was the name of the constitution!

***

Justice had retreated into the house, and reclaiming his seat at the edge of the deck, Messiah stared down at the diamonds in his hand. *Blood diamonds!* He thought of the lives stolen behind them. Sighing heavily, he poured them back into the red bag before pushing it back into the *safe*. And suddenly, he burst into manic laughter. Not merely because his mother had bought the book for the sole purpose of stashing her drugs inside of it, but because of the irony of the game. *Murda!* That nigga he'd used as a decoy to deliver the money for his wife's ransom had been one of the snakes in his garden the entire time! And not only had he got away with treachery, but also with the bag! The bag of hundred-dollar bills wrapped around cut up newspaper clippings. Messiah laughed until tears fell from his eyes—he cried and laughed, until the heart break and shock of it all became a distant whisper, and with tears staining his face, he opened the black book to the last entry his mother would ever put inside.

***

*Last Entry:*
*There's a reason the crocodile is at peace with the hippo sharing its waters, and it's the exact reason pimps, playas, and hustlers can coexist. Predators, respect predators, Messiah. Yet, never mistake respect for love, baby, nor understanding for fear! Your only way of being a success in the game is by understanding that everyone goes, outside of the ones that don't, and the ones that don't have to be few! Love should always be rare to you, baby, because it's when you begin to view it as normal that it loses its value. Know this: every man needs a diamond in his life, 'cause only something that the pressures of life has tested will survive the shit that the type of nigga you are will take it through! That diamond is a thorough bitch! A women that understands you, so she'll never misunderstand your ways. See, all fairytales involving a bitch; Snow White, Beauty and the Beast, and even the tale of King Kong, all had something in common. Each one of those women fell for a street nigga! Someone everyone else viewed as unworthy or savage! Yet, it took those bitches to look beyond the physical to recognize the playa within their dudes! Messiah, Snow White kisses a frog! Sleeping Beauty smooched a beast! And King Kong's gal kissed an ape! Nigga, a bitch has to see some powerful shit in Mr. Wrong for her to believe that with a kiss he'll become Mr. Right! Point is, baby, those kisses were metaphors for those bitches' minds! One kiss with the lips; the same things words are formed with, and the only way a woman's thoughts can be given to you is from her words that must come from her kissers! Lol! Messiah, a simple bitch only sees what a nigga projects…a bad bitch only sees how a nigga can compliment her…But a boss bitch sees what she can mold a nigga into! That's why every boss nigga you know has an even bossier bitch as his backbone! So, if you ever meet the typa bitch that sees more outside of you than she sees in you, you're better off without her 'cause she's a surface bitch! The type that looks up a person in the phone*

*book by their first name vs. their last! And when you find a bitch like Snow White, you better pour your all into her, 'cause if a bitch meets a frog and can see that there's a prince lurking...just imagine what she'll see in you!*
—Mama—

## Lock Down Publications and Ca$h Presents
## Assisted Publishing Packages

| | |
|---|---|
| **BASIC PACKAGE**<br>$499<br>Editing<br>Cover Design<br>Formatting | **UPGRADED PACKAGE**<br>$800<br>Typing<br>Editing<br>Cover Design<br>Formatting |
| **ADVANCE PACKAGE**<br>$1,200<br>Typing<br>Editing<br>Cover Design<br>Formatting<br>Copyright registration<br>Proofreading<br>Upload book to Amazon | **LDP SUPREME PACKAGE**<br>$1,500<br>Typing<br>Editing<br>Cover Design<br>Formatting<br>Copyright registration<br>Proofreading<br>Set up Amazon account<br>Upload book to Amazon<br>Advertise on LDP, Amazon and<br>Facebook Page |

***Other services available upon request.
Additional charges may apply

**Lock Down Publications**
P.O. Box 944
Stockbridge, GA 30281-9998
Phone: 470 303-9761

# Submission Guideline

Submit the first three chapters of your completed manuscript to ldpsubmissions@gmail.com. In the subject line add **Your Book's Title**. The manuscript must be in a Word Doc file and sent as an attachment. Document should be in Times New Roman, double spaced, and in size 12 font. Also, provide your synopsis and full contact information. If sending multiple submissions, they must each be in a separate email.

Have a story but no way to send it electronically? You can still submit to LDP/Ca$h Presents. Send in the first three chapters, written or typed, of your completed manuscript to:

**LDP: Submissions Dept**
P.O. Box 944
Stockbridge, GA 30281-9998

*DO NOT send original manuscript. Must be a duplicate.* Provide your synopsis and a cover letter containing your full contact information.

Thanks for considering LDP and Ca$h Presents.

# NEW RELEASES

BLOODLINE OF A SAVAGE **BY PRINCE A. TAUHID**

THE MURDER QUEENS 4 **BY MICHAEL GALLON**

THE BUTTERFLY MAFIA **BY FUMIYA PAYNE**

KING KILLA 2 **BY VINCENT "VITTO" HOLLOWAY**

BABY, I'M WINTERTIME COLD 3 **BY MEESHA**

THESE VICIOUS STREETS **BY PRINCE A. TAUHID**

TIL DEATH 2 **BY ARYANNA**

CITY OF SMOKE 2 **BY MOLOTTI**

STEPPERS **BY KING RIO**

THE LANE **BY KEN-KEN SPENCE**

MONEY GAME 2 **BY SMOOVE DOLLA**

THE BLACK DIAMOND CARTEL **BY SAYNOMORE**

CRIME BOSS 2 **BY PLAYA RAY**

THUG OF SPADES **BY COREY ROBINSON**

LOVE IN THE TRENCHES 2 **BY COREY ROBINSON**

TIL DEATH 3 **BY ARYANNA**

THE BIRTH OF A GANGSTER 4 **BY DELMONT PLAYER**

PRODUCT OF THE STREETS **BY DEMOND "MONEY" ANDERSON**

# Coming Soon from Lock Down Publications/Ca$h Presents

BLOOD OF A BOSS VI
SHADOWS OF THE GAME II
TRAP BASTARD II
By **Askari**

LOYAL TO THE GAME IV
By **T.J. & Jelissa**

TRUE SAVAGE VIII
MIDNIGHT CARTEL IV
DOPE BOY MAGIC IV
CITY OF KINGZ III
NIGHTMARE ON SILENT AVE II
THE PLUG OF LIL MEXICO II
CLASSIC CITY II
By **Chris Green**

BLAST FOR ME III
A SAVAGE DOPEBOY III
CUTTHROAT MAFIA III
DUFFLE BAG CARTEL VII
HEARTLESS GOON VI
By **Ghost**

A HUSTLER'S DECEIT III
KILL ZONE II
BAE BELONGS TO ME III
TIL DEATH II
By **Aryanna**

KING OF THE TRAP III
By **T.J. Edwards**

GORILLAZ IN THE BAY V
3X KRAZY III
STRAIGHT BEAST MODE III
By **De'Kari**

KINGPIN KILLAZ IV
STREET KINGS III
PAID IN BLOOD III
CARTEL KILLAZ IV
DOPE GODS III
By **Hood Rich**

SINS OF A HUSTLA II
By **ASAD**

YAYO V
BRED IN THE GAME 2
By **S. Allen**

THE STREETS WILL TALK II
By **Yolanda Moore**

SON OF A DOPE FIEND III
HEAVEN GOT A GHETTO III
SKI MASK MONEY III
By **Renta**

LOYALTY AIN'T PROMISED III
By **Keith Williams**

I'M NOTHING WITHOUT HIS LOVE II
SINS OF A THUG II
TO THE THUG I LOVED BEFORE II
IN A HUSTLER I TRUST II
By **Monet Dragun**

QUIET MONEY IV
EXTENDED CLIP III
THUG LIFE IV
By **Trai'Quan**

THE STREETS MADE ME IV
By **Larry D. Wright**

IF YOU CROSS ME ONCE III
ANGEL V
By **Anthony Fields**

THE STREETS WILL NEVER CLOSE IV
By **K'ajji**

HARD AND RUTHLESS III
KILLA KOUNTY IV
By **Khufu**

MONEY GAME III
By **Smoove Dolla**

MURDA WAS THE CASE III
**Elijah R. Freeman**

AN UNFORESEEN LOVE IV
BABY, I'M WINTERTIME COLD III
By **Meesha**

QUEEN OF THE ZOO III
By **Black Migo**

CONFESSIONS OF A JACKBOY III
By **Nicholas Lock**

JACK BOYS VS DOPE BOYS IV
A GANGSTA'S QUR'AN V
COKE GIRLZ II
COKE BOYS II
LIFE OF A SAVAGE V
CHI'RAQ GANGSTAS V
SOSA GANG III
BRONX SAVAGES II
BODYMORE KINGPINS II
By **Romell Tukes**

KING KILLA II
By **Vincent "Vitto" Holloway**

BETRAYAL OF A THUG III
By **Fre$h**

THE MURDER QUEENS III
By **Michael Gallon**

THE BIRTH OF A GANGSTER III
By **Delmont Player**

TREAL LOVE II
By **Le'Monica Jackson**

FOR THE LOVE OF BLOOD III
By **Jamel Mitchell**

RAN OFF ON DA PLUG II
By **Paper Boi Rari**

HOOD CONSIGLIERE III
By **Keese**

PRETTY GIRLS DO NASTY THINGS II
By **Nicole Goosby**

PROTÉGÉ OF A LEGEND III
LOVE IN THE TRENCHES II
By **Corey Robinson**

IT'S JUST ME AND YOU II
By **Ah'Million**

FOREVER GANGSTA III
By **Adrian Dulan**

GORILLAZ IN THE TRENCHES II
By **SayNoMore**

THE COCAINE PRINCESS VIII
By **King Rio**

CRIME BOSS II
By **Playa Ray**

LOYALTY IS EVERYTHING III
By **Molotti**

HERE TODAY GONE TOMORROW II
By **Fly Rock**

SON OF A DOPEFIEND 4 | RENTA

REAL G'S MOVE IN SILENCE II
By **Von Diesel**

GRIMEY WAYS IV
By **Ray Vinci**

# Available Now

RESTRAINING ORDER I & II
By **CA$H & Coffee**

LOVE KNOWS NO BOUNDARIES I II & III
By **Coffee**

RAISED AS A GOON I, II, III & IV
BRED BY THE SLUMS I, II, III
BLAST FOR ME I & II
ROTTEN TO THE CORE I II III
A BRONX TALE I, II, III
DUFFLE BAG CARTEL I II III IV V VI
HEARTLESS GOON I II III IV V
A SAVAGE DOPEBOY I II
DRUG LORDS I II III
CUTTHROAT MAFIA I II
KING OF THE TRENCHES
By **Ghost**

LAY IT DOWN I & II
LAST OF A DYING BREED I II
BLOOD STAINS OF A SHOTTA I & II III
By **Jamaica**

LOYAL TO THE GAME I II III
LIFE OF SIN I, II III
By **TJ & Jelissa**

IF LOVING HIM IS WRONG…I & II
LOVE ME EVEN WHEN IT HURTS I II III
By **Jelissa**

SON OF A DOPEFIEND 4 | RENTA

BLOODY COMMAS I & II
SKI MASK CARTEL I, II & III
KING OF NEW YORK I II, III IV V
RISE TO POWER I II III
COKE KINGS I II III IV V
BORN HEARTLESS I II III IV
KING OF THE TRAP I II
By **T.J. Edwards**

WHEN THE STREETS CLAP BACK I & II III
THE HEART OF A SAVAGE I II III IV
MONEY MAFIA I II
LOYAL TO THE SOIL I II III
By **Jibril Williams**

A DISTINGUISHED THUG STOLE MY HEART I II &
III
LOVE SHOULDN'T HURT I II III IV
RENEGADE BOYS I II III IV
PAID IN KARMA I II III
SAVAGE STORMS I II III
AN UNFORESEEN LOVE I II III
BABY, I'M WINTERTIME COLD I II
By **Meesha**

A GANGSTER'S CODE I &, II III
A GANGSTER'S SYN I II III
THE SAVAGE LIFE I II III
CHAINED TO THE STREETS I II III
BLOOD ON THE MONEY I II III
A GANGSTA'S PAIN I II III
By **J-Blunt**

PUSH IT TO THE LIMIT
By **Bre' Hayes**

BLOOD OF A BOSS I, II, III, IV, V
SHADOWS OF THE GAME
TRAP BASTARD
By **Askari**

THE STREETS BLEED MURDER I, II & III
THE HEART OF A GANGSTA I II& III
By **Jerry Jackson**

CUM FOR ME I II III IV V VI VII VIII
An **LDP Erotica Collaboration**

BRIDE OF A HUSTLA I II & II
THE FETTI GIRLS I, II& III
CORRUPTED BY A GANGSTA I, II III, IV
BLINDED BY HIS LOVE
THE PRICE YOU PAY FOR LOVE I, II ,III
DOPE GIRL MAGIC I II III
By **Destiny Skai**

WHEN A GOOD GIRL GOES BAD
By **Adrienne**

A GANGSTER'S REVENGE I II III & IV
THE BOSS MAN'S DAUGHTERS I II III IV V
A SAVAGE LOVE  I & II
BAE BELONGS TO ME I II
A HUSTLER'S DECEIT I, II, III
WHAT BAD BITCHES DO I, II, III
SOUL OF A MONSTER I II III
KILL ZONE
A DOPE BOY'S QUEEN I II III
TIL DEATH
By **Aryanna**

THE COST OF LOYALTY I II III
**By Kweli**

A KINGPIN'S AMBITION
A KINGPIN'S AMBITION **II**
I MURDER FOR THE DOUGH
By **Ambitious**

TRUE SAVAGE I II III IV V VI VII
DOPE BOY MAGIC I, II, III
MIDNIGHT CARTEL I II III
CITY OF KINGZ I II
NIGHTMARE ON SILENT AVE
THE PLUG OF LIL MEXICO II
CLASSIC CITY
By **Chris Green**

A DOPEBOY'S PRAYER
By **Eddie "Wolf" Lee**

THE KING CARTEL I, II & III
By **Frank Gresham**

THESE NIGGAS AIN'T LOYAL I, II & III
By **Nikki Tee**

GANGSTA SHYT I II &III
By **CATO**

THE ULTIMATE BETRAYAL
By **Phoenix**

BOSS'N UP I, II & III
By **Royal Nicole**

I LOVE YOU TO DEATH
By **Destiny J**

I RIDE FOR MY HITTA
I STILL RIDE FOR MY HITTA
By **Misty Holt**

LOVE & CHASIN' PAPER
By **Qay Crockett**

TO DIE IN VAIN
SINS OF A HUSTLA
By **ASAD**

BROOKLYN HUSTLAZ
By **Boogsy Morina**

BROOKLYN ON LOCK I & II
By **Sonovia**

GANGSTA CITY
By **Teddy Duke**

A DRUG KING AND HIS DIAMOND I & II III
A DOPEMAN'S RICHES
HER MAN, MINE'S TOO I, II
CASH MONEY HO'S
THE WIFEY I USED TO BE I II
PRETTY GIRLS DO NASTY THINGS
**By Nicole Goosby**

LIPSTICK KILLAH I, II, III
CRIME OF PASSION I II & III
FRIEND OR FOE I II III
By **Mimi**

TRAPHOUSE KING I II & III
KINGPIN KILLAZ I II III
STREET KINGS I II
PAID IN BLOOD I II
CARTEL KILLAZ I II III
DOPE GODS I II
By **Hood Rich**

STEADY MOBBN' I, II, III
THE STREETS STAINED MY SOUL I II III
By **Marcellus Allen**

WHO SHOT YA I, II, III
SON OF A DOPE FIEND I II
HEAVEN GOT A GHETTO I II
SKI MASK MONEY I II
By **Renta**

GORILLAZ IN THE BAY I II III IV
TEARS OF A GANGSTA I II
3X KRAZY I II
STRAIGHT BEAST MODE I II
By **DE'KARI**

TRIGGADALE I II III
MURDA WAS THE CASE I II
By **Elijah R. Freeman**

THE STREETS ARE CALLING
By **Duquie Wilson**

SLAUGHTER GANG I II III
RUTHLESS HEART I II III
By **Willie Slaughter**

SON OF A DOPEFIEND 4 | RENTA

GOD BLESS THE TRAPPERS I, II, III
THESE SCANDALOUS STREETS I, II, III
FEAR MY GANGSTA I, II, III IV, V
THESE STREETS DON'T LOVE NOBODY I, II
BURY ME A G I, II, III, IV, V
A GANGSTA'S EMPIRE I, II, III, IV
THE DOPEMAN'S BODYGAURD I II
THE REALEST KILLAZ I II III
THE LAST OF THE OGS I II III
By **Tranay Adams**

MARRIED TO A BOSS I II III
By **Destiny Skai & Chris Green**

KINGZ OF THE GAME I II III IV V VI VII
CRIME BOSS
By **Playa Ray**

FUK SHYT
By **Blakk Diamond**

DON'T F#CK WITH MY HEART I II
By **Linnea**

ADDICTED TO THE DRAMA I II III
IN THE ARM OF HIS BOSS II
By **Jamila**

YAYO I II III IV
A SHOOTER'S AMBITION I II
BRED IN THE GAME
By **S. Allen**

LOYALTY AIN'T PROMISED I II
By **Keith Williams**

SON OF A DOPEFIEND 4 | RENTA

TRAP GOD  I II III
RICH $AVAGE I II III
MONEY IN THE GRAVE I II III
By **Martell Troublesome Bolden**

FOREVER GANGSTA I II
GLOCKS ON SATIN SHEETS I II
By **Adrian Dulan**

TOE TAGZ I II III IV
LEVELS TO THIS SHYT I II
IT'S JUST ME AND YOU
By **Ah'Million**

KINGPIN DREAMS I II III
RAN OFF ON DA PLUG
By **Paper Boi Rari**

CONFESSIONS OF A GANGSTA I II III IV
CONFESSIONS OF A JACKBOY I II
By **Nicholas Lock**

I'M NOTHING WITHOUT HIS LOVE
SINS OF A THUG
TO THE THUG I LOVED BEFORE
A GANGSTA SAVED XMAS
IN A HUSTLER I TRUST
By **Monet Dragun**

QUIET MONEY I II III
THUG LIFE I II III
EXTENDED CLIP I II
A GANGSTA'S PARADISE
By **Trai'Quan**

SON OF A DOPEFIEND 4 | RENTA

CAUGHT UP IN THE LIFE I II III
THE STREETS NEVER LET GO I II III
By **Robert Baptiste**

NEW TO THE GAME I II III
MONEY, MURDER & MEMORIES I II III
By **Malik D. Rice**

CREAM I II III
THE STREETS WILL TALK
By **Yolanda Moore**

LIFE OF A SAVAGE I II III IV
A GANGSTA'S QUR'AN I II III IV
MURDA SEASON I II III
GANGLAND CARTEL I II III
CHI'RAQ GANGSTAS I II III IV
KILLERS ON ELM STREET I II III
JACK BOYZ N DA BRONX I II III
A DOPEBOY'S DREAM I II III
JACK BOYS VS DOPE BOYS I II III
COKE GIRLZ
COKE BOYS
SOSA GANG I II
BRONX SAVAGES
BODYMORE KINGPINS
By **Romell Tukes**

THE STREETS MADE ME I II III
By **Larry D. Wright**

CONCRETE KILLA I II III
VICIOUS LOYALTY I II III
By **Kingpen**

THE ULTIMATE SACRIFICE I, II, III, IV, V, VI
KHADIFI
IF YOU CROSS ME ONCE I II
ANGEL I II III IV
IN THE BLINK OF AN EYE
By **Anthony Fields**

THE LIFE OF A HOOD STAR
By **Ca$h & Rashia Wilson**

THE STREETS WILL NEVER CLOSE I II III
By **K'ajji**

NIGHTMARES OF A HUSTLA I II III
By **King Dream**

HARD AND RUTHLESS I II
MOB TOWN 251
THE BILLIONAIRE BENTLEYS I II III
REAL G'S MOVE IN SILENCE
By **Von Diesel**

GHOST MOB
By **Stilloan Robinson**

MOB TIES I II III IV V VI
SOUL OF A HUSTLER, HEART OF A KILLER I II
GORILLAZ IN THE TRENCHES
By **SayNoMore**

BODYMORE MURDERLAND I II III
THE BIRTH OF A GANGSTER I II
By **Delmont Player**

SON OF A DOPEFIEND 4 | RENTA

FOR THE LOVE OF A BOSS
By **C. D. Blue**

KILLA KOUNTY I II III IV
**By Khufu**

MOBBED UP I II III IV
THE BRICK MAN I II III IV V
THE COCAINE PRINCESS I II III IV V VI VII
By **King Rio**

MONEY GAME I II
By **Smoove Dolla**

A GANGSTA'S KARMA I II III
By **FLAME**

KING OF THE TRENCHES I II III
By **GHOST & TRANAY ADAMS**

QUEEN OF THE ZOO I II
By **Black Migo**

GRIMEY WAYS I II III
By **Ray Vinci**

XMAS WITH AN ATL SHOOTER
By **Ca$h & Destiny Skai**

KING KILLA
By **Vincent "Vitto" Holloway**

BETRAYAL OF A THUG I II
By **Fre$h**

SON OF A DOPEFIEND 4 | RENTA

THE MURDER QUEENS I II
By **Michael Gallon**

TREAL LOVE
By **Le'Monica Jackson**

FOR THE LOVE OF BLOOD I II
By **Jamel Mitchell**

HOOD CONSIGLIERE I II
By **Keese**

PROTÉGÉ OF A LEGEND I II
LOVE IN THE TRENCHES
By **Corey Robinson**

BORN IN THE GRAVE I II III
By **Self Made Tay**

MOAN IN MY MOUTH
By **XTASY**

TORN BETWEEN A GANGSTER AND A
GENTLEMAN
By **J-BLUNT & Miss Kim**

LOYALTY IS EVERYTHING I II
By **Molotti**

HERE TODAY GONE TOMORROW
By **Fly Rock**

PILLOW PRINCESS
By **S. Hawkins**

SON OF A DOPEFIEND 4 | RENTA

SANCTIFIED AND HORNY
by **XTASY**

THE PLUG OF LIL MEXICO 2
by **CHRIS GREEN**

THE BLACK DIAMOND CARTEL
by **SAYNOMORE**

THE BIRTH OF A GANGSTER 3
by **DELMONT PLAYER**

# BOOKS BY LDP'S CEO, CA$H

TRUST IN NO MAN
TRUST IN NO MAN 2
TRUST IN NO MAN 3
BONDED BY BLOOD
SHORTY GOT A THUG
THUGS CRY
THUGS CRY 2
THUGS CRY 3
TRUST NO BITCH
TRUST NO BITCH 2
TRUST NO BITCH 3
TIL MY CASKET DROPS
RESTRAINING ORDER
RESTRAINING ORDER 2
IN LOVE WITH A CONVICT
LIFE OF A HOOD STAR
XMAS WITH AN ATL SHOOTER

www.ingramcontent.com/pod-product-compliance
Lightning Source LLC
Chambersburg PA
CBHW071148260626
47162CB00003B/963